To the one who made us all

‘Yet I hold this against you: You have forsaken your first love.’
REVELATION 2:4

1
BEGINNINGS

Grimsby, ages ago

Being kissed by Suzanne Devlin was the best thing that would happen to Joe Belton for nearly fifty years. He didn't realise this at the time because how could he? Does anyone think much beyond the next day or two when they're ten? Oh, you might long for Christmas, or for snow, but Suzanne kissed Joe on a warm dinnertime in the first truly sunny week of March. The snow had melted into slush a month before and Christmas was impossibly far off whichever way you looked at it.

This dinnertime Joe was flying through the low hills at the back of the playground. He was alight with the thrill of the hunt, hearing the first notes of the delicious theme that obsesses, delights, and ruins so many people over their lives. Kiss Chase was his favourite game, and it had been for a week now. It was simple enough: the boys chased the girls. If they caught them, they could kiss them on the cheek, more daringly on the lips. Joe was an outsider, uninterested in most of the other children for most of the time, but he wanted to play this game, and for once they let him.

At this minute the excitement was high. Because the real magic, the treasure that jolted Joe's stomach with pleasure, was that sometimes the game switched round and the girls chased the boys. This was gold, because if a girl chased you that meant something. And this playtime Joe was being chased by Suzanne Devlin.

Like every boy, Joe was in love with Suzanne, and he had been all year. She was the prettiest, everyone knew that, and she was too pretty for Joe. If he saw her in the school corridor, he walked the other way. Once she asked him if he had seen her friend Corinne and he shook his head and blushed dark red, for which Sean Garner and Michael Bluff had mocked him for days. Yet when he was walking home, or watching telly waiting for his tea, or shivering in his bath before bed, he escaped into daydreams. In those dreams he was the only one who realised she had been kidnapped, so it came to him to rescue her. Sometimes he scored winning goals while she watched. Sometimes he simply walked up to her and took hold of her hand.

So today he was on fire. First the thing on the bus. Then Kiss Chase. A great day, and it made him bold. Rather than escaping, he slowed as cleverly as he could so Suzanne could catch him without realising he was letting her – and then her hands were on his arm, and she had him and she was pulling him toward her.

He froze, waiting in a glorious terror …

For Suzanne the playground was an ever-changing adventure. One week everyone would be skipping. Ropes made of knicker elastic or hundreds of rubber bands swarmed across the tarmac. Another week they'd all be singing. The winter she was six her best friend Corinne Ayr taught her the whole of the song 'Two Little Boys'. They stood in the playground by the railings, and line-by-line Suzanne got hold of the words. Then it might be hopscotch. You'd find a chunk of chalk, mark out the squares, and use the chalk as a marker as you hopped and jumped up and back down the grid. Some girls spent hours playing at horses, skipping round and pretending to hold reins. Some stood and talked all they could. That was Suzanne. In those first few years at school it was so exciting to talk to each other. You'd get up early on school days because you couldn't wait to be there, you'd be excited to see your friends walking up the road, and when you got chance you'd laugh for a whole playtime.

The boys were different. Suzanne watched them sometimes. They didn't do so much talking. They did more shouting. Spent more time in motion. Sean Garner would get his gang going, and they'd start a war. Soon all the boys and half the girls would be involved every playtime in a battle that ebbed and flowed round the old Victorian school buildings for a day or two. The biggest crime you could commit was not taking your shots. If someone bren-gunned you and they got you fair and square, you had to die – and you couldn't lie down for a moment and then jump up, you had to do it properly.

Suzanne understood war because singing 'Two Little Boys' so many times had shown her what happened. It was sad, and heroic, and about being the best friends you could be, helping each other through to the end, whatever went wrong. You did have to watch Sean Garner and his friends though. Sometimes while you were talking, or singing, in your group, and you thought the boys were off somewhere shouting and fighting, they surprised you by running in and lifting up your skirts.

It wasn't all one way. Helen Lacey flashed her knickers at the boys, and there were stories she once even took them off in the field of dock leaves next to the school. Suzanne's mum sucked hard on her cigarette when Suzanne told her that and said Helen needed a good slap. Suzanne nodded, yes, she did, but Helen's family weren't around much and when they were, they were loud and rude and worried about running their hardware shop. Suzanne understood why Helen did that – it was a very exciting idea – but Suzanne knew it was wrong. Besides, if she ever felt like that, there would be far better ways to get what she wanted.

Suzanne had her first boyfriend around then. A Londoner called Glen. As an outsider, a southerner, he was exotic, his family somehow washing up in this remote northern fishing town. He was also the sweetest, kindest boy Suzanne had ever met. When he was around her, she felt better. He clearly felt the same about her.

They were six, so their entire relationship was a set of five-minute moments stripped across one autumn of infant school. Every morning the class had to line up in pairs before assembly. That involved each pair holding hands. Then one day Suzanne realised she was different. The custom was for the boys to walk hand in hand with boys, girls with girls. Glen didn't go along with this. He'd find her and take her hand and hold it as the class walked in pairs out of the classroom, along the corridor, into assembly. They never talked – Suzanne couldn't remember ever having a single conversation with him – but they didn't need to, because there was nothing which couldn't be said by holding hands. She knew she was very special to him, and he was certainly very special to her. Over that autumn, she became sure that the one thing she could rely on was holding hands with Glen.

When she came back after the Christmas holiday Glen wasn't there. No-one knew where he was. This hurt, a lot. She cried, and her mum couldn't comfort her. She eventually found out his dad had got a new job in Boston, forty-five miles away in South Lincolnshire, and the entire family had moved down there on Christmas Eve. Suzanne never saw Glen again, but the faint, growing ever fainter, memory of how it felt to hold his hand and walk into assembly with him beside her always warmed her, no matter what else was happening in her life.

This didn't do her good. From then on, in all the boys she liked, she would always be searching for uncatchable echoes of Glen.

Suzanne didn't notice Joe in those first years at school, but when they were eight their mothers ended up working together as telephonists in the hospital, and that made the first connection. Suzanne would walk home through the hospital grounds after school and wait outside the main door for her mum to finish work. If she was early, Suzanne could go into the switchboard room. She'd find a stool and watch the cigarette smoke drift through the shafts of sunlight. Mary and Janet, Joe's mum, spent their days in there, chain-smoking Players Number 6, cackling at each other's jokes, commiserating over each other's problems, while plugging and unplugging a fiendish nest of cables into the giant dark wood plugboard which flashed and buzzed and filled the side wall of the little room.

One afternoon Suzanne came in and saw the mood was different. Janet was crying. Her mum had her arm round her and was doing her best to comfort her. Janet had a suitcase next to her and Suzanne's mum caught her looking, so she took her out and gave her some pop and a biscuit. She told her Joe's mum was having problems at home, and they didn't have enough money, and Joe's dad sometimes wasn't very nice to her, but it would be alright – and then, feeling guilty at having said too much, she swore Suzanne to secrecy. Suzanne wasn't to say anything at school because poor Joe had it hard enough already.

That intrigued Suzanne because it hadn't occurred to her that Joe was poor anything. She thought he just liked being on his own.

After that she kept half an eye on him. She'd notice him, on his own by the fence, or playing with toy cars in the mud. Reading an American comic as he walked to school. On the edge of one group or another, smiling too much, not sure what to say. Even at their age Suzanne knew there was something about his pale face and his grubby mustard-coloured cardigan which set him aside, which made him forgettable to most. She noticed when he got caught for stealing from the tuck shop at the Christmas Fair, and she was sitting nearby when he explained the secret about burgling his uncle had told the night before.

A little crowd had gathered, and he talked fast, thrilled to be in the spotlight: you could get into a house so easily. First off, you stick a rubber sucker on a back window. Then you scrape a circle on the glass with a diamond ring and tap the window with a hammer. The glass circle breaks out of the glass of the window. The sucker on the glass stops the glass falling and so there's no noise. You pull the circle out with the sucker, and put your arm through the hole to open the window catch …

Suzanne noticed people had stopped listening, which she thought was strange, because it sounded pretty interesting to her. Joe realised his audience was slipping away and talked louder, doing his best to hook them back in.

The problem was, he explained, if the police found you walking down the street with a sucker in your pocket and hammer in your bag and a diamond ring on your finger, they might guess you were going to burgle somewhere. The real trick was – and Suzanne never forget how pleased Joe was with his clever uncle – to forget about carrying any sucker or hammer. When it came to it, you'd use a rock you could find in the back garden of the house, and you'd put your lips up against the glass, like this, suck the glass with your own mouth, like this, and it would come out fine …

She wanted to clap, but by now almost everyone else had gone. She felt sad that they had left him, but she did understand the impulse. There was something about Joe that meant, even when he was telling a wonderful story, it was hard to be around him. Sometimes she'd find him staring at her. He'd look away, and pretend he was looking somewhere else, but it still made her uncomfortable. And then, even when she heard him speaking to other people, he didn't get it right. When people were listening to him it seemed like he was showing off, but he didn't seem to believe in what he was showing off. It was always the same. After a while everything Joe said flew off somewhere, went past your ears without ever bothering them. What he said didn't count because of his dirty clothes, because of the way his hair stood out, because he was made to be ignored.

Nevertheless, Joe's story, and what her mother said, had hooked her a little. Suzanne was usually surrounded by a laughing crowd, so it bothered her how he could be so alone. It made her curious, sometimes even envious, so, over the next year or so, whenever she was bored, she'd check on Joe. She was always disappointed that he didn't do much. He'd keep silent in class, stay on the edges of the playground, walk home alone. He'd always be reading. And then he started to draw. Every chance he got he'd draw spaceships, goblins, wizards, aliens. The teachers told him it was rubbish, and he should draw proper things, which annoyed her, but even so, she never saw how, or why, she should talk to him.

Then, on that warm March day when they were both ten, there was the bus ride, and the kiss, and things between them changed for ever.

. . .

Earlier that morning, just like every Wednesday, the entire school had climbed into three double-decker buses and gone the half mile from the school playground to the local swimming baths. The drive took ten minutes, but the noise was always epic. It might be songs they'd learned at scout camp, or songs the older kids had taught them, but the best times were when Michael Bluff stood up at the front of the bus, punched the air with his black and white Grimsby Town FC scarf tied round his wrist, and led the chant in the standards they sang down the Pontoon on a Saturday afternoon:

G R I
M-S B Y
Grimsby's the pride of the Humberside

The whole bus roared into this, even Joe, and for a few minutes it was eighty children chanting as one, in a way the drivers hated, but could never silence, no matter how much they bellowed over their shoulders.

Na na nah, na na na
Na na nah, na na na na
Na na nah, na na na
We are the Grimsby
Boot Boys

This morning, Suzanne and Corinne were sitting a few rows behind Joe on the top deck, when the bus stopped at roadworks. Out of nowhere Joe got up in his seat and started banging on the window, looking at something below them. The boys around him saw this, but most of them rolled their eyes and carried on with what they were doing.

Until he started shouting, 'Dad! Dad! Up here. Dad!'

The kids nearby broke off from singing and scrambled over to see what was there, then Sean Garner fell about pointing and laughing.

Corinne looked out the window. 'That's never his dad.'

Suzanne couldn't see. 'Why?'

'He looks like my grandpa'.

Suzanne got up and looked down past Corinne. Two old men stood in a hole in the road. One of them used a pneumatic drill while the other shovelled the debris. Unshaven, in dirty donkey jackets, they were grey, lined, hollowed out by years of hard work.

Up ahead Joe was frantic, banging louder on the glass.

'Dad! Dad! I'm up here. Look up here.'

The men weren't looking up; banging on the window wasn't loud enough to get above the sound of the road drill. Joe broke off to look round the top deck at the other children. Suzanne saw how his face was messy with joy and pride.

'That's my dad down there!'

The kids round him broke off singing long enough to sneer at him, 'He's a road digger!'

Joe looked round them and saw the contempt. The light in his face collapsed in on itself, and Suzanne couldn't stand it.

When the bus moved off past the traffic lights and they got past the road works and the other kids had turned back to what they were doing, Suzanne got up and walked over to Joe.

He looked up, startled.

'Budge up.'

He obliged, alarmed, and she sat next to him, ignoring the 'Wooh's from the kids around her. She looked at him properly, for what was probably the first time in her life. He dropped his eyes. She could tell she terrified him, and that flattered her, but it also touched her. She realised he had a sweet face.

She was genuinely curious. 'Was that really your dad?'

'Yeah. So?'

Suzanne shrugged. 'He looks like a fine man.'

'Yeah?'

'Digging the roads looks hard. Does it make him tired?'

'He's alright. He gets a bit mardy sometimes,' she said.

'So does my dad. And he never says owt. He never speaks to me or mam. And him and our Malcolm are always off down his lockup. They never invite me.'

Not used to a flow of conversation aimed at him, Joe didn't know what to say. He smiled a snaggle-toothed smile, which touched her even more.

'Anyway. I wanted to tell you that.'

He nodded.

'What's his name?' she said.

'Eddie.'

'Mine's called Bill.'

He nodded again and looked out the window. The conversation had ended.

Suzanne went back to her seat.

Corinne was alive to this amazing breaking of protocol. 'What did he say? Was he upset? What's he like?'

'He's alright. Normal, you know.'

That wasn't what Corinne had wanted to hear, and she switched her attention to the front of the bus.

'Look at Michael!'

Michael Bluff was standing on his head on the front seat, his legs splayed, and his feet braced against the roof. The bus lurched on the kerb and then turned sharp right as it pulled into the swimming baths car park, but Michael kept it going around the corner, finally toppling forward over the back of a chair, ending up on his feet for applause like a circus acrobat.

Corinne clapped and cheered him with the rest of the lads, but Suzanne was looking at Joe sitting on his own, with his ratty hair, in his dirty blue anorak and his mustard cardigan. Same old, annoying old, Joe. For a moment she had a pure sense of him. It was overwhelming, as though she could see through to something more real. She knew for certain he was someone, there, living, and alive, and she loved him. It made no sense. She'd worked out what it would be like to be in love with your boyfriend, and what she was feeling right now for Joe was something else. She couldn't take her eyes off him. She realised she desperately wanted to help him. To give him something. She didn't know what.

So, later that day, after swimming, in the playground at dinnertime, out of all the boys Suzanne could chase – and she loved to chase the boys just as much as the boys loved to be chased by her – she chased Joe.

It didn't surprise her when she caught him. She was beginning to realise she always caught the boys she chased.

Held by her, Joe stopped running and twisted round, pretending to wriggle free, as she pulled him round and leaned in. He saw the freckles on her cheeks, and her eyes blur as they came so close. He caught the smell of Bazooka Joe; and then she kissed him. Her lips were softer than he had expected, and her mouth was open. He felt a flash of foolishness. He'd had his lips pursed like he was going to kiss his mam, but she was kissing him like he'd seen grown-ups do in films, with her mouth open, with something that felt like hunger.

She kissed him, and he felt his body liquify, like he was plunging over distant water, like his heart and his mind were reaching out to the sky far, far above.

Then she was backing away from him, pulling a strand of her long dark hair out of her mouth, grinning as always — yet for all her energy and laughter she was a hint less confident, even a little confused. He looked back on that moment many, many times over the following years, wondering why that could have happened. It always felt to him that something in the kiss had surprised her.

She turned and ran. He watched her as she went. And saw to his wonder how, when she got back to her friends, she turned away from their conversation to look back at him. She locked eyes with him for a long moment across the playground, until he had to break it off, overcome by the knowledge of her.

All that day his heart was the size of the sun, and that massive heart soaked up the happiness of being alive. He felt tall, and proud, and brave, and complete, like he was a proper person who would have friends and walk tall and take part in the world. She washed away all that held him back, all that made him scared and weak. He felt filled by light and knew total, self-sacrificing love for her.

All this, from one moment in a long life. But this glimpse of light formed him. Elevated him. Oriented him. So, even though he was only ten when they kissed, through all the dark times in his later years it was never a surprise whenever he found her living still in him.

Suzanne never did become Joe's girlfriend, and in many ways that kiss was the closest they ever got. They were still too young, and it would take another couple of years for those first boyfriend/girlfriend relationships to bud. What's more, a year later, Eddie died in bed. It was a quick end for Eddie, but the family was never the same. Janet was smoking next to him when it began, looking at the new Grattan's catalogue. By the time it finished she was screaming blue murder in the bathroom.

Joe surprised Janet, and himself, by crying for three days solid. The shock turned him in on himself far more than he ever had been. Janet wasn't available to help. She had fought with Eddie every day of their marriage and had always fantasised of being free of him. Now it had happened, she had no more purpose. They had married when she was 17; he was all she had known, and the scrapping was part of her. His death took a vital part of her confidence, and she diminished from then on, growing hollow and frustrated.

The fact Joe and Suzanne didn't connect also had much to do with Suzanne. She was always friendly to Joe, and cared what happened to him, but the minor curiosity and tenderness she felt for him could never be enough when she had so much else calling for her attention. Though she wasn't unkind, she had her own needs, and there was far too much to do in the world besides be patient with Joe. That didn't hurt him as much as he expected, because he never for a moment thought he deserved love from someone so alive as her. For Joe's part, he was happy enough to be around her: unrequited love was better than no love.

So he stood by and watched her as they went through the rest of their time at school. He understood when she was sad, was happy when she did well. He managed to be pleased for her when she got her first proper boyfriend, and he worried for her later on when she got into a habit of treating boys carelessly. Throughout it all he remained faithful to that moment of the kiss. His overriding feeling through it all was a simple happiness, a glowing joy she existed.

As it turned out, Suzanne died the summer they were eighteen. She was caught, alone, in a fire in the holiday chalet her dad had bought for the family when she was six. The chalet was one of many on a pre-war holiday camp called "The Fitties" at the edge of town. It was a scrappy old thing, made of wood and plasterboard, parched dry by the summer sun, and intensely flammable. It stood away in a corner at the far end of the park, nestling among the sand dunes and the seagrass, and by the time people realised there was a fire the flames were too much. The fire brigade came quickly, but a butane gas canister had exploded in the chalet and it was all far too late.

There was an investigation, but in the absence of any prosecutions the newspapers moved on to Prince Charles and his wedding to "Lady Di". Yet in the real world, among the grief, some questions wouldn't go away. Why was she alone out there in the first place? How did the fire start? And why, when it was just a single-story four-room chalet, hadn't she escaped? The coroner eventually put it down to misadventure, but there were rumours she'd been drinking, and there was enough suspicious about it that the police didn't let it go until every single avenue was closed.

They questioned her family, Mary, Bill, and her brother Malcolm, and, frustrated by the sombre silence of the men in particular, went hard at them. They questioned the people who said they were friends with her at school, of whom there were many, and they went around her inner circle of close friends, of whom there were surprisingly few, but no-one knew anything.

Eighteen months later the police boxed up Suzanne's file and put it away, although it nagged away at the investigating officer for the rest of his life. One by one, everyone who knew her moved on.

Except for Joe Belton.

They'd locked him up on remand in Freiston borstal a couple of months before the fire, so he couldn't be around the town to hear first-hand what happened. When he got back to town eighteen months later, he raged around demanding answers, but did no better than the police. No-one could be bothered to talk to him at the best of times, and now that he was borstal scum few talked to him at all. Plus, by then it was old news, so people who had buried the trauma of Suzanne's death could use the gap as an excuse not to remember.

Joe realised there was confusion over what had happened to her, but he never did find out the details. Back then there was no internet, people only existed in one time, in one place. You talked to the people in the same room as you, or maybe on the phone. You read the papers, but once you threw them away, that was it. The TV news came and went, and cast a light for a while, but soon vanished in a fog of distance. So, if you weren't there, on the scene, around people who could be bothered to tell you, you'd never quite find out what happened.

It stopped hurting eventually, but Joe never quite put her behind him. He lived a long life, that went increasingly wrong. It was only when he had walked his own road for further than he could ever have imagined that an intervention from the greatest love of all gave him the chance to go back home and find out what really happened to Suzanne…

2

THE HAUNTED ABYSS

Brighton, recently

On his bed in the hostel all day, in the queue for the food slopped out on the plates, watching crap in the TV lounge in the evening, smoking any spliff he could get out by the fire escape, it didn't matter where he was, what he did, Joe Belton couldn't get away from the sign.

Two simple lines that cross.

They say if you know how to worry you know how to pray, but he stuck with the worry. From every angle he broke this cross apart, and considered it, and jammed it back together in different ways and none of it fitted with him. He gnawed at it, and it gnawed at him, and he tried to digest it but while he did that it ate him right up.

Start with nothing. Out of that comes a dot. The dot becomes a line. Then two lines. Then they meet. A cross is the fourth most simple thing in the world.

Yet everywhere Joe turned his gaze this simple symbol leaped out at him.

It was in shadows made by the blind across his ceiling at night. *(How come it only came with the street lights, only at night when he was scared? Why couldn't he see the shape in the slats in the daytime)* It was in the crack on the wall of the smoking shed. The scar on the neck of the old boy who doled out the dinners. The way they laid out the trestle tables in the dining hall. The breaks in the glass in the mirror he shaved in. In silver and gold on the necklace of Ginny who worked on reception. The tattoo on Ant's arm. In the logo on the poster of the smiling teenagers at the bus stop. The interweaving tyre tracks in the mud on the grass verge. Two crossed syringes in the gutter. The carving on Ronnie's brand-new gravestone last November. Birds forming intersecting rows in the branches above the grave. Silver contrails in the frost-blue sky. Everywhere he looked, everything made the sign of the cross.

The most powerful cross of all? The mark made on his forehead on Christmas Eve.

Swaying into midnight mass, the whole church spinning, his belly bubbly, feeling pukey from the lagers and the kebab, his heart banging in his chest from the brandies, in there for no more reason than something childish and long-forgotten and soft and warm-hearted had led him, Joe had knelt at the altar rail, his head bowed low, his arms folded in front of him.

He had folded his arms because even through the booze he remembered he couldn't take proper communion. Unconfirmed at his age, the mumbling shame of it. Never confirmed meant a mam who hated God for her own dad who walked out, and her own mam who died way too young. Who hated God for how the kind older man she picked as husband could only give her one single weird kid before he turned out to be weak and buffeted by all he should have saved her from, to the point he could barely keep a roof over their head let alone excite her. Never confirmed meant a dad who wanted Joe out playing football, or fighting, or breaking and entering, or smashing stuff up, or doing anything but going to church on a Sunday and sitting with the posh kids who mocked him.

Never confirmed. Unconfirmed. The story of his life.

Preparing to give him the wafer the vicar noticed Joe's folded arms and changed his approach to give him a blessing. He touched his middle finger to a vial of oil and then marked a slow cross on Joe's forehead.

So tender his words.

'May God bless you and keep you. Make his face shine upon you'

The cross he marked on Joe was 2,000 years old, and Joe felt every day of its weight.

A week later, as he woke up in his pit on New Year's Eve, Joe could still sense the cross on his forehead. He lit his first rollie of the day and considered why this might be. Not many people touched Joe these days so that could account for a lot, but there was more. That touch had mattered. It was the touch of love. The tenderness of it burned. The fact such a thing as this ceremony existed. The penetrating compassion with which the vicar spoke the words.

How could two crossed lines on his forehead make him want to cry so much seven days later?

On his phone on his bed all the day long, but this day was not normal. Bored with Instagram he had a look at Facebook, scrolling through a group created for his old school. He did this more these days, flicking through the feed, spotting marriages, divorces, hair loss, weight gain, children, grandchildren even. Gate-crashing holidays and getting drunk at family birthdays by proxy. Seeing which of the teachers got love, and which were remembered bitterly. Seeing holidays in Canada, the Grand Canyon, Ayers Rock. New kitchens and boat trips and houses in Cornwall. Football teams, netball trophies, school shows. Glimpses of lives he could have had, and one or two of the deaths. Time spent on Facebook never ended well, and this day was no different. He saw they were planning a school reunion in May. Funny no-one had invited him.

For a moment he fantasised. Get lucky on the horses and keep the money for once. Get a haircut, hire a suit, a Merc, get back up to Grimsby, put on a show and rub their noses in – what? The rubbish of his daily life? How bad would that make him feel?

He played it out for a moment, saw the old faces, imagined how it went. He'd go in, get a drink, find someone he recognised, and go over to talk about – what? Maybe he could fake it. He could have a wife. Say they met in Cyprus on an 18-30. Two kids, hell, maybe a grandkid or two by now. If he stayed away from the fine detail, he could blag a good history. He could bang on about the holidays in America, the businesses he'd set up, the – but there Joe stopped stuttered, and eventually stopped. He couldn't think of anything else. It rang fake, every word of it.

The rage hit him. Who was he kidding? He choked even trying to blag himself. He'd had five years living on the street, two turns in prison, twenty years as an addict. You can't hide what that does to you with a suit and a haircut. He wouldn't last five minutes. He could see the smiles fading, the frowns, the smug gets starting to mock, the jeers starting, till they ran him out of the place.

Sick to his stomach, beginning an anxiety sweat, he got off Facebook fast. Stupid, stupid, digging that up. When would he learn?

The kid in the room upstairs started blasting drill out from some antique sound system. Joe dug his head back into his pillow and tried to go back to sleep.

. . .

The day passes quietly enough, but it's about waiting, getting ready. This evening is a big evening. New Year's Eve is the biggest night of the year, it's a given, any kid on the pull knows that, and Joe is still very much a kid on the pull, even though he should have long learned his lesson, but where else is he going to find the woman he's been seeking for the past forty years?

And he's right, it's going to be great because at ten past seven the pub is already rammed. He gets past the bouncers without a second look, which makes a change, and from the first step inside the glee bursts out of him at the full-body blast of the crowd. The Irish girl is behind the bar, Jamie is next in line to be served so it's perfect timing, the jukebox is playing *I Feel Free* by Cream, top tune from way back to get him in the mood, and Rob is working on three girls by the window who are laughing and flicking their hair.

He bares his teeth at these six hours of pleasure that's his. He's saved for weeks so he'll get a couple of drinks from Jamie, they'll get over to Rob and the girls, have a laugh. There's one girl each and they're fit, things will be good.

He gets his first pint down and the jokes come in. Endless gags, the lagers fizzing in his brain, him bouncing off Jamie and Rob, the three of them doing the old routine, but they're on fire tonight, the other two are faster than him but even so he's well on form too and he's hanging on in there, he's got a good few sparks in him, he's leaping and jumping with them, and everyone is laughing so hard at the bar and the Irish girl is laughing with him while she serves the crowd, she's appallingly beautiful and her smile jabs at the need in him so hard it wounds, yet she's laughing so much at his jokes he can't get it wrong, it's like playing pool with each ball on rails to the pockets, like ten-pin bowling with the bumpers up.

Later and two flash twenty-five-year-olds have pulled the flicky-hair girls, and the Irish girl is off down the other end of the packed bar so it's more lagers and shots and then a few wines because you have to don't you it's New Year's.

Later and it's gone to shit. The music's too loud and the crowd's thinned out and the Irish girl is huddled in a corner with Jamie who's smiling a filthy smile and whispering in her ear, and Rob's AWOL, gone off hunting with that blank look in his eye, but it could still be OK because at least Joe's got himself huddled up in a corner too, and even if it's not the Irish girl it's the remaindered flicky hair girl, left behind by her better looking mates. She's definitely not so clever up close, but she'll do. But something's off. Too much booze maybe. Whatever it is he can't talk no more, his tongue's too thick. His lines stopped landing a while back, she's trying to keep it going on her own but she's getting bored. He knows he shouldn't have got on the Kraken but he can't see an obvious moment when he should have stopped drinking; it was one long conveyor belt to this point.

He tells her how he's being haunted by the Cross; she says yeah OK but it's obvious she thinks it's a line and really he just wants to shag her. He surprises himself because he did, but he doesn't want to now, that would take him away from the Cross, now all he wants is to talk to her, why can't they just talk why does sex always come in they might really love each other if they could just get to know each other first.

Later and he's on his own by the toilets. He should have eaten before he came out, not saved his money for the booze, stupid, so stupid after all these years' practice, how can he still mistime it so badly? And the music is banging on his head and his stomach is turning over and he's sweating and he can't hear properly but now he thinks he can hear bells ringing and everyone is kissing everyone else except him and everything's aching and he feels he's got the flu of a thousand years, a flu from the tomb, an Egyptian flu, a flu from back before history. He aches so bad and now everywhere he looks is light and blur and jagged colours and the kissing has stopped and the faces are coming and going and they're full of fear and sharp teeth and the people are hungry and there's a rush coming and they'll swarm at him and fall on him and tear him apart and the mouths will feed on him and he'll be done and that's going to be it, once and for all, finally the end of him, is this all he came to?

Later outside in the cold and the air is biting at him, and he's down on his knees in mud, and he's sprawling and scrabbling for his money. He knows he's miles from the pub now, but it's even more miles home to the hostel and he's put his fists in his pockets to find what cash he has left, see if he has enough to mumble his way to a kebab, a strip club, a cab home, a car to a new life, a way out, some hope, but he's only left with coins and they slip through his fingers, jump away from him into the dark, land in the mud.

He'd bent down, couldn't reach them, tipped forward onto his knees. It's ice cold through his jeans, but it's only mud it'll warm up soon anyway who cares. Then he's collapsing forward, smack onto his hands, plashing about in the slop, now he's fallen he wants to stay there, even though the ice in the mud is killing him and he's panting and he lets out a sob because it's not that comfortable and his legs are cold and his belly's getting in the way and there's such a long walk home and it all hurts so bad. He lifts his head, realises he's by the side of the church, and moans, 'not again', because up above him is a big banner – it's got Bear Grylls on it for some mad reason which defeats him entirely – and red next to it hanging like blood in the night is the biggest cross of all.

In the morning Joe would be sober, and he'd look back at this moment in disbelief and fear, but for now he's too drunk to do anything but groan. This cross has got the killing grip on him so he groans good, groans deep and low and agonised, groans in pure, shameless terror of the light cloaked in dark and the infinite and final knowledge of a newly birthed yet eternally patient world of love that calls him out of himself.

3
THE WIND IN THE TREES

The wind plundered the Scots pines above their heads as they ran. They raced along the towpath and the branches bowed and swayed, the needles in motion in a slow-rolling sigh. Coniston water lapped black and icy at the jetty, but Sean Garner was on fire, chasing his son Callum along the lakeside path to the second mile post, and, subtly, letting him win.

He arrived second, pleased he still had it in him to beat this 28-year-old, who, even with his illness, was a fierce competitor. He high-fived Callum, who, flushed and grinning with his victory, turned to jog back to the car. As he went, he threw out a winner's challenge to his old dad: 'Last one back to the car washes up for mum'.

'No chance. It's your turn and you know it!' Sean yelled after him.

Sean was watching the pines. The motion of the trees was compelling, and disturbing. The rushing force that shook these enormous branches was invisible, came from who knows where, yet produced such dramatic results. And then he saw it happen. A high-up branch, rotten inside no doubt, pulled too far by the wind, finally gave up. It splintered free, toppling downwards, breaking a slow-motion path through the foliage, coming to a stop lodged in a fork where it would rest indefinitely. The trunk left behind wore a flash of raw yellow. Sean knew the sap would bead soon, sealing off and protecting the tree against the rest of the winter, but he still didn't like it. That healing would be too small. The outline of the tree was spoiled for this coming season, and for many years to come.

More upset than he expected to be, he turned to follow Callum.

He loved running with his son. It had started when Callum was six and wanted Sean to time him as he raced from tree to tree in their garden. It had gone on through training for track events, through athletic clubs after school, through the years away, and had lasted till now, when Callum was 28, and a doctoral student at Glasgow University, studying something important to do with organic chemistry which Sean accepted he would never understand.

Home for the holidays, Callum and his younger sister Billie usually brought life, energy and wholeness. Yet this Christmas Sean had felt something more fractured about both children. Their happiness was brittle, their focus split, they were both more subdued. They were both rowing in a way they hadn't done since they were teenagers. Callum disapproved of Billie's new boyfriend Thomas for being too possessive, and Billie disapproved of Callum in general. Christmas Day, usually joyful, had been particularly scratchy. Rebecca had been combative over cooking the lunch, at sea in her new kitchen although she'd never admit it. One oven was too hot, the other too low, and when she burned the gravy and discovered Billie had forgotten to buy the cranberry sauce all hell let loose, leaving Billie shut down into silence. Callum had just been moody throughout. As the day had gone on a cord of irritation had tightened around them. The tension only built, pulling tighter, and thinner. As the afternoon rolled on into the evening and the wine came out Sean felt more and more detached from them all. The kids' constant checking of their mobile phones was aggravating, the escalating bickering between them less and less endurable, and the board games interminable. They all felt it. Billie gave up first and went to bed to call Thomas. Callum and Rebecca followed soon after, because without Billie the whole dynamic, bad as it was, had evaporated. Sean had ended the day alone, watching an old film on through midnight into Boxing Day as the house settled. Despite his family in the bedrooms above his head, his family home of twenty years around him, he had felt the noise of the family turn into solitude, the solitude turn into loneliness, until he was abandoned, derelict, lost in a rubble-strewn landscape.

He already knew there was something wrong with him. On the outside he was warm, energetic, and (perhaps too) competitive, but there was a vacuum at the heart of him, and there had been for years. However, this sharp peak of self-pity was new. He had told none of it to Rebecca. What could she do? And it would incentivise an already painful situation. Her latest course was an Open University Introduction to Psychotherapy, and she had been testing her new diagnostic ideas on Sean in an alarmingly energised way. Protecting himself from the unsettlingly accurate intrusion, he sabotaged each questionnaire as it came, and fabricated an inner life of happy abundance in the free-writing experiments. But keeping consistent was tricky work, and from the increased puzzlement on her face as she worked out his latest results it was clear the wheels of his fraud were coming off. He thought it was her pushing and probing that was bringing him down. He wished she had stuck with the dressmaking. Or the Roman History. Or the lake-swimming.

. . .

It finally came out soon after they got back from the run. Billie picked on Callum once too often, and Callum snarled back at her, and Rebecca yelled at them both with a note of frustration which was far deeper than the squabble in front of her.

Sean sat them down and demanded to know what was going on, and so became party to what the others knew already. Callum's girlfriend Jess was pregnant, but Callum didn't want to be a dad, didn't actually want to be with her. In fact, he didn't want to go back to Glasgow. In fact, he wanted to jack all it in and come home to his old bedroom 'to rethink'.

Hurt at being kept out a conversation which had been in play for weeks, Sean surprised himself by keeping calm. Which was good because he was suddenly furious. With Callum mainly. The way he was slouching in his chair made him look sulky, far too young to be having this conversation. He was acting like he'd done the hard bit in bringing it out into the open, and now he was going to sit back and let everyone else solve it for him. He looked bored, and Sean could swear he was about to reach for his phone. Then he remembered him lying on his back and screaming in Tesco because no-one would buy him an ice lolly. Like most two-year-olds there had been a phase of this, and Sean couldn't help smiling at the memory, so he asked his next question more softly than he might have.

'Do you love her?'

Callum shrugged, 'I think so.'

'Then marry her.'

'Dad! I've told you. It's just not an institution we want to be part of.'

Billie cut in, 'He's basically making her get an abortion because he can't make a commitment. He's pathetic.'

Rebecca was furious, 'Billie, please! It's a huge step to get married.'

'It wasn't too huge a step to make her pregnant.'

Sean couldn't believe it. 'An abortion? Is this true?'

That stung Callum, 'Of course it's not. Thanks Bill. Now shut up?'

Rebecca tried to soothe, 'We're discussing Callum's options, Will you please give him some space? It's very unlucky –'

'Oh yeah, having all that unprotected sex was real unlucky,' Billie said.

'Contraception wasn't only Callum's responsibility and I feel sorry for Jess, but it's Callum's life and we must respect his choice.'

Billie said, 'He isn't making a choice. He wants you to bail him out like he always does.'

Rebecca didn't back down. 'We're lucky we live at a time where there are simple ways to sort this out.'

'Have you booked it?' Sean said.

Callum was desolate. 'She won't have one. Whether we're together or not, she wants to have the baby. I can't believe it. I'm only 28. I'm not ready for this. Will you speak to her, Mum? I'm sure you can talk her round. She loves you.'

That startled Rebecca, 'I – er – yes of course.'

Billie was red-faced, 'You are so pathetic.'

Sean wasn't angry any more. Instead, he felt gigantic, and strong, and clear-headed. He knew without doubt he could help.

Sean stood up. 'Come outside Callum.'

'What?'

'I want to talk to you.'

'To say what?' said Rebecca.

Sean was gentle, 'You can't rely on your mum, Callum, this is down to you. Come on, lad. Let's get outside and straighten this out.'

. . .

They walked up the path to the bottom of the garden. Far away across the lake Sean could see Carron Crag striding away from them. He soaked up the dark green of the hills, the scatter of snow on the higher levels, and the deep blue above. On the run from his past, he had wanted to come to live here so much. He could remember the first time he had left Grimsby, on a school holiday to the Yorkshire Dales, and realised there were hills, even small mountains in the world. Tired of the coastal plains which stretched between the Wolds to the North Sea, tired of the big sky which domed the land whichever direction you looked, he had been hungry for variety, for a landscape that had something more human in it, a landscape with curves, and drops and corners, valleys and peaks. The fact none of that existed in North East Lincolnshire had added to the strange sense of deprivation which he'd carried through his childhood. His parents were poor, for sure, but that wasn't the point. It was the fact they lived poor that he had reacted to, and he had always told himself what pushed him away from Grimsby was the hunger for something more. It wasn't even money. He wanted to taste more of the beauty out in the world.

He had found a spot which fulfilled that hunger, and he had found a wife and built a business and bought a house. They had children and filled the house with an expectation of happiness. It should have been perfect, but it had been hard, harder than he could ever have expected. Though they lived surrounded by beauty, it had proved so difficult to grasp, so he and Rebecca had given up big ambition and hunkered down. Even then it had kept slipping away from him, and now his son was about to fall.

Sean stared at the skyline. He was sure of one thing: He couldn't let Callum damage his life by killing his baby.

He sat on the old bench, and looked at Callum, who was standing in front of him, uneasy and beginning to shiver. Sean took off his coat and handed it over.

'No, dad, I'm OK. You'll need it.'

'Take it. I'm fine.'

'Can we go in?'

Sean looked searchingly at Callum, who dropped his eyes.

'Come on. Sit.'

Callum struggled into the battered old Barbour, and sat down, careful to look out into the far distance.

'Parkamoor's clear today. We should go fishing.'

Sean took his time. 'Callum, I need to ask you this. It's something you should think about.'

Callum closed his eyes, knowing the worst was arriving. 'Go on?'

'What kind of man do you want to be?'

'Oh, what? Are you serious?'

'And what kind of father?'

'How should I know?'

'Haven't you ever wondered?'

'Of course I haven't. People don't do that sort of thing these days.'

'It's time you did. Tell me one thing though first. Honestly. Do you love her?'

Aghast, Callum fell silent. Sean looked at his son. He was wide-eyed, staring at the horizon, his face unformed and watery from this unexpected ambush. He was desperate for a chance to change the subject, yet Sean held on. There was far too much at stake.

In the kitchen Rebecca washed up, one eye on her husband and her son at the bottom of the garden. She was in agony.

Oh, Callum, my precious son, the child I bore. The son I dedicated to the future, what can you be thinking? Don't waste your strength on this woman.

She couldn't help it, she blamed Jess. Why didn't young

couples wait till they got married? Sean and she had waited – he had been surprisingly strong-minded – and that had made those first few years of their marriage bed so very sweet.

Even if they couldn't wait – and, Lord knows, no-one seemed to any more – there was something sharper there. Jess was a smart young woman, how could she not have taken any responsibility for contraception? There was no way on earth Rebecca would have been caught out with an unwanted pregnancy, so Rebecca had to wonder: had Jess trapped Callum?

She tried to bury the thought as supremely uncharitable. It kept returning. She would understand if Jess were trying to hang on to Callum. Jess's family were wealthy, so it wasn't money. It could only be to do with the life force within Callum. Her pride as a mother discounted, there was no avoiding it. He was so bright, driven, so full of light. Jess had to understand; he had much to do in life, he could help so many with his work, the last thing he needed was a drag on these crucial years.

A smart young woman, if she could sense his love for her was waning, might she take a secret step to get on board his ship as it sailed? Jess was smart, no question, but she was young. Too young to know that once love had switched into withdrawal – and Rebecca knew her boy, knew what he felt for Jess was surely on the wane – this joint voyage could only be a shipwreck.

She watched Sean and Callum talk and hoped against hope he could do something. That soon she'd see Callum walk back up the path, happy, settled and fortified, with a winning strategy to win Jess round.

So when they got up and headed away off into the woods, her stomach knotted. She hung up the tea towel and went to sit by the fire. Billie was in her bedroom, talking to her boyfriend, so Rebecca tried to read, but her mind was far away, out in the woods with her son, the love of her life, as he made the decision of his life so far.

When they clattered back into the porch, they were both shivering with the cold, but they had the weighty air of men to whom something momentous had happened. It was clear they had decided something out there, and what they had decided had brought them peace.

It relieved Rebecca. She knew she could rely on Sean, in the end, to do right. She waited to be told, happy even to call Jess when Callum was ready.

Later that evening, and Sean worked at his laptop in his study. He became aware Rebecca stood at the door of his study.

'Hey love, how's it going?'

Her voice was quiet, 'What did you say to him?

'Rebecca?'

'He's just told me he's going to marry her.'

'But that's great!'

Sean had a blaze of pride. He was proud he'd known the right things to do. Pleased he'd kept calm, and strong, and led Callum into making the right choice. Delighted that he had inspired his son and kept him safe and on the path. That his life's wisdom had saved the situation. That he'd been a good father.

He looked at her, expecting congratulations for a peaceful resolution. 'Isn't it?'

'He's going back up to Glasgow tomorrow to ask her,' she said.

'Oh, that's incredible.'

Rebecca took a step into the study, and the light from his desk lamp caught her eyes, and he could see they were wet.

She shook her head. 'He doesn't love her enough for that.'

'He loves her. He's just scared. I get it. It's a big deal. But he'll be OK.'

'He's too young!'

'We were 22!'

'That's the rest of his life gone phut. He'll be tied to her forever. And the poor baby, if its parents feel like that. What the bloody hell did you say to him?'

'It's between us. And it'll stay between us.

'Seriously?'

She waited. Then she saw how he had set his face, the determined squaring of his jaw.

When she spoke, her voice was bleak with pain, 'I'll never forgive you for this.'

'Rebecca –'

'Never.'

She went. The study door closed behind her and, for the second time in a week, there seemed nothing left to connect them.

Yet, despite everything, Sean knew that wasn't the end. Whatever happened, it was never the end, and he knew how it would play out too. Cold, grey silence, then a stuttering back into life with a row or two, and then at some stage in the next week things would settle again to something more endurable.

He turned in his chair, got up to look out the window. It was a clear night, and the stars were bright over the dark hills across the valley. There had been such joy at their wedding. The sunshine and the new suits and haircuts, the dresses, the people he hadn't seen since college. The sheer pleasure of finding Rebecca there at his side at that season of his life, at a point where he felt the darkness could have swallowed him.

'Do you, Sean Garner, accept your salvation from this woman?'

'I do.'

The redemption of her open, upturned face, lovely in the surrender of her love for him.

'Do you accept she will lift you from your filthy sin and seat you high and unimpeachable in the light of her innocence and her faith in you will carry you until death do you part and beyond?'

'I do accept that so very very much please God thank you I do.'

He had done, for so long now, and he would no doubt go on doing forever.

The warmth of those memories brought him back to common sense, and the coldness he felt for her receded. Over the years he'd let her down so much. There was something in him that wasn't up to the challenge. He'd watched how the love in her face had hardened over the years into something far duller and more resigned. Yet, even after everything, he trusted their marriage. There was so much anger laid out between them, but she still had a practical faith in him to turn up, more or less, and he still had the strength to trust her, more or less, and, for all the arguments and the disappointments and the boredoms over the years they both still had commitment to the thing.

It was settled, done, never to be upset. Their bed made; they would lie in it till death indeed did them part.

His laptop pinged, and saw an email, from a name he'd long filed away: Terry Mullion.

He opened it with trepidation – what was the past doing lurching into his path?

It seemed that Terry lived in Canberra, and he had been trying to find Sean for a while. There was going to be a school reunion. Sean skimmed it, had a gut reaction of 'Not likely' and deleted it.

But then he sat back and thought about it. Why was he so anti? He'd never done a school reunion before. It could be interesting. Mick Bluff was bound to be there for one. He smiled. It would be great to see Mick. See if he had calmed down.

He pressed Ctrl-Z to undelete the message. Read it again more slowly.

A school reunion first weekend of May. In Grimsby, in the old school building, 7.30 till 9.30, pub afterwards.

It felt weird after what, forty odd years. But if not now, then when?

There'd be drinks, which would help.

Teachers? Not all good news, but most out to pasture by now? And he'd done pretty well for himself, so he'd hold his own if things got competitive.

Then again, what on earth was there going to be to talk about? Two hours could be a very long time.

It would either be amazing. Or hideous.

He followed the fast-weaving thread of his thoughts until he hit the inevitable knot. The last he'd heard, Corinne Ayr still lived in Grimsby.

What did that mean? Did living there make her more or less likely to go to a school reunion? If you lived in the same town, walked the same streets, were you bored stiff with the town and with everyone you still saw? Or would a reunion hold such a promise of old times that you would be curious?

He didn't know.

If she went, and if he, Sean went, what then?

He'd never actively look her up again. She was bound to be married, and he was a little scared of her anger, even now. But running into her at a school reunion? That would be OK, wouldn't it? Time heals all, and forty years is a whole chunk of time.

He opened up his old Facebook account for the first time in months. He'd never really used it, hadn't even added any photos, but it was sometimes useful for local groups. Corinne had changed her name when she married, but he found her in the end. She had locked off her account so he couldn't see much, but she had a profile picture.

He gazed for a long time, mystified, trying to see the shy teenager he'd known in the confident face of the middle-aged woman smiling at the camera. Slowly the past came forward to inform the current picture. It was still Corinne Ayr. And frankly she still looked great.

Would meeting her again be a good or a bad thing? There was no clue about any husband on the profile. Would going back there be a happy turn towards the light? Or a fierce unravelling into darkness?

He loved Rebecca, was committed to Rebecca, so he was surprised to recognise how, despite everything on his mind, this new unknown produced a long-forgotten spike of excitement in his belly.

4
THE LIGHT

It was the light off the faces that bothered him. Painted faces, somehow shedding light, on a sidewall of the church, hanging in a gap between two columns.

Joe had ended up in the soup kitchen a few times since New Year's Eve, but he couldn't get the hang of any of it. He certainly didn't believe in God, and, apart from Christmas Eve, he couldn't remember the last time he'd been in a church, but this one was nothing like. It was too loose. They cooked the meal out the back like you'd expect, but they turned it round so you sat at a table while the volunteers served you with the free food – which was good stuff – and you got to sit and eat it as though you were in a café. When you'd finished you could go through into the main church bit where there were sofas and bowls of sweets instead of dark wood pews and tatty old prayer books, and you could sit in the warm and eat the sweets and read the papers as long as you liked. Obviously, it was a trap, and they were looking for you to join the cult, but Joe was way ahead of them, so it was fine him being there for now.

In the quiet session after they'd served the food they'd sit around and chill. He had noticed the circles of chairs faced forward, so whatever you were doing, when you were in this part of the afternoon, one way or another you'd spend a fair bit of time looking up at the cross above the altar.

Some of the men would sit and look at it, most would get on with the *craic* of being off the streets somewhere warm with their mates and ignore it. It was only Joe that actively turned away from it. More and more he needed a break from the cross. But that had led him to the painting. Which had its own problems. It showed an old woman and a younger man walking together along a track through green fields. The young boy was carrying an earthenware pot on his shoulder. They were obviously happy to be with each other. The younger man was speaking, and the older woman was looking at him, smiling as she listened.

Joe sat and stared at the painting until he couldn't stand it any longer. The sun was setting behind them as they walked, the fields looked too green, the sky too blue. And the pot was spilling water all over the shoulders of the boy. He called over one of the volunteers, who was crossing with a plate of cakes.

'Oi.'

The volunteer turned, smiled, 'All right?'

Joe looked at the volunteer, looked at the cakes. Mr Kipling crap as always. The volunteer's name badge said 'Daniel'. He was just a boy, maybe twenty-two, and he looked so innocent. Joe didn't get it. Why did people like him who should have been out chasing skirt and smoking weed come down to hang out with old dossers like Joe?

'What's going on with that picture?'

'What do you mean?'

'Looks like Walt Disney? And how comes it's leaking?'

'Eh?'

'The bucket thing. Are they going to the well?'

Daniel turned to look at the painting and realised what Joe had seen. 'Oh, no, no, it's not water. It's from the Bible. Corinthians.'

'What's that?'

'It's a letter written by St Paul. This bit is about how we're like chipped pots. We get knocked down but not broken.'

'Chumbawumba isn't it?'

'What?'

'You know.' Joe sang a few lines of the old song, about getting drunk, getting knocked down, getting up again. It had meant a lot at one time, that song, but the volunteer didn't look like he recognised it.

Joe looked closer at the picture. He could see now that the jar was cracked, and what he had first thought was water running down the sides was actually a flood of light.

'What's happening with that jar then?'

Daniel hesitated, then chose his words carefully. 'There's a light inside us. It heals us where we hurt, then it shines through the broken places so people can see what happened.'

'You what?'

'Not a light light. It's God. The Holy Spirit. Inside us, if you believe in Jesus.'

Joe looked at the picture again. The way the woman was looking at the boy. The way the boy looked so young, and fresh and happy. It turned Joe's stomach.

Daniel sat on the arm of the sofa, 'The bloke who painted it is such a good artist. The way he's got it so real. You can feel the way they love each other.'

'Are you one of these Christians then?'

Daniel thought, 'Yeah. Yeah, I suppose I am.'

'Ah, for godssake.'

What was in him was growling out. It was only a hint of what there could be, but Daniel had clearly felt it already and Joe guessed he would be getting uncomfortable right about now.

Yup. Daniel stood up again, 'Can I get you a coffee?'

'You're all right, mate.'

'OK then.'

Daniel left the plate of cakes on the low table in front of Joe's sofa and headed off.

Joe watched him go, amused. He watched him cross the church, sit at the painting table, pick up a brush, talk to the street guy next to him.

Joe couldn't believe the painting table. An old girl set it up every week. She pulled out a box of paint brushes and put out pots of water and kids' painting sets, and every week homeless guys went over and painted with her. Joe had been coming three weeks, and every week there were more guys at the table, all busy painting more crap. Junior school stuff. Clumpy trees. Houses like dolls houses. Mountains with a thin line of blue sky above them at the top of the page. Just absolute rubbish. One guy sat there and painted his paper black every time. Joe had to laugh: every week for the last three weeks, a whole sheet of paper painted completely black. But the old girl didn't mind. She collected it up with the rest, the clumsy trees and childish pictures of houses. The scrawls in blue and purple, and the scary faces in garish yellow and red. The stick figures with guns and knives and blood dripping out, as well as the beautiful pale flowers from the young Indian kid. She talked about the rectangle of blackness like it was a real painting, and every week she'd come in, start the painting table up, and talk about Jesus.

But now, as he watched Daniel dab away at his piece of paper and saw how he listened to the guy sitting next to him rabbit on about something mad, Joe felt a pang of affection for him. Shaking off a sense of guilt, he got up and walked to the side of the church for a better look at the painting.

Close up the picture got powerful. The way the woman looked at the boy, it should have been too much, but it wasn't. He saw she had her hand on his arm. Just the lightest touch, guiding him along. Joe realised Daniel was right, whoever had done this was a good painter. He'd managed to get the light on the two figures, the light from the cracked pot, that somehow came out of them too, a light that shone out of their faces and their clothes, a light that changed everything, showed up any bad thinking as a lie.

'Hello there.'

Joe whirled, surprised someone had got close, and saw it was the head woman, the one who actually ran the drop-in.

'Hi, we've not met. I'm Shannon. I'm the curate here. I was wondering how you were getting on.'

That jagged hard in on Joe. He was taking free food from a soup kitchen and begging on the streets to pay for a skanky hostel bed. How did it look like he was getting on?

Something pulled Joe's gaze back to the picture. But Shannon didn't go away. She kept on standing there at his side.

After a while, Joe gave in, and turned to her. She had stopped smiling and was now watching him.

'We're glad you're here.'

'What?'

She kept on looking and waiting. He wanted to shove her away, get out from under her look. Anyone else, he would have decked by now, but you'd have to be a real crazy one to do that in a church. Nevertheless, she was properly pissing him off. When she looked at you, she seemed to look right into you. Like she could really see you. Like she could see how messed up and broken you were. There was such kindness in her face. But why didn't she say something? What was she waiting for? What was she looking at? Was she waiting for him?

Joe couldn't take it any longer. 'Ah, just sod off, will you?'

He turned his back on the vicar, got his bag, and left the church. Back on the street he lit a rollie and looked around him. The sky was blue, and it wasn't so cold as the morning had been, and he felt a lot better.

But that didn't last.

5
VALENTINE'S DAY

Corinne Ayr packed the blood pressure monitor and her testing kit into her health visitor's bag and watched Pat the Hat carry the tea tray through from the kitchen. Along with three mugs, a basket of warm croissants, and the milk bottle, it had a little vase of snowdrops and a gift in red paper. Pat put it on the coffee table in front of Rosie, his wife.

'Here you go, love. Happy Valentine's Day.'

Rosie's face wrinkled in pleasure, but, aware of her manners, she turned to her guest before she opened her present.

'Isn't he sweet?'

She offered Corinne the basket of croissants. 'He makes these himself. Did Paul get you owt nice, love?'

Corinne found it so easy to lie these days. 'The usual, you know. Chocs and a book I wanted.'

'Aw, lovely.'

Rosie unwrapped her gift: two old *Blake's 7* VHSs. She couldn't hide her pleasure.

'Thanks, love. We can start these tonight.'

Pat grunted his assent, and, groaning at his knees, got down to poke at the smoky log fire.

Rosie read the back of the VHS boxes, and Corinne sipped her coffee and watched the two of them, trying, once again, to work out how they were so happy when they had so little to shout about.

Pat was overwhelmingly fat. Overwhelmingly filthy. Not overwhelmingly bright, but generous, welcoming, and sublimely good hearted. Always a black beanie over his thinning grey ponytail, he wore oily denim, wide belt, tee shirts, and boots. Rosie was small, skinny, chatty, with long grey roots in her long dark hair. She wore old cheesecloth, battered gypsy skirts with beads and glass stitched on, loose knit woollen jumpers and a stack of bangles and necklaces.

Corinne had never met anyone who disliked either of them.

'When did you two get together, then?'

Rosie looked at Pat for confirmation.

'I was fifteen, Pat was 17, so that's what, oh, too long ago now.'

Pat threw another log on and stood up. 'It were 1971. At a Country Joe and the Fish gig at the Winter Gardens. A proper long time ago.'

He saw Corinne had packed her bag and was reaching for her coat. 'I've finished the Triumph. Fancy a look before you go?'

Corinne never wanted to leave Pat and Rosie, so she gladly followed him out the front room, along the dark, stone-flagged corridor, out through the split-panelled Dutch door and on into the back yard.

After the heat and smoke from the fire it was fresh outside. Far away across the coastal plain she could see the Triton Knoll wind farms sitting in a thin strip of salt blue sea. The wind gusted in her face, sharp, and pinching, and it was good to get into the lean-to at the back of the cottage.

Refusing to take benefits, they lived off what Pat could do for other bikers. The workshop was lit by bare bulbs, and there was no furniture apart from two car seats. Pictures of motorbikes torn from magazines covered the walls, and there was an old stone sink in one corner. The magic came from the grotto of classic bikes. Immaculate Harleys, old Nortons, Triumphs, a field of shiny chrome. Wheels, chains, handlebars like antlers hanging, rusting frames in one corner, a stack of old parts in the other.

Pat could fix most machines, but his proper gift was his painting. He took requests and made them his own. Most bikes that left the workshop were newly decorated. Works of art on their fuel tanks, on the forks, on the engine cowls. Naked women in thigh boots wrestling with serpents. Hairy barbarians slaughtering dragons. Winged horses, demons' heads, ancient runes for speed and war.

Pat showed Corinne the Triumph. Covering the fuel tank were a serpent and an eagle, locked in dreadful battle over an amber sea, a sun of pure gold rising behind. It was savage, and beautiful.

Rosie came in behind them and slipped her hand into Pat's as they looked at the bike. She caught Corinne's appreciation and smiled. 'He's dead clever, isn't he?'

Pat put his arm round Rosie and gave her a squeeze. 'Give over, will you? What do you reckon then Corinne?'

'I think it's lovely. Just lovely.'

Pat and Rosie were her last call of the day, so Corinne drove home along the coastal roads. Twenty miles across flat, waterlogged countryside in the gathering dusk, back roads all the way, then on into the outskirts of Grimsby. After the best part of an hour, she pulled up outside their bungalow and opened the car door, the wind whipping it out her hand and bending it back, threatening to pull it off its hinges. She climbed out with her bag, battling the wind to close the door, getting a clear taste of salt spray as she did so. This grey blast had swept across the bleak plains of Northern Europe, come all the way from alien Russia, and now it was hitting Corinne and her house.

Paul had given half of everything to his wife and kids when he got together with Corinne, so the last six years had been tight. They'd ended up buying a tiny box of a bungalow off Taylor's Avenue, a long, mostly treeless road of 1960's housing which ran north-east to the North Sea. Corinne didn't mind. There was no glamour in any of it, but she'd realised a long time ago that glamour was for kids. They had a freshly painted front door, smart PVC windows, and a little boat in the drive under a tarpaulin. The small garden was nice and tidy, with cropped plants obedient and small in the scrupulously weeded beds. Low privet hedges faced the road, grown as markers rather than obstacles, for who would have the bad manners to intrude?

Pat and Rosie had given Corinne renewed hope as she walked in through her front door. But there was no need for hope. There was no card, there were no flowers, no home baking, no gifts in red paper for her.

She got out of her Health Visitor's uniform, showered, then went into the kitchen and got on with making tea.

She and Paul spent the evening together as usual. Beans on toast at the table, her telling him about Pat and Rosie. She'd had an email about a school reunion and tried to talk about going. She got non-committal interest from him, which quickly turned into his battles with both sets of neighbours, and from there to pushing through the planning permission for a higher garden wall, whatever anyone else on the bloody street thought. Then he went through to wash up while she put the telly on.

They didn't talk. He read his book; she watched a Corrie double episode, *Bake-Off* on catch-up, then the news, depressing as ever. The evening wore on, and the hands on the clock on the fireplace wound each slow hour on, and she got more and more cold, more and more angry.

At 10.30 he got up. 'Right then.'

He went out to the hallway, on into the bathroom. She rummaged around on the TV. Nothing to watch, but she'd have to find something as she wasn't going to lie next to him while he snored.

She heard the rustle of him getting into the bed and for a moment she felt grey, washed away. Memories of a time when she was young, when love was like fresh water, came over her. She had a sense of how much she had lost, and she thought she was bound to cry.

But then he called through, 'Corinne?'

'What?'

'You coming to bed then?'

'In a minute.'

She waited. What did he want?

'It's Valentine's Day you know.'

She raised an eyebrow. Finally.

'Is it? I'd forgotten,' she said.

'You little liar. Well, I never forget.'

'You did last year.'

'No, I never. But you wasn't being very good last year.'

She frowned. No way was she going back over that. She let it pass. She continued to search for something to watch.

'Cos?'

'What?'

'I went shopping at the weekend. Over in Hull. I brought summat back for you.'

She let that sit for a moment while she thought it through.

'Is it nice? I'm not having it if it's not nice.'

'You'll find out.'

She smiled, despite herself, and said nothing. They were

playing their game now, and she knew he would be smiling too.

He called again, 'I should think you'd say it were very nice.'

She bit her lower lip, and waited, shy now, even here on her own.

'Don't be too long, there's a good girl.'

'We'll see. I might find a good film.'

But a warmth hit her. Who was she kidding, trying to keep annoyed with him? It was a sparse, hard love, but it was theirs.

She couldn't wait any longer. Feeling once again that electric mix of excitement and fear she got up, put the lights out, locked the front door and went to the bedroom for her Valentine's treat.

6
EATING FOR FREE

Joe had been going back to the church more often. He told himself it was for the free food. In fact, it was because it was the least scary alternative. He had started to hear, not voices exactly, and not with his ears, but the effect was the same. Constantly with the same message: 'Get back in there'.

Besides the voices, he'd started having nightmares about dogs. One dog in particular, to the point that he was getting nervous about sleeping.

The nightmare was an old one, back from his childhood, and he hated to go through it again. It was always the same. Him, as a little boy, eating beans on toast at the back table in his old home. He was alone, and the table was pushed up against the glass door into the front room. On the other side of the glass door was another identical table. At that table, sitting upright like a human, using a knife and fork to eat the same tea as Joe, was a large, smooth-furred dog. Every time Joe lifted his fork and took a bite, the dog did the same. Every time he took a sip of tea, the dog did the same. A sense of intense dread would drop on Joe as he realised the dog was mimicking his every move. In the dream Joe could keep eating for a while, but he always knew the dog was going to attack. Sooner or later the dog would leap down from its chair and run for the door. Joe would whimper and try to scramble down from his chair, but he was too slow, and the dog was too strong. It would run down the corridor, its claws clicking on the tiled floor, and run into the back room. It growled as it jumped, its dreadful teeth wet with slaver, drool dropping from its gaping mouth in thick ropes as it leaped up for Joe's throat.

First the cross, now the dog. So, after everything, now he was cracking up? But there was no arguing with the fact that the church was making him better. It was only on the days he'd been in there that the voices stopped, and he didn't dream about the dog, and he got peace of mind.

The first time he'd gone back to the church after walking out on Shannon he'd stood at the edges. Watching the street guys pick up their food, he couldn't join them. He felt bruised with awkwardness.

Then Shannon crossed the room and caught Joe's eye. Joe nodded, awkwardly waved her over.

'How are you, Joe?'

Joe buried his surprise that she knew his name. 'I wanted to apologise to you for last time. For being gobby.'

'Not a problem. It's fantastic to have you back. How have you been?'

Joe looked at her and couldn't see any sign she was putting him on.

'Not too good as it happens.'

'I'm sorry to hear that. What's been happening?'

'I, er … '

Joe didn't know where to go with it. He'd made a terrible mistake coming back in. What could he possibly say? That he'd spent the last five years making bad deals and thieving and blowing his money on booze and ketamine and lap dances? That he was doing pretty well thank you very much and having a real laugh until his best mate Ronnie had died last November completely out the blue and that he couldn't quite get past that? That there was this guy in Vauxhall who said when he found Joe he and his boys would cut Joe in half unless Joe had fifteen large for him in cash there and then. That he wanted some of what this bird Shannon had got? Please? Any of it? Just a piece of it? Cos if he even had a crumb of what this was, he absolutely knew he'd be able to go back out onto the street and sort himself out and get straight and get a job all that bollocks the same as ever. Please? How he needed it, Jesus Christ how he needed it, please God, he needed it.

Shannon waited. Did the eerie, silent, watching thing again. But this time Joe wasn't so freaked out. He saw more in Shannon's face. He saw tenderness, and concern, and compassion.

Joe welled up.

He couldn't help it, and he couldn't stop himself, and then he found he was openly crying.

Shannon stood by, and it embarrassed Joe. He wanted to turn away, but Shannon's face held no judgement, and anyway, who cared about being judged by this chick?

And Joe cried, and he cried, and it got worse and worse.

After a while Shannon spoke, 'Is it OK if I put my hand on your shoulder?

Joe nodded, and Shannon put her hand on his shoulder, and that did it. At the touch of her, the weight of her arm, her closeness, Joe started to howl. Really howl. Raw sobs and yells, tears sprouting and drenching his face.

Shannon led him to the back of the church, away from the guys, and in this semi-privacy Joe could let everything go. Crying replaced by coughing, and shaking, choking and shuddering, convulsing in his grief for … it turned out he didn't know what, exactly, but it felt fundamental, ancient, geological.

When he was done, and he had finished wiping the snot

away with his sleeve, Shannon asked, 'I'd like to pray for you. Would you mind?'

No chance. No taking advantage of him while he was down. 'No offence, mate. It's not my thing.'

Shannon considered him. 'You've been coming to a few services lately, haven't you?'

Joe shrugged, alarmed they had noticed this, 'Yeah, I sat in the back a couple of times. That's OK, isn't it?'

'Oh, yes, that's very OK. But look. Why don't you come to one of our groups? We run one on a Wednesday evening that I think you'd enjoy.'

'I don't know.'

'People get here at 7.00, and we serve food. Then it starts properly at 7.30. It's a kind of a course thing. It lets you talk about this more. You don't have to be a Christian to come. In fact, it's great if you're not.'

'Yeah, OK. Maybe. Let me see, OK?'

'Sure. No problem. But I do think you'd get a lot out of it.'

Shannon left him to it. Joe watched her go over to help pack up the tables and chairs. The faintest memory surfaced, the impression of a life from long ago. He had been part of a world like this once, a world when the people around him worked together. Where they didn't argue, and fight, get drunk, and stitch each other up and rob each other. Where they all had that clean look. He had to work hard to remember when, like grasping the thinnest smoke, and when he got it, it stunned him. He hadn't felt this since he was at junior school. That year he was ten. The year before his dad died.

He felt he might start crying again, so he looked round him at the church. He watched the volunteers packing away the chairs and tables, and how they laughed with each other. He saw how a few of the other homeless guys joined in, and then his gaze went beyond them, and he looked at the columns, the slabs of fluted grey stone which reached up and combined into high arches. He saw the painted plaster circles far above their heads which crowned each arch with flowers and angels. He looked up at the great stained-glass windows, made when people had time and care enough to spend on hand-painting intricate pictures on pieces of glass, and through which the sun was pouring onto his face.

And, of course, he looked up at the cross high on the wall at the front of the church. The fourth most simple thing in the world. The thing that was still appearing to him wherever he went.

Joe wasn't quite so bothered by it as he had been. It had stopped being so threatening. But more: in the constant appearances he was sensing the approach of something simple, and good. And simultaneously very complex. An approach which created a soft, unfurling desire for warmth, and closeness, and support.

Wednesday, seven o'clock. Why not? Besides, the way these suckers threw food at you, if he played it right, pretty soon he'd be eating for free all week.

7
CLOSING TIME

Five in the morning and the night had been hard in Walking Street. The bar girls' faces were pale and tired in the pools of light as they picked their supper off the food vans. Wasted and sweaty from the heat and the demands of the night, still they kept coming, circling the corners and the doorways, prowling in and out of the bars, always with a watchful eye for the next wealthy ex-pat. These guys weren't too hard to spot in Thailand: grey hair, sun-reddened Western faces, floral shirts tight over big bellies, and wallets that opened wide for the right smile.

The *Johnny l'Americain* bar doors were flung open onto the street, and there, bang centre, shaven-headed, wearing his favourite old *Triple Five Soul* vest and cargo shorts, with jacked-up muscles and beaten-up tribal tattoos, Mick Bluff cranked up the volume for the last set of his slot. Old school techno, late in the night now and a bit of a rarity round here, but it was what he loved, and it always got this crowd back up on its feet. He saw Rahul, the old Indian owner, looking at him. In a minute he'd tell him to turn it down, always fearful of having to increase his bung to the local police, but in the meantime, Mick could nudge it up another notch and keep on dancing in the booth.

Mick knew this was a good time. He was coupled up, so far as he ever got, and mostly happy. Mainly because he'd been smart enough to stay out the marriage trap. A mate of his had made the mistake of getting married last year. Six months in they found him in a pile at the bottom of his tower block. Pati, his inconsolable wife, said he had jumped from their condo balcony. She had told the stone-faced detectives how she had begged him to stop, but he'd been too determined. She showed how she had reached out for him while he was sitting there, yet he had pushed her away, and slipped off the balcony in front of her. When they'd calmed her down, she talked for hours: how poor Carlton had been so sad, how he kept on missing England and what he'd given up there to come here to Pattaya, and how, try as she might, she couldn't cheer him up.

Mick knew with certainty that Carlton didn't have a suicidal idea in his head. In fact, exactly the opposite – he was loving life. An overweight tax inspector out of Scarborough, Carlton had finally had enough of being bossed around by the government. He'd sold his house and flown business class out to Bangkok while he was young enough to have fun. He'd certainly enjoyed it, though not in the way he expected. He'd got his stomach stapled, lost a lot of weight, tried to party – which was how he'd met Mick – but his heart wasn't in it. He wanted something quieter, and that's where Pati came in. Carlton, silly sod, too vulnerable after ten years on his own, had fallen head over heels.

Mick guessed, and the stone-faced detectives would almost certainly know, that Pati's three brothers paid the couple a visit that night. Maybe for drinks on the balcony, more probably getting straight to the point, but either way Carlton wouldn't have seen it coming. The brothers would have left in a hurry after Carlton hit the pavement, leaving

Pati time both to wash up the glasses, and get worked up and emotional for the police.

Except for Mick, no-one cared. Soon enough Pati would sell the condo, reassign his pension, and split the money between herself and her brothers. So long as they looked after the police, they wouldn't be too interested. Carlton was far underwater now, the waters breaking overhead, another ex-pat drowned in a foreign country where, whatever the size of his money clip, he'd never quite belong.

Mick hadn't married Amita, but he did kind of love her, despite everything. He'd tried not to, because that was how you went wrong. But you couldn't not like a woman who turned up regularly and slept with you every night, whether or not you wanted sex (and lately he wasn't so bothered, he just liked the company), who did your laundry, who cooked, cleaned, who made you laugh, dressed up good when you went out, who had a banter with your mates without stepping over any lines. He'd found her sitting in a bar six years back, and he was still paying her 40,000 Baht a month to keep her on board, so in theory he could pull the plug any time, but she'd outsmarted him in one way: Florence, their daughter, was going to be five soon, and no doubt about it, leaving her was going to be hard.

Shift over, back up in his rented condo on the 15th floor, Mick looked in on Amita. She was sleeping in bed with Florence in her arms. Frowning at a dream, Florence wriggled a little, and Amita gathered her up in her sleep without waking. Even at forty Amita was a good-looking woman, and the two of them made a real sweet picture.

Not wanting to get caught up in all that he opened a beer, grabbed his robe and went out on the balcony to think. This was the morning it was supposed to happen, and he had to be sure. He had a woman who would stick around, his own little daughter, a decent place to live, and all the nightlife he could handle – what was there not to like?

The opal sea far below threw back a thousand trembling fragments of the early morning light, and for a long moment he wavered. This place, this life, it was beautiful. Maybe he could move up country with Amita and Florence, get away from the city, get away from her family. Maybe even buy some land and hire the guys to work it.

Then a cool breeze from offshore hit him. He pulled his robe around him and got real. This wasn't his country, never would be – and Florence and Amita? On hire. He could kid himself that Amita genuinely liked him – and maybe she did – but she'd always been clear: without her monthly payment, she wouldn't stick around too long. Mick was 58, so 60, 65 were round the corner, and even with the best sniff in the country, how long would he have the pace to keep on fronting up the DJ booth? More to the point, with all the sniff he'd been taking lately how long could he keep out the hospital? His days on the Saudi oil fields had left him with a bankroll, but they'd also given him injuries which meant big medical bills down the line. It's a cliché, but it's no less true for all that: you get to a certain age, you can't help realising how much you love the NHS.

So, even without this latest thing, the writing was on the wall, and he knew it. It had been a banging party, but the sun was rising, the street cleaners were sweeping round the casualties, and the kids were coming up harder and faster than ever. He'd had a great run, held on longer than anyone else he knew, but there was no fooling himself any more: he'd had his lot. Time to get packed up, and get off home, Mickey boy.

The breeze was cool, comforting, and he crashed out on the lounger. When he woke up the condo was empty: Amita had taken Florence to nursery. He had a couple of hours before she was back, as she'd always go to the gym with her friends after that. He wondered what she'd be saying about him and decided he didn't want to know.

He wandered through the condo, had a bite at the breakfast she'd laid out for him – he had to smile, she would keep trying to feed him this healthy crap – and went into their bedroom. He saw Florence had left her teddy behind, dropped down the side of the bed. She wouldn't be happy she'd done that. He'd bought her a teddy because in his view you couldn't be a kid without one, and at the moment she took it everywhere she went. He picked it out and put it on her little bed where she'd see it as soon as she ran in. He remembered how she looked in her red pyjamas. How her thick black hair got so tangled. How she stretched her arms out for a cuddle when she was sleepy. How he'd scoop her up and feel her go to sleep on his chest. How he put her to bed and tucked her in with her *Masha and the Bear* cover. How the skin on her face looked so perfectly smooth, fresh, untouched, like it was lit from the inside with her love for him.

So anyway, yeah, this latest thing. Had to be done. He found a pen and a Post It pad and wrote her a note:

Your a good lass Flo, be good and do well at school and look after your mam. Your daddy loves u and will think about u lots on his travels.

He pulled out his bag. Leather, brass and ornamental bronze trim, handmade by a guy up the coast. Mick enjoyed the good stuff, and in Thailand he could afford it. It had never been like that in England for him, but that was no longer an issue. This latest thing, the Facebook thread about the school reunion, was the final straw. It had delivered a call from an old, persistent spirit. It had sent him spinning into a sea of memory, and his own waters were closing overhead fast. But, unlike Carlton, he wasn't sinking. He was going home, and these were the waves that would save him.

He grinned as he considered what he had in mind. Nice bit of fun. Hit the clubs in Istanbul, then on for a few weeks with mates in Düsseldorf, see if that stacked up as well as they reckoned. Then a flight to Stansted, pick up a nice car, hit the A1, A46 all the way back home. See his mam for the first time in a good while. Bit of Grimsby fish and chips, look round the old town and a night out or two, then the main event: the school reunion. Yeah, it would be interesting to see Sean, but that was definitely secondary to seeing Corinne. Sean had had his chance and blown it way back, so it was over to him now. It was probably not going to be that straightforward – most things weren't, Mick had found – but this was last-chance territory so they were all going to have to be real about it.

Mickey Bluff and Corinne Ayr, eh? After all these years, finally make or break.

He put on his headphones, turned up the sounds, started to pack.

What's a forty-year gap between you and the woman you never forgot?

8

ATTACKED ON THE ROAD

Though it tested him severely, Joe kept on with the course. Obviously, it was a conversion thing, and obviously the whole point was to brainwash him and get him to say 'Yes sir' to Jesus. If it hadn't been for the constant visions and general weird stuff that was happening to him, he'd have had real trouble keeping a straight face as they told him some of the more out-there rubbish.

In fact, he did walk out of the first session. Well, he tried to. He was sitting in the group, waiting for things to kick off, feeling like a spare part. He'd not been so much on edge for a long time. There was something weird about this church. The way they threw everyone together and expected it not to go wrong. So on his left he was being ignored by the middle-class women talking about school fees, and on his right he was being ignored by two northerners bantering about the footie. A crustie-looking kid drooped unhappy in the corner, and the leader of the group was sitting in silence opposite him, looking vacant, obviously thinking he'd rather be anywhere else.

He thought, forget this, got up, and headed out of the church, on his way to the wine shop. But he got no more than a hundred yards down the road before the voice in his head exploded at him, 'Get back in there!'.

That was when Joe realised things had changed. Two months previously that voice would have freaked him out, but now it was no more than what he expected. He did what he was told. He turned around, and went back in, put up with feeling bad, and got through the first session.

Once he was over feeling stupid and imagining what his mates would say, it wasn't so bad. He'd done a few stints in AA, been in full-on residential rehab twice in his life, so the process wasn't too strange. They showed you a video about Jesus, and then they talked about it. The talking was surprisingly familiar. He was used to sitting round while people shared the most God-awful stories about their lives, and, you name it these people had been through it, even (especially) the middle-class women. Abusive grandparents, husbands, children. Rejections, drugs, affairs, deaths, beatings, robberies, self-harms. He found when it was his turn, he could talk on the things he'd been through pretty simply, so he ran through a few bits and pieces. Secretly he was a little disappointed: for a church group they weren't very shockable. No-one disapproved, even when he described the lap dancers and the scams he and the boys got up to in London.

The first real turning point came three weeks in. He wasn't sure how it happened, but he got talking about Ronnie. How they'd met five years back, how they weren't loved up, but were amazing mates, like she was the best kind of sister. How they'd had such a laugh, and how she was the only one who gave him somewhere to hide when things went bad with the gang. He described how he had bought the pills that Ronnie had used that night back in October, and how the gang had got the dealer to spike the package without him knowing. How the cleaners had found her on the floor in the kitchen in the morning, and how the ambulance had taken forever to come.

He stopped crying and finally looked up at the group. Expecting contempt, even disgust, he was prepared to leave. It shocked him to see how they were all listening, and how one or two of them had tears in their eyes too. One of them explained how when you said you believed in Jesus, everything you had done wrong up till then got forgiven.

'Everything?' Joe had asked.

'Everything', they had assured him, their faces open and vulnerable.

'Everyone gets this? Doesn't matter what they've done?'

'Everyone gets this. For free '

He nodded, tried not to let on how much he wanted to laugh. Scammers always came on with an offer like that.

Yet he was slowly realising that the leaders genuinely believed in magic. They kept on bringing it back to God, and Jesus, and this weird thing he couldn't get a hold of called the Holy Spirit.

'You are loved.'

'Loved by who?'

'Jesus. Our Lord God.'

The thing within Joe growled out, 'You are having a laugh, yeah?'

'You are loved, you are loved.'

The leader turned to the rest of the group, 'What does anyone else think?'

People shrugged. The unhappy kid in the corner started talking more about pyramids. And aliens. And so it went on. They'd watch a video, or hear a speaker, and then have cake and a coffee, and then they'd have a talk. Joe had a good few questions, but there was never a straight answer. Everything got deflected. Except there was always someone else saying something surprising, 'When I talk to Jesus …' Or 'I felt God saying to me … '

Soon Joe clocked more of the people in the group were Christians than Shannon had let on, but instead of feeling ambushed, or tricked, he got curious. Why did they waste time in the group if they'd already got the message? He'd look around at the different faces, hear the weirdest stories of times they 'met' God, and try to work out how these different people could all be mad in the same way.

Week by week some of the non-Christians dropped out, including Pyramid Kid, but Joe hung on. They gave him a Bible, and he even started trying to read it. He battled the old-style language, but when they showed him how there were phone apps with modern translations, he finally got going.

One night he stayed up till three in the morning reading a book in the Bible called 'Luke'. It told the story about Jesus that Joe recognised from when he was little. Reading the book, a feeling dawned on him of what it must have been like. How it must have felt if you were in that stable, in the temple, going around in that gang of mates. How weird if it were happening to you. How incredible to see Jesus heal people. How exciting it must have been.

'You are loved, you are loved, you are loved!'

The constant message from the group – and it was dynamite. It reminded him of his mam. She'd died maybe fifteen years back and Joe hadn't seen her for years before that. He never went to the funeral, didn't see the point. But those three words took him straight back to Monday mornings when he was tiny, before he'd gone to school even. He'd go out in the back yard after breakfast. He'd be playing with his football, the birds would be tweeting, he'd sit on the step with a biscuit and watch the clouds. Later on, his mam would put the washing out, and then maybe he'd go and have a look at the dog violets she liked to plant. When it got later, the smell of cooking would come out the kitchen window, then she'd call him in for dinner and they'd have bubble and squeak.

All the time at the course he kept wanting to cry, and

that's what kept him coming back. Something was untangling inside him.

Thing was his mam was only nice when he was little. By the time he'd got to junior school things had changed. She'd smell of wine by the time he got back from school, be drunk as a rat by six, shouting at him and his old man by seven, passed out and snoring wherever she fell by eight.

He and Eddie never talked about it and looking back Joe reckoned they had both just hoped she would miraculously straighten out. No chance. Every now and then she'd have a quiet spell, but before long she'd start back on the wine, and then hit the vodka. Eddie would empty her bottles down the sink, which caused battles every time, but she was clever, and there was always a new hiding place, and the war went on.

Even now it twisted at Joe's belly to think of that, let alone the yelling and the beatings and the apologies he took from her in the years after his dad died.

The first time he suspected there was more to the church stuff than met the eye, that it could be real, was one Wednesday evening while he was on his way to the meeting. At six pm he was on the bus on his way into town along the coast road from the hostel. The bus was packed, as per, but he'd got a seat, and he was minding his own business, reading the Argus. The bus stopped by an office complex and a load of young women spilled on. They'd been drinking, and they were laughing and talking loudly. They were office workers, late twenties, early thirties, top end, looking great. There was one just his type. Bit posh, but not too posh. Quietish, but you could see she liked a laugh. Great skin and hair and looked real smart. His dream type, to be fair. The kind he fell for far too fast. And who never showed him more than polite interest.

The women were noisy, talking about some conference

they'd been at all day, and a faint pang of jealousy hit Joe. How come some people got jobs where they could drink with attractive women all day? The closest he'd been to that was the mugs of midnight tea with that security guard when they were watching that derelict office block in Stepney. He'd bring in a flask full of tequila and some mixers and they'd have a wild time all shift. She'd tease him about how old he was getting, and he'd prove he wasn't old at all by chasing her round the dusty board room, and the evenings would pass very pleasantly indeed. But that was hardly the same as suits and white wine, and an expense account you could blow at the bar.

The office women had quietened down. He looked over, wondering idly if he could catch an eye, but it was pointless: their gaze skated over him without friction.

The old Joe would have felt bad that he was invisible to them, and annoyed how, even when he was younger, they would never have looked at someone like him. If he was in the mood, back then he might even have followed them off the bus and had a go anyway, crash and burn, why not? The new Joe couldn't say he wasn't bothered but for some reason watching them wasn't the priority it would have been even a few weeks ago. The fact of what they looked like seemed to make less of an impression, create far less of a need in him.

He went back to his paper. It was going to be a long journey. The bus was crawling along the coast road, and for a time he bounced between reading and looking out at the rain on the windows and the black of the sea on his right. But it was peaceful enough, the old man sitting next to him chuntered peacefully into his shopping bags, and time seemed to slip away.

At one point the bus stopped dead. There were horns from ahead, and then a siren and blue lights from behind, as an ambulance squeezed past them into the gridlock.

He folded his paper, shut his eyes, tested whether he

could sleep, but more noise from the office women cut through the sound of the engine. One of them was on her phone now, broadcasting loud and clear like everyone on the bus was interested. He wished they'd tone it down. What was wrong with people these days? Why was everyone so noisy? He pulled out his own phone. He'd got more into the Bible recently, and he was trying to read the old-fashioned translation, the James one, on his phone. He'd give it another go now, though he doubted he'd get far.

He was right, it always gave him a headache, and pretty soon he realised today was going to be no different. The words made no sense at all, and he couldn't be bothered. Plus, the heating on the bus was on high. He was sitting over the engine, and the seat was too warm against his legs. The heat, and the bouncing up and down was getting to him, and when he thought about the course at the church he got hit by a wave of nausea. The prospect of watching another video about Jesus, and having to talk about forgiveness, or healing, or whatever delight they had in mind this evening, all seemed too heavy.

He thought about how good it would be to have a pint right now. Super cold, that first taste, it would cut right through all this crap. Maybe he could get one in before the meeting. One or two. There was this little place he'd found in North Laine which was cheap enough, and the beer wasn't bad either. Maybe he should sack the meeting off, have a proper drink. Maybe he was done with church, anyway. Those people in the group, they wouldn't miss him. Who was he kidding to think otherwise? They talked about love all the time, but they didn't love him. How could they, people like them and a geezer like him?

He did nod off for a moment, because when he came to the bus was moving slowly again and the crowd on the bus had thinned right out. Half the seats around him were empty now, and he realised with a shock that the hot office worker was looking at him. She was still standing up front, but she was on her own now, her friends must have left her. She had been looking at her phone, but right now she was staring at him.

Puzzled he stared back at her. But she didn't drop her eyes, just met his gaze and kept on looking at him.

The sudden intensity rattled him. Gruff, he lifted his chin at her, 'All right?'

She looked coolly at him, then through him, then back to her phone, and just like that the moment was gone. He nodded, gave a bitter laugh to himself – predictable – except then she was coming over, heading for the empty seat next to him.

'Is this free?' Her voice was even, educated, calm, *nice*. An echo of a distant age came back in the phrase. She was a nice girl, definitely. His mum would have liked her. He smiled to himself at the randomness of that thought. Thought she was too good for him, more like.

She settled in next to him. After a moment he glanced sideways at her, but she was staring away across the bus, like she'd forgotten him already. The bus continued rolling. He looked back out the window, washed in a sudden flood of self-hatred. She was no more than 30 and he was pathetic.

But then he realised the side of her shoe was touching the side of his shoe.

That slight contact was microscopically small yet felt so evident.

Suddenly he was fully awake. Things were clear and sharp in him. He felt alert, the beat of his heart more obvious in his chest. The touch of her shoe, through his own shoe, like the cross on Christmas Eve, had a weight far beyond what was actually happening.

He sat and wondered how stupid he was to get so worked up over something so small. Something that, if she had ever noticed, she would have felt was like a fly landing on her.

The bus jolted, and they both bounced, and moved a little. They settled, and he realised they were closer. Now he was sure their thighs were touching. He waited for her to move away, to get the space back between them. To his amazement she didn't.

He looked quickly sideways at her – she was gazing straight ahead. But she must have noticed. The bus jolted again. Now their legs were touching all the way along.

Reckless, momentarily aggrieved – did she want all the seat to herself? – he pressed his leg back against her. She shifted a little on the seat and slid her leg away – then she brought it back against him.

Returned the pressure.

Unmistakeable now.

Yet she was still staring up the bus, apparently oblivious to him.

He froze. Desire colliding with his battered self-image. How could she possibly be doing this?

More urgently – what should he do about it?

The bus bounced along. An out-of-season fly buzzed against the steamed-up window. Two flies, three flies. Flies all over the window. Her thigh was soft against his. He could feel the warmth of her. Time stretched, and yawned, seconds taking years.

And then she sighed, and relaxed, fell against him with a soft yielding, so their arms were touching, her head nearly on his shoulder.

Too, too much. He couldn't stand it. He pulled away, turned to her.

'Hot on here, i'ntit?'

He could have punched himself. He sounded thick, guttural, so stupid, like he came from the wrong part of the world for her.

But she was smiling at him.

'Aye, that it is,' she said, mocking him very gently.

'You lost your friends then?'

'They've giving a seminar tomorrow, so they've gone back to their hotel to get it ready. Which leaves me high and dry in this strange town.'

'Ah,' he said. He didn't know what else to say.

'That conference was hard work. I don't know Brighton, but I could do with a drink. Fancy buying me one?'

Yeah, he did fancy that alright, but then his own pig-headedness barged in. He couldn't help it – he hated that attitude so many good-looking women had. He'd been caught out so many times when he was younger. They'd smile all night at you over the dance floor till you bought them a drink, the minute you put it in their hands they'd turn back to their friends, and you'd stop existing.

He hated himself for being so gruff, but he wasn't going to be the same old idiot.

'Nah, I can't. I've got plans,' he said.

'Change them.'

He laughed at her cheek, despite himself.

'I'm supposed to be going to this meeting.'

'What kind of meeting?'

'It's at the church.'

'Church?' That caught her attention. 'You don't seem the sort.'

'What sort am I then?'

'Calm down. It's pretty hot, actually. Are you corruptible?

'Am I what?'

'Never mind. Well, I want to go out this evening. Are you sure you won't come?'

'You're alright. Thanks though.'

She opened the bag on her lap and took out a bottle of mineral water. He watched her hands as she unscrewed the top. Good hands. Good nails. Unlike her friends, she didn't seem drunk, just happy. And she was so, so attractive. So fresh, and careless. She reminded him of someone from a long time ago. Occasionally when he was young, someone like this crossed his path. He'd work hard, and through a miracle it would come together, and he would get her into his bed for an evening or two. Or maybe not. Maybe this whole thing reminded him of someone from a time from before even that. A time on a bus. Someone with long, straight, dark hair. He couldn't think straight, she'd knocked him so badly off balance.

'Cheers!' she said, mocking him with a faint smile.

She lifted the bottle to drink. He watched her throat as she swallowed, and the way the crisp lines of her white shirt lay against her skin.

She caught him looking and smiled at him again.

'Will you come back to my hotel with me?' she asked.

'What?'

'You heard.'

She drained the bottle, put it back in her bag, and leaned gently into him.

'I'd really like that.'

'What are you –?'

She turned and looked at him gravely. She was beautiful. It was painful to see her.

She was soft, intimate in the way she spoke. 'Look. I'm in town for one night. They've given me a hotel room round the corner from the Pavilion. I don't want to be lonely. I really want you to come back with me.'

Something was way, way off. Joe had been around enough situations to know this never happened. It was a rule of Nature: hot young women like this never, ever approached old guys, let alone knackered old homeless guys, to ask them back to their hotel room.

'I've got no money.'

She shrugged, 'I'm not a hooker. I just like you. Come on. You don't want to go to this church thing, whatever it is. Let's go and have fun.'

Joe looked round. The bus was waiting to slip into the bus rank where he had to get off. No-one was listening. Time to decide. Make or break.

What was his problem? Why was he even hesitating?

She smiled again and calmly, carefully, took his hand. Her skin was cool, soft, and for a moment he was utterly lost. He flashed a sideways look at her. He couldn't help it; he felt so grateful. Like she was a sign of goodness to come. Like things were finally changing for him. He tried to smile back at her, even managed a thin, awkward grin, a grin that made a crack in the tension of his life, cracking the years of loneliness.

But then she licked her lips. It was just a flicker of her tongue along her lips, but it was wrong somehow, and it broke the spell. And then he caught the feral hunger behind her eyes and caught a whiff of raw lust. He felt her hurry to pull him into her, and he realised there was a darkness there.

'Oh, man! No way!' He wrenched his hand away from her, recoiling back. Even in her surprise she looked sweet, desperately desirable. Yet now he could feel the darkness of a cold, inimical mind, a malevolence behind the whole thing, an evil swarming out of her.

'What's wrong?'

'No way. Get away from me!'

He stood up. She looked so hurt.

'I thought you liked me –'

The bus stopped and the doors flew open. He grabbed his jacket and pushed past her. Stumbling down the aisle he knocked into an old man and crashed his way around a mother struggling with a pushchair on her way to the door.

He ran all the way to the church, and the terror did slowly lift once he was in there. But he had realised something: that there might be something out there that didn't want him to go to church, something that had sent that woman to him to tempt him to miss the meeting.

The implications exploded in his head. Was that true? Was there really a thing that wanted to stop him going to church? Because if that mad idea were true (*How could it possibly be true? Seriously? Surely, she was just a weirdo slumming it?*), then what other mad ideas were true? Prayers got listened to? (*By who? By what?*) Healing worked? (*Oh, come on.*) Even that dusty morning 2,000 years ago, with a man on a cross, on a hill called Golgotha? Him dying, then coming back from the dead? *(Was even that true too?)*

When he eventually told the group about the woman, when he was brave, or foolish, enough to say he suspected the Devil was behind it all, no-one raised an eyebrow. Daniel said it was written in the Bible that Satan could come as an angel of light. That Joe would find there were many people in the church who would have had similarly weird-sounding experiences.

Going home that night to the hostel Joe realised he'd crossed the line. Now he believed this stuff more than he disbelieved it.

So, the next step was no surprise.

9
THE DOG

Part of the church course was a free weekend at a hotel in Eastbourne. There, surrounded by people eager to believe, bombarded by a message he couldn't fault, (*what IS so funny about peace, love and understanding?*), Joe accepted it was worth a try. He prayed, properly, on his own for the first time, and in his prayers, he accepted the story as the truth. He told God he accepted Jesus was the way. That Jesus had been born the son of God, and had died for his, Joe's, sins. That Jesus had been resurrected and would come again.

Nothing happened.

He felt so stupid. He could hear the blokes at the hostel laughing at him, laughing long and loud. Typical loser Joe. What did he expect to happen? Another con, and he'd fallen for it.

He did feel calmer. The torment of the always-pursuing Cross had somehow left him. In his head he saw a picture of a high hilltop. He was there at the summit. He was walking along the side of a low stone wall, which ran along the crest of the hill and divided it into two. At the moment of acceptance in the prayer he stepped over the wall, and now he was on the other side of the wall, and the grass down the hill stretched away from him. He was now in a different field, his old life lay behind him, and all he had to do was keep walking down the hill into this new country.

He coped with the social evening in the bar, even the silly games, in a way he wasn't used to. Normally on the edge of things, he joked with Daniel, who was turning into a proper mate, and laughed with the group. He slept better that night than normal too.

It was the Sunday morning that sealed his fate. It happened during the final prayer session of the course, in the conference room, among the crowd of people. He held out his hands in a posture of prayer. Daniel put his hand on his shoulder and waited.

They waited, and waited, to the point Joe felt uneasy.

Then Daniel spoke, 'Come Holy Spirit.'

Joe waited. Nothing. Half-opening his eyes he had a quick squinny around. The people from his group were there, hands out in front of them, being prayed for. It looked like a cult. Definitely a cult.

He turned his attention back to Daniel. Still nothing. He kept on saying, 'Come Holy Spirit … Come Holy Spirit …'

Joe felt foolish. Wondered what was supposed to happen. Because he felt nothing.

Daniel kept on, 'Come Holy Spirit …' and broke off. Joe felt the arm on his shoulder tremble.

Joe threw him a sideways glance. Daniel had his eyes clenched shut. And now his legs were shaking. Joe was embarrassed for him. This was nuts. He'd give him another minute, then say thanks and stop it.

Daniel went on. 'More power Lord, we need more of you … come now Holy Spirit …'

Joe felt nothing, and Daniel could tell that. He calmed down, stopped shaking.

'Are you OK'

Joe considered. 'Yeah, good.'

'Is there anything in particular you'd like me to pray for?'

A thought came to Joe. Of what it would be like to have a girlfriend. Someone sweet and funny, who felt good to be around, who he could look after, who looked after him, who he could be with, who loved him, who he could love back. Yeah, he could well get on board with that.

'I'd like a bit more love in my life. Definitely.'

Daniel nodded, more solemnly than Joe felt. Joe had half been flippant, to let up the tension caused by the prayer not happening. Yet having said it, he felt differently. Admitting such a thing had opened him up.

Daniel said 'Thank you Lord for Joe. He wants you in his life, please pour your love upon him. Fill him with your light. He hears you knocking on his heart Lord, the door to his heart is wide open, please come through, please pour your Spirit on him so that he knows your love.'

Joe stood and waited, and Daniel's arm started shaking again, even more violently than before, and his leg started twitching, and his foot started banging on the floor. Joe noticed this with a rising alarm – he still felt nothing.

And then things went weird.

Joe was in a grassy field, and a dog's head floated up in front of him. It was so vivid Joe opened his eyes for a moment to check he was still in the hotel room.

He was, and Daniel was still calling in the Holy Spirit, and his arm was still shaking, so Joe closed his eyes again.

The dog growled and fumed in front of him, pressing his dreadful face close in on him until Joe was sure he was done for. He could have laughed. He asked for a girlfriend, and this is what God came up with? But he wanted to know what would happen next; this was a trip, alright. So, in his mind, he said, 'OK, go on then God. Bring it on. Show me what you've got.'

Slowly, the dog's face transformed into the snarling face of a demon. It was terrifying in its hatred, invincible in its power - yet as Joe watched, it began to sink down in front of him, tilting upwards as it lowered. It touched the ground, and slowly sank lower, somehow vanishing into the grass. Sunlight poured down into the vision, the demon's head was still half visible in front of him, but new green grass was fast growing up through and around it, shoots entwining and covering it until it lay hidden beneath a mat of fresh, green vegetation.

Joe looked up, and he saw how the field was on a clifftop overlooking a deep blue sea. He looked down at the water. It reminded him of a long-ago family holiday, when he was a little boy, and his mam and dad had hired a caravan down in Devon. It had been that rarest of things, a happy fortnight, and they'd gone for long walks along the cliff tops.

And now, there, ahead of him along the clifftop path, walked his long dead old man and his long dead mam.

He watched, spellbound, as they turned and smiled at him. His dad looked great. Old, but restored, and full of life. His mam stepped forward and smiled at him, a happy, peaceful smile. She was an old woman now, but she looked well. There was no sign of the bloating the drink had given her by the end. Her eyes were clear, and her smile was genuine, happy. She looked at peace with herself, and with the world.

At that moment Joe felt nothing but love for them both.

They waved at Joe, then his dad took his mam's hand, and they walked off together ahead of Joe. He watched them head off into the distance, walking along their own path into eternity.

Joe felt a thing within himself, some *thing* uncoiling, lifting a baleful head, unwrapping itself from his spine, his nerves, his essence. He felt a darkness lift, a light pour in. There was a wrench, an uprooting deep inside him, and he got the sense of a shadow fading, flapping off into the daylight, as if something dark, and old, and evil was leaving him.

The vision faded, and Joe was back in the hotel conference room. He fell to his knees, knocking into the chairs in front of him, sending them spinning and banging into each other. He sprawled forwards, fell over a chair, landed hard on the floor. Winded, he rolled over, tried to get his breath, gasped, and noticed how people were still ignoring him. Lying there, a wave of warmth blasted through him, and he began to laugh at how mental it all was, his tears *(again with the tears, what the f- was it with all the tears?)* mixing with belly laughs, as he lay and shook and thanked God with the outpourings of a newly opened heart.

He lay there for a time; he wasn't sure how long. But when he finally lifted his face, he saw the same thing had been happening across the room. Many people had left, but isolated people remained around him, some in twos and threes, talking in quiet voices. One or two were in tears and being comforted by helpers from the church. One older woman lay curled up on the floor, a younger woman had her hand on her shoulder, mouthing the words of what could only be a silent prayer. The mood was peaceful; a wave had passed.

They got back from the weekend, and Joe slept twelve hours straight, too far gone to heed the barrage of the hostel.

He woke with a freshness in his mind he'd not felt for years. He reached for his phone, driven to search, for something he wasn't sure what.

Twitter was the usual pit of anger and despair; mad people slinging dung at each other. Without thinking, he closed his account and deleted the app.

WhatsApp had the usual string of messages from the people in the church, mostly an ever-growing stream of Bible verses and memes. One caught his eye. It was from the book of Revelation – a part of the Bible he still privately considered Nutter Central – but the words punched him in the gut:

"Even so, I've got this against you: You walked out on your first love."

He looked it up in one of the modern translations on his Bible app and found the surrounding verses. Turns out it was Jesus talking, and he didn't sound too happy:

"You walked out on your first love — why? What do you think you're doing? Have you got any idea how far you're gone? Lucifer had nothing on you when he fell from Heaven! Go back! Save your early love. You've not got much longer, because it won't be long before I cut my losses and take your light out the golden circle."

Time stopped for Joe, and he stared at the words. Written two thousand years before, this message chilled him. Was he so, so far off track in his life? Had he really fallen so far? A Lucifer fall? That didn't sound good. In fact, it sounded terrible. And whatever that golden circle was, he definitely didn't want to be taken out of it.

The whole thing sounded awful. He felt cold. Sick. Closed WhatsApp. Put the phone down.

Who or what was his first love?

One moment she wasn't there. The next, Suzanne Devlin stood in his imagination. Solid and as real as if the years in between had never happened. It was as if a shattered glass was in front of him, a hundred, a thousand shards in the frame, each one holding a memory of her.

~ Suzanne aged sixteen. Joe watching her play her violin in the school orchestra, her frown as she struggled to follow the score, her hand flashing along the fingerboard, her sound lost among the strings leaping out into the audience. It being so obvious to Joe that Suzanne, who he knew never practised her violin unless she was chained to the music stand, was miming.

~ Suzanne bouncing out of school past him with Wayne Dillon, the two of them laughing as flirting fifteen-year-olds would laugh, Wayne looking at her the same way nearly all the boys looked at her. She saw Joe and broke off the conversation with Wayne to ask Joe to settle the burning question: 'Hey, Joe, you'll know. Do you say it 'Mustash', or 'Mustosh'?'

~ Thirteen and finding her sobbing in the cloakrooms when her first boyfriend broke her heart. Sitting with her till she calmed down. The two months afterwards he feared she might die of misery. And the way she flitted from boy to boy ever after, never quite landing, always out of their grasp.

~ The school trip to Flamingo Land when they were eleven. The two of them teaming up to play the grabber machine in the arcade, and the joyful hug she gave him when she won a shiny Zippo lighter.

~ Walking her family's Red Setter one early morning across the playing field behind the Rose & Crown. She was nine, alone and suntanned, gym shoes and no socks, her long hair tied back, walking tall and straight without parting the morning.

~ And the time she caught him when they were playing Kiss Chase.

If she was his first love, how had he left her? Anger churned in his belly. It was she who had left him. He had always been there – far, far too much, to the expense of his entire life – but he stopped, realising he had abandoned her in one big way. He had never found out the full details of how she had died. There was something uncovered there, something wrong with the story as he had been able to scrape it together. He had tried to get to the truth, and he had failed, and had given up too easily, leaving Suzanne Devlin buried somewhere, alone, frozen, abandoned.

He found himself back on his phone, back on Facebook, flicking around to calm down. Which led him to the school Facebook group.

With a dawning sense of inevitability, he checked what people were saying in there.

As ever, many posts from people whose names he recognised and whose faces he didn't. Then he found it: the crossroads in his life. A long thread of posts talking about the school reunion. It was going ahead, two weekends from now, up in Grimsby, in the old school building itself, and the organisers had posted the details. His year, all past students and staff welcome.

He searched for the agony he'd felt last time, but it had gone. Replaced by calm. He felt sure of himself in a new way which he liked.

In the end it was easy. He was a child of God, right? Loved by Jesus? Guided and protected by the Holy Spirit? That made him as good as anyone. He could easy handle a poxy school reunion.

10
GOING HOME

In early May it was time. After the weekend away with the church, a lot of things had come together for him. Out of the blue the council had started talking about housing for him, and he had no idea how he'd jumped a list that took most single men several years or never to clear. Plus, he'd landed a barrow job, basically sweeping up on a building site, but good long days, at a miraculous £14 an hour, and, best of all, paid in cash. He saved every penny for three weeks, got himself rigged out at TK Maxx and bought a train ticket for Grimsby Town.

All the time he pushed the broom on the building site, he remembered, and the memories grew more and more vivid, until they felt more real than the hard world of work and hostel, the past more real than the battle around him. In his excitement he forgot the bad, remembered only the good. Remembered how Grimsby, in those days before the internet ruined everything, was a place of close community and faith in things getting better. How, even if you weren't close friends, you'd recognise all the children from your school. He forgot about being a loner and remembered only the times he'd been invited to play in different gangs and bands, either in the old streets and the 1930's housing estates or roaming through the fields and ash coppices which stretched south from the edge of town.

He remembered that growing sense, as you moved up the school, of life how was broadening out for everyone. One year Sean Garner's dad had a big win on the pools. He splashed out on the first colour TV anyone had seen, and Sean invited a roomful of kids round to watch Doctor Who. The next winter they were all hit by the blackouts when the miners went on strike. Suzanne Devlin had told him that her dad was driving his pickup truck in Bristol, but most evenings she, her silent older brother, and her mum would play candle-lit board games in front of an eked-out open fire. (Joe couldn't help comparing that picture to his house, where his mum and dad got drunk and resentful on pale ales and fags and cursed the miners for the empty coal scuttle.)

The spring always came, and the evenings pulled out. The kids rode Chopper bikes round the streets, played games of squarecles, or rounders, or mass games of football and cricket on the field behind the Rose & Crown. When school finished for the summer, they built dens in the corn after the harvest and led raiding expeditions on other gang's forts. They hollowed out giant snowballs to make igloos in the winter, mooched along soggy dyke paths in the late autumn, in summer when the evenings were long, they might go on expeditions in gangs to explore the woods in Bradley – or even the far side of Waltham, some two miles distant across the ploughed fields – all the time with a weather eye for any of the tougher kids who could always want to beat them up. One memorable day Sean Garner and Michael Bluff started cycling south and never stopped. They ended up going to Mablethorpe. This was a ten-hour bike ride, a fifty-mile round trip at the age of eleven, and their parents yelled at them when they got back.

Getting on with living for boys like Joe was a full-time

job: simple, yet immeasurably rich. It was reading Spiderman and Mighty World of Marvel comics. Walking to school. Learning about the Anglo-Saxons and learning how good and true Jesus was. Making papier mâché pigs in art. Singing hymns in the school hall in the morning. It was wishing your dad wasn't so tired, and your mam would be nice. It was liking Mr Trenton because he was kind and ran rock-and-roll bops in his classroom every Friday dinner time. It was singing the Match of the Day theme tune as you ran onto the field for the games lesson. It was waiting ten years for playtime, and fifty years for dinner time, and having nightmares about a dog.

In those days Father Christmas always came at Christmas, even for Joe. The shops closed on Sundays, and the streets were quiet at night.

The vivid past built, and built, turning into a fever, until, as he waited at Brighton Station early that Friday morning there was just one thing on his mind: finding out what happened to Suzanne Devlin all those years ago. Thirty-five years after blowing out of town in a rage-tangled knot of mess, he was going home.

He got on a train, then another train, then another, and six hours later he was back in Grimsby.

The church bell chimed nine in the distance. Leaves rustled and chattered around Joe. Hidden in dusky and dusty bushes at the bottom of the garden, he gazed at the lights of his old house.

He'd spent the first, discomforting, hour in Grimsby walking lost amid a scatter of new buildings, walking down streets which didn't exist back then, looking for landmarks which, even if they were still around, now had a different meaning.

The station was the same, but the road out of the station was wider than he remembered. And then things got tricky. Crossing at the first junction, falling back into a muscle memory it amazed him to own, he stepped out only to have a near miss with a car coming the wrong way along the road. They had changed the traffic flow and what was once a one-way street now had cars going in both directions.

That was the first knock, and they kept coming. Everywhere was familiar, yet strange. New buildings, new shops, new businesses, and yet the distances were so small. He could walk everywhere if he wanted, and, used to walking, he wanted to walk, very much. He spent a long time looking for familiar faces amid the sparse crowd, but the streets were empty compared to Brighton, the shopping mall deserted. He was half scared of who he might see, half desperate for connection, surprised he recognised no-one. Until he realised he'd made the mistake of searching among the faces of people twenty years younger than him. It shocked him to realise the grey-haired, anonymous old people who had been so easy to ignore were the ones he should have been looking at. Anyone he knew back then was old now. And he was old too.

He found the Salvation Army and paid for three nights. The woman on the desk was friendly as she ran him through the assessment. He hadn't signed off from benefits while he was working the barrow job, so he was OK on that score, but things got sticky when she asked him about his local connection. He told her he didn't know anyone in the area, and she looked dubious – but then he mentioned how he had grown up here. Carried away for a moment, his old accent came out and she relaxed. When they realised that they'd both been at the same school, but ten years apart, she opened up. She admitted she had never lived outside Grimsby and wanted to hear about Brighton – and what brought him back.

He didn't tell her. He had nothing he could tell normal people. In fact, he was starting to worry about what had brought him back. It was starting to feel like he was on a madman's mission.

He dumped his bag in the room. He was tired and his feet ached already, but the town drew him back outside. He walked along streets of pebble-dashed terraced houses and ended up in the old Victorian People's Park. He circled the lake, walking the path he knew so well, the Mandarin ducks jostling on the water reminding him of trips to feed them when he was a little boy.

He left the park and walked down quiet residential roads which made him feel calm and safe. The old playground looked the same, still with the grass tennis courts. He went on into the cemetery.

The May sun beat down, the trees were thick and green blue in the distance. He found his grandad's grave and said a prayer for his soul. Then he saw a marble statue, an angel, which rushed and burst out of the past at him.

He sat on the verge to study the angel, and the tomb on which it stood. The smell of cut grass tipped him back in time. One Friday afternoon art class the teacher had sent them out with paper and pastel crayons to find something inspiring. Coming into the cemetery to get away from the other kids, Joe had seen the angel, and become entranced. He remembered how it felt to be there back there, wearing his battered school blazer, threadbare grey trousers, his tie in a fat knot loose at his collar. He had spent the entire afternoon trying to trap the angel on paper. He could even remember the blues and greys he had used to capture the look in the angel's face. This afternoon Joe looked at the play of light that softened the severity of the stone, and the grace in the carving that made the statue both gentle and approachable. He wondered if, on that afternoon all those years ago, God had been speaking to him. Was this a call that had gone on all his life, and he'd only just heard?

He walked on through the cemetery, past the old gatehouse, and along the long straight path out onto the main road.

The closer he got to Scartho, his village on the edge of Grimsby, the more every street corner, every single building, brought back memories. Of course he went back to look at his junior school. He peered through the tall metal gates, new since his day, and took a long look at the school buildings off in the distance. He shook his head at the unclimbable eight-foot steel fence which now surrounded the place. It disappointed him to see new buildings on the site of the 1950's hut that had been his first classroom – but the wall where they'd kick footballs and hit tennis balls for hours was still there. He recognised the curve of the playground itself and filled it with the faces of his childhood – and there, just visible behind new climbing frames, he saw the ground zero of this entire mission. The playing field they used to call "the hills".

These hills were big enough to lose yourself in when he was eight. They hid among them, pushed toy cars up vertiginous roads in cliff faces they had carved in the sandy soil, made friends and alliances and fought bitter wars. Now he could see the hills were nothing more than gentle undulations in the grass that would come no higher than halfway up his shin. He stared at them, eyes wet with memory. He could see a blowy March day half a century ago. See children running in gangs. See himself, grey shorts, tatty cardigan – and he could see Suzanne Devlin chase him, and catch him, and kiss him.

The caretaker came out of his house to sweep up, taking the chance to give him one heck of a tough stare, and Joe moved on.

. . .

He walked on into Scartho, past his old scout hut, past the roundabout. Expecting to see the old cherry tree in flower, it shocked him to see it had gone, replaced by a sapling no bigger than the stake holding it upright. He walked on past the shop where his dad had bought him his first bike, and then he came to an arcade of shops, standing back from the road in a car park. He knew every inch of this car park. For years it had been the centre of his village life. He tried out the names on the facades. It hurt that not a single one was familiar. Also, the gang of teenagers on the corner intimidated him. They were only kids, as he and his mates had been, but they were far smarter, far more worldly. He watched as they rode their bikes in lurching wheelies around the car park. They all wore black, and they seemed brutal, fearless, too wild. The big lad who led them opened the supermarket doors and rode in. They followed, riding out minutes later laughing. They yelled at him, and sprinted off down the road. He was shocked. He had thought his home town would be soft compared to what he'd seen of the world, and that it would be easy for him to tame, that he could come in and dominate at last, but these kids felt too tough for that, with a confidence that could only come from total certainty of their place.

Joe moved on, feeling the first pang of an anxiety he had long forgotten. Next to their muscular energy, he felt precarious. These teens would have jeered, or worse, if he let them, like people always used to jeer at him in Grimsby, and far from dominating, he was beginning to feel unarmed.

He turned off the main road and walked down into the estate. Tucked away at the back, still looking out onto open fields, he found his old house, standing in a row of white-painted houses. He stood for a long minute, taking it in.

Again, how small it was, how anonymous for such a momentous location.

The sun was getting low. Figures moved inside the front room. In the house next door, a woman switched on a lamp.

He walked down the grassy track at the back of the houses, counting as he went. At the right place he climbed up so he could see over the new wooden fence. He looked at the back of the ordinary brick semi that was once his entire world.

He had to be nearer. He hopped over the fence and advanced up the well-kept garden.

He looked into the kitchen to see a couple with their young son. The boy was showing the man card tricks; the woman was cooking. The light of the room glowed warm.

When Joe could no longer stand it he turned to go. But then he saw a tree in the corner of the garden. A tree which held a tree house high in its branches.

A dog a few gardens along barked, loud in the silence. Startled, he looked around, but it was dark now and there was no-one to see him.

The branches to the tree were low, and the leaves were thick. He climbed the ladder. The door stuck. Joe remembered there was a trick to opening the catch, and the door swung open. He stared at the inside of the tree house. He couldn't contain the smile that flared across his face.

He risked the torch on his phone to scan the roof of the tree house. There, on the planks, still visible under battered layers of paint, was a war-cry of hope and expectation. He'd carved it nearly fifty years ago, and he'd long forgotten how he'd felt that day. When he wrote it, a secret part of him had believed life to be only a matter of waiting for all the good things of the world to unroll in front of him.

He traced the letters with his finger: *Joe Belton rules the world.*

He had to cry at that.

. . .

Back in the hostel, he got talking to the woman on the desk. Her name was Mel. Late forties. Like so many of the women in this town she had long blonde hair. She was funny, with a warmth that broke through. He looked more closely. Noticed her tight jeans, tight jumper, no ring, but an air around her that said, 'Don't even think about it'.

Not that Joe ever thought about it these days.

He went halfway up to bed before he recognised what he'd sensed in her. He went back down to check and caught her as she was putting her coat on to go home.

'I'm looking for a church for Sunday. I don't suppose you know where's good?'

'There's the Minster, I suppose. It's not bad.'

'Are people friendly?'

'It's a good place. I usually go in the evening.'

He was right. She was a Christian.

'Yeah?'

'Come along. I'll introduce you to people. Anyway, got to go. See you.'

She let herself out, but she looked back at him before she shut the outer door. She caught his eye and held it; her face serious as she studied him.

That night Joe dreamed he was a new-born baby, seconds old, in the first moments of purity, before any life in this world.

He had floated forever in the primal landscape, wandering amid the clouds of light and noise, the fierce hungers, the yearnings and the comfort. Now time coalesced, he was squeezed and crushed and in motion, surrounded by light and booming that pressed on him. He felt the feverish activity of his brain coming together; he felt pulled, battered, there was a sheet lightning of pain.

Noise and cold surrounded him in floods. Time was everlasting yet started to move. He soaked up good and bad, agony and joy, and the storms in between. He understood how there were moments, how moments could connect to other moments, and he lived a lifetime in every one.

He felt himself lifted, placed on a place of softness and safety, and felt warmth, rightness, security.

There, then, held at his mother's breast, he felt the very first kiss of all. The first kiss from the mother to the newborn, the kiss at the time when everything is possible, and all is potential and, for a moment, there is nothing but love.

11
THE DOORWAY

At 8.30 on a fructuous green evening, with mayflies in the air, with peach clouds in a dahlia sky, with tabby cats basking on doorsteps, with the mossy old bricks of the garden walls warm from a day full of sun, Joe Belton walked up the road to the school, walked up the drive to the school, strode through the door of the school, into his second innings.

In fact, he'd walked all the way from the hostel, which was a mistake. One and a half miles was enough for his new shoes to hurt him, and his new suit break him out in sweat. His neck itched from his haircut and his bitten nails and fingertips were raw and embarrassing. But his heart was full of hope, and he very much wanted to see people again.

He hesitated outside the hall. Through the glass doors he could see men in casual shirts and trousers, and he regretted the suit. Plus, he had decided to be an hour late, and that may have been a mistake – people looked to be having a big old time, laughing and talking in tight groups he knew he'd have trouble breaking into.

He thought about going back out for a roll-up but, remembering what Daniel had taught him about praying, closed his eyes and said a few words instead. 'Heavenly

Father, thank you for this get-together. Keep me safe. I know you love me, so please give me good things to say, and make this evening joyful. Let it be a celebration, a happy time. And let me find out more about how Suzanne Devlin died. Help me do right by her. In Jesus's name. Amen.'

And then he went in.

12
OVERLOADED

He spent the first twenty minutes alone, but he didn't mind. It gave him time to handle the shock. He recognised so many of the people – but their faces, their hair! Afflicted with age, their flesh had melted. Their faces were drooping, their bodies sagging. Standing by the trestle table bar, he couldn't shake the idea that there had been a fire in a waxworks. Drinking his pint far too fast, he found a spot in a corner and scanned the room, alienated, looking for the good, but struggling.

That changed when an elderly lady asked if he would like some wine. A bottle would have been more like it, but he took the glass.

He watched her cheerful face as she nodded and chatted and described the plans to close the school and rebuild it as an Academy. Typical Tennyson, last to do anything, never got past its comprehensive school roots, she blamed the governors … As her words blurred past him, he wondered who she was. Maybe part of the staff. Someone's mother, maybe, brought along out of curiosity. She obviously had the same worry as, after a while, she asked him his name.

'I'm Joe Belton.'

He didn't expect a reaction, but she stopped talking mid-sentence, looked at him with fierce interest.

'Joe? Joe! I didn't recognise you! I'm Jane. Jane Anson. Do you remember me?'

He remembered that name. Of course he did. They'd been in the same class for pretty well all of the eleven years he'd been at school. He had known her most days of the year from the age of five until they were sixteen. Now he looked, he could see it was her. Just so changed. Never would he have known it was her without her telling him. And how was it she didn't recognise him? Could he really have changed that much?

She was waiting for him to speak.

'Did you get to Oxford?' he managed.

'You've got a good memory. I did, yes.'

'I knew you would. You were well clever.'

'It nearly killed me though, so I dropped out in the second year and came home.'

She started a story about getting on the wrong course, feeling out her depth, missing home, boyfriend troubles, maybe Oxford wasn't the right place for people from Grimsby, but he wasn't listening. He couldn't get over the shock of not recognising her. Although, from the way she struggled to hide her fascination with his face and his clothes as she talked, she felt much the same about him. He didn't like that. Had he got so old too?

She was talking too much, the type of woman who worried about a lot and tried to pretend she didn't.

'… it was the first time I'd failed at anything, so when I look back it's a wonder I didn't jump in the Isis. Well, I did try through other means, of course. But that was years ago. All better now. I've been working for the council for years. Trying to make things happen. Though that's never easy. "Vested interests" they say. I call it laziness. Sheer laziness. Anyway, we've finally got things moving, the council have put proper money into our *Revive and Rebuild* initiative. We're starting to get the place stripped back, clear out the junk, so it's not entirely embarrassing when you think it's the 21st century …'

She caught that his interest was waning, 'But that's very boring. What have you been up to? Silly question Jane, it's been forty years, how's he going to answer that? Where do you live now? Not Grimsby, surely, I'd have seen you. I'm trying to think – you didn't come into the sixth form, did you?'

That made him laugh. 'I wasn't sixth form material.'

'You did the smart thing and went out and got a job!'

'I got a few jobs. I've been round and about. Worked on the roads. This and that. I live in Brighton now, though. Near the sea.'

'I love Brighton! I go down there a lot to see my sister. It's so rakish!'

'"Rakish?"'

'You know. They keep trying to do it up, pretend it's glamorous, but it's got that real dark side to it, don't you think?'

'You reckon?'

'Definitely. All those hipsters and coffee bars and eco cereal bars and whatever you call them, but it keeps going back to the criminal element. There's something quite sinister about it. Devilish. I do relish that. Grimsby is so boring. Not nearly enough sin.'

Joe watched her as she picked over the buffet, how jolly and light she looked, and how desperate and forced the conversation seemed, He thought about Jane Anson being in a place where she'd tried to kill herself. That took him back to Ronnie, and then how things had got so bad for him when he moved to Brighton. Could Brighton be devilish? Maybe. Maybe not. There were devilish people there alright, but you got that anywhere. In fact, in the last month he thought

Brighton was better than most. Lately he'd been having visions of the church sitting in the middle of the town, and he saw a tidal wave of goodness. In his vision the Holy Spirit, whatever you wanted to call it, was rolling in off the sea. It reared up and came to a crest and broke over the town. It met with a beam of light that dropped from the sky at the church and erupted out again over the city, splashing in a clear deluge up the hills, flooding each street, washing out the grime and the filth and the pain and the sadness, washing the city clean.

He realised he didn't want to talk to Jane Anson about sin.

'Maybe. Look, I better do the rounds. See who's here. Have a good evening, yeah? It was good to see you.'

Jane's face fell, 'Oh, OK. Yes, you too. It was amazing to see you, Joe. I love things like this reunion. It's so good to catch up.'

He looked back at her as he crossed the room. Her smile had gone, and she stood alone, head down, picking at the food. He recognised how lonely she was and felt a sharp pang of empathy for her.

He didn't know where he was heading. He'd finished his wine and wanted more, but Sean Garner and Michael Bluff were by the bar, laughing too loudly and punching each other's arms, and he could see a woman who he guessed was Corinne Ayr with a crowd who used to be girls who played netball. He'd never got on with any of them then, so how would that be any different now? Dan Kerry and his mates were over there, and they were always scary back then and looked terrifying now. Gary Lawson and the maths geeks were over there, and he'd never understood a word of what they said so why would that have changed? The trendy kids were on the sofas, still looking like they owned the place, suntans and smarter clothes, distinctly better looking than anyone else even now – they'd take one look at him and swap glances about his haircut and see how he wasn't used to wearing a suit.

What was surprising was how fast they had fallen back into the same groups. What wasn't surprising was how he was on his own.

Then he ran into Tony Smith, who he remembered as quiet and kind. He stood in chinos and brown anorak, having an earnest conversation with Simon Connelly. They both looked more or less the same – untouched by the years – how did that happen?

Tony saw Joe and held up his hand to interrupt Simon, 'It's Joe Belton! Hello Joe, how nice to see you! How have you been all these years?'

Tony smiled at Joe, honest and interested, and Simon turned to smile a kind smile at Joe, and he too looked genuine, and there was something so open and caring in the two of them that Joe knew he'd have to answer their questions truthfully and he discovered that was no good either. He didn't have the will, because any real look at the last forty years went something like: 'Basically lads I got proper screwed up as a kid and so I never got going and I've been crapping over my life for decades now and in fact it's caught up with me recently real bad and so at the moment I'm doing a bit of living on the streets and a bit of living in a hostel in Brighton where I get a room that stinks of weed and old sweat but I can't ever get off to sleep because if I do I'm worried that someone will break in and do me or at least nick my shoes and oh yeah, there's men who want me dead and I lost my best mate, sod it, my only mate, last November, and I've got into Jesus lately so I've probably gone mad too, but at least it stops me feeling sick with the fear all the time.'

What he did say was, 'Great mate. But I need a wazz. Are the bogs still in the same place?'

Simon nodded, happy to help, 'Yes, and they've not

changed a bit. It's so good.' He and Tony rocked back on their heels, pleased to be in a world so constant.

Joe wasn't so sure about toilets that hadn't changed a bit in 40 years, but he knew he had to get out. He turned and immediately banged into Corinne Ayr, knocking her glass of wine down her front.

'Oh, man, I'm so sorry.'

He grabbed a napkin from a table and started dabbing away at the wine on her shirt. She recoiled. She wasn't angry, more amused he would do this.

'Hey, hey, it's OK.' She took the napkin off him and saw how embarrassed he was. 'Don't worry, it's not so bad.'

Then she recognised him.

'Joe? How are you?'

He was pleased she knew him, but it was obvious she saw his embarrassment, and her poise made that worse, so the boiling in his head grew louder and he had to run.

'I was on the way out – I'll catch you later yeah? Sorry about the shirt.'

He hurried out the hall, and turned down the corridor, furious with himself for being so clumsy. Why was he getting so twitchy? And why oh why did he feel so apologetic about joining the church? About the only good thing that had happened in the last few years, and he was getting ready to run it down? What was wrong with him? He had to go somewhere and pray. Say sorry. Shape up.

He turned a few more corners, and as the noise of the reunion damped off behind him, he ducked under a cordon that said *'Renovations: Closed to the Reunion'*. He pulled open one heavy set of fire doors, and then another, and then turned into the breeze block corridor which led to the old sports hall. The corridor was long and bare, and his heels clicked and echoed, as they had done back then, and then he remembered where he might get some peace, maybe even some safety. He went all the way to the bottom of the corridor, pushed open a heavy door, and found himself in the old, cavernous sports hall.

He reached around and scrabbled along the wall in the dark, and found the switches for the overhead lights, and he flipped them on, one by one. They were dim orange at first, then warmed up and got brighter, and Joe blinked as he looked around. The hall was full of … stuff. This wasn't renovations, this place was a dumping ground. Jane Anson's *Revive and Rebuild* campaign made real. There were piles of old desks, chairs, old gym equipment, packing cases, lathes, groundsman's tools. One old motor mower, two old motor mowers, petrol cans, a stack of lumber, an entire tiled – and rotting – roof complete with carved wooden gables which Joe was sure used to be on the cricket pavilion.

Joe moved among the debris in wonder. There were old stage sets, netball hoops, a wire cage full of empty violin cases, half open cabinets over-flowing with years of children's artwork: paintings, some funny-looking papier mâché pigs, mosaic walls, photo montages. There were spades, rakes and two wheelbarrows from the gardening club, boxes of Bunsen burners, shelves of Pyrex measuring flasks, filing cabinets and teachers' desks, rolls and rolls of old cabling, and piles of ancient computer monitors. It went on and on, filling a good half of the gym.

Joe wound his way through the stacks and found the changing rooms. The lights didn't go on and the whole place smelled stale, but the taps still worked so he had a pee and washed his face anyway. It calmed him down a little. Then he came out and found a corner, far away from the doors, where he could see nothing but history, hear nothing but silence, feel nothing but stillness. At the end of a maze of packing cases, he knelt on a stack of old carpet tiles. He felt hidden, and safe. Putting his head in his hands, he began to pray.

He thanked the Lord for the loving creation that had made him, and which had brought all these people back together. He asked for a blessing over the evening. For himself he prayed for strength, and courage, and freedom from anxiety.

Most of all, he prayed he would do God's will and uncover the truth about what had happened to Suzy Devlin.

And then he heard the main doors to the gym bang open, and a gust of laughter echo off the walls.

13
COLLISIONS

Paul had dropped Corinne off at the school gates and she'd walked up the drive on her own. She knew he'd be watching her into the building, but she didn't turn to wave goodbye before she went in through the doors. There was something about going back to school that made her skip along feeling just a little rebellious. She put her phone in her bag, her bag and coat in the cloakroom. For once, she wouldn't worry about Paul.

She so nearly hadn't come. The building itself held no fascination. She'd been back to the school many times over the years; there had been badminton, netball and aerobics classes early on, which had turned into yoga and the occasional classical concert as the years went by. Also, she had kept up with the local people she wanted to see. In the end, what brought her was the curiosity about those who had gone out into the wider world. Paul wasn't keen, obviously, so she'd had to work on him for weeks. After some thought, and an evening spent with a nice bottle of wine in which she showed him everyone from her school she could find on Facebook, he was relaxing to the idea. After all the bald heads and beer bellies, even Paul had to realise he was being paranoid to think she could run off with any of these guys. Then, once she'd pointed out that the evening clashed with the golf finals, he'd finally said that he would take her, of course he would, but would she mind if he didn't come?

The secret she didn't like to admit, even to herself, was that everyone from her school she could find on Facebook didn't include Sean Garner. Then again, who cared about him? It was possible he would be there, but so what? She was far more interested in catching up with the girls. She couldn't wait to find out how they'd been doing.

She looked around the room again. She had heard nothing about Sean since a couple of summers after school. They had bumped into each other in the pub when he came back from Loughborough and had fallen out within twenty minutes. She'd removed him from her life at that point, ripped his page out of her address book, thrown away the paltry three post cards he'd sent her, and since then she had never once asked anyone else to find out what he had been up to. She knew nothing about where he lived or what he had done with his time, and she cared even less. All that had been buried long, long ago, never spoken about, only rarely remembered.

Standing there in the old school hall with the girls, catching up with years spent in Southend, California, Italy, even South Africa, was amazing. She couldn't get over how some people had changed – makeup and procedures and weight gains and losses had done incredible things – and how some people hadn't. The stories in her gang were vivid and funny, with everyone laughing and drinking and talking at once. One woman had her own PR marketing agency and worked mainly for movie clients at the bigger studios in Los Angeles. She'd even been to the last Oscars with a famous director (whose name Corinne didn't know). She had a sharp sense of humour, and a steely side to her character which hadn't been there at school. It fascinated Corinne for a while, but in the end, she decided she may as well have been telling stories about Martians for all the sense in the behaviour of film people.

Another friend worked for a web-development business in Johannesburg and had a streetwise edge that came from living in a big city in conflict. One had become a criminal barrister and had married a police officer in the Met, so she was very funny about how he nicked them and she got them off. Another had dropped out of a job in the city to buy a decrepit old farmhouse in northern Italy, and nowadays she and her husband were hanging on by the skin of their teeth to what sounded like a barely viable wine business. This held Corinne's attention, as she showed round photos of an appealing family, all suntans, relaxed smiles and sweet looking grandchildren.

Standing there and listening to all this while getting light-headed from the wine, Corinne could have felt envy for all the life she had missed. In truth, she felt nothing but exhilaration for them all. She'd spent her twenties travelling to various countries as a holiday rep, so had quenched a lot of her basic need to see the world. Then, even though she was shy about admitting she'd lived in Grimsby ever since, even though she and Paul had their moments, she would have said she was actually deeply content here in this little town, her own little town. There had been no children, but that was OK, she couldn't remember ever having really wanted any. She loved being a community nurse in the day; she had her quiet life with Paul in the evenings, weekends and holidays. She felt secure in all that, which left her free to feel nothing but happiness that her old friends had been out so far and done and seen so much.

So it frustrated her when each time she took a sip of wine, or when each fresh face came in the door, or even when she heard a bark of male laughter over the other side of the crowd, a reflex made her scan the room – and to realise that each time she scanned the room she was checking for Sean Garner.

Mainly out of curiosity, just to see what he looked like these days. Who wouldn't be curious?

So, when he came in (tall, slim, distinguished and serious faced, looking like she'd have described him if she'd had to) it was no surprise she felt a soft blow inside her.

There he was. After so, so long, there he was.

They had been in love for what seemed like ten minutes, then estranged for what felt like ten lifetimes. And now they were back in the same room. Only twenty feet away. How strange it was.

As she watched him, she felt a subtle shift in her centre of gravity. She wondered what would happen after so long. Would he come to find her, or should she go over? She had yelled at him to get out of her life – was it up to her to fix that?

And then Mick Bluff walked in like a gangster. She watched him scan the room. Leather jacket, shaven head, broken nose and vivid tattoos peeking out of the neck of his too-tight shirt, he looked like a real thug. He caught Corinne looking at him, and winked broadly at her, fist-bumped some men she didn't recognise, and went straight over to Sean. Tapping Sean on his left shoulder, he ducked round his right side to put him off balance, but Sean was wise to that, and turned to meet him. Corinne watched the moment. Saw how they stood, looking each other up and down. Then – and they couldn't have helped it – they both burst out laughing. Mick threw his arms out wide, and they locked together in a hug. Arms round each other, they headed off to the bar and got down to telling jokes like they were still in the fourth form.

Absurdly thwarted, Corinne wondered – should she have done the same as Mick? Or maybe not. What did she want out of tonight, anyway? Did she even have to talk to

Sean? That wasn't why she was there. Besides, maybe he'd forgotten all about her. It had to be a bad idea, raking over something that died nearly forty years ago. If they did bump into each other, it would be best to stay in the present.

She turned back to her gang of friends, trying hard to catch up to where they'd got to. But somehow the conversation seemed a little less interesting than it did five minutes before.

It happened simply enough. The girls went for top-ups and Corinne tagged along without thinking. Before she realised the only empty slot at the bar was next to Sean and Mick she was close enough, and trapped enough, that turning away would have been ridiculous.

Mick saw her, reached out, grabbed her hand, and pulled her into conversation with him and Sean.

'Alright Cos?'

His big smile was a little loopy and very infectious, and so his yanking her about amused her rather than annoyed. She pulled her hand out of his grip as he looked her up and down and clocked her damp shirt.

'You're supposed to drink it, not chuck it down yourself.'

She pulled a face at him. 'Michael Bluff. Long time no see. And is that Sean Garner?'

Sean turned to consider her and, she noticed, didn't miss a beat. 'Hey Corinne. Wow. So good to see you. What's been happening?'

It surprised her she didn't recognise Sean's voice. He had lost any Grimsby accent, smoothed it all out, and then added a lilt which had to come from the North West somewhere.

'I could ask you two the same.'

But Mick wasn't having any of this, '"So what have you done with your life?" "How old we all are." "My rheumatism is really bad". Come on, don't be boring. We're here to have a laugh, not get morbid.'

Sean reacted, 'Who's getting morbid?'

'I give it ten minutes at this rate. I've got one for you. What's the difference between a G-Spot and a golf ball?'

'Oh, mate.'

But Corinne knew the answer. 'A man will look for a golf ball.'

Mick looked impressed, 'Not bad.'

Corinne pointed at herself, 'Nurse skills. You can't shock me.'

'I haven't started, believe me.'

'Please don't encourage him, Corinne.'

While they talked, she took every chance to study Sean. There were care lines on his face, and his blond hair was thinning and greying. He'd kept the weight off, but his face had changed shape and his skin was rougher, paler, like it would burn in the sun instead of tanning. His manner was so much more polished than the boy she remembered, so much more relaxed and affable. There was a moment of dislocation. She wondered for a moment if they had all made a mistake and she was talking to a complete stranger. But then he stood up to offer her his stool, and the size of him next to her, the way he ducked his head to the side as he moved the stool, the way his eyebrows curved, his arms went, his legs, feet – all the angular geometry of him, it all broke back through the illusion of age, and she knew without doubt it was him.

Then someone slammed Mick hard on the shoulder, and he spilled his pint halfway to his mouth. He turned fast; his fist cocked out of instinct before he realised who it was. The Dillon twins, looking rough and wild like they ever did, grinned back at him. Wayne Dillon winked at Mick. 'Alright, old man? Been a while. Are you coming outside for a smoke or what?'

'Nice one.' Mick turned and said to Sean and Corinne, 'I'll be back.'

As he headed out after the twins Sean called after him, 'Be good.'

Mick yelled back over his shoulder, 'Never doubt me.'

Corinne watched Sean watching him go. He had a strange smile.

'We might as well be back at school. Plus drugs,' she said.

'We didn't do much of that back then, that's for sure.'

'You're such great mates, aren't you? Do you see a lot of him?'

Sean thought. 'I haven't seen him for over thirty years.'

'No way!'

'Yep.'

'How did that happen? You couldn't get enough of each other when I knew you.'

'We drifted apart.'

She waited for more, but nothing came. She broke the silence. 'So, what *did* you do with your life?'

He exhaled, in a way that made her look up.

'Was that a sigh?'

'Where to start.'

She shrugged, 'Wherever you like.'

Sean looked across at the stage, where the head teacher and a few of the junior staff were getting up. 'This looks dangerously like speeches will be made.'

'It's a reunion, Sean. There's going to be speeches.'

The head teacher tapped on the microphone and peered at the stressed-looking sixth-former fiddling with sliders on the mixing desk at the side of the room. People stopped talking and turned their attention to the front. There was a screech of feedback, more stress from the sixth former, and two men from the crowd went to help.

Sean rolled his eyes, 'I'm not sure I'm up for this. It's not as if she was our head mistress. And I haven't seen the school yet.'

He darted her a glance. 'Do you want to get out of here for a while? Have a look round? See what it's like to go back in time?'

That was a question all right. And she noticed he couldn't quite hold her gaze. She tried to hesitate, but her answer was inevitable.

'If you like.'

14
THE BLACK MUSEUM

The ice began to thaw properly as Sean and Corinne walked around the arts room, and it was running like a river by the time they'd finished geography and history. Science got them on to who remembered what, and the unaccountably moving view of a particular lamppost outside the window of their first-year classroom made Corinne cry, which made Sean dab at a tear or two himself when he thought she wasn't watching. The music rooms, and memories of a lesson that compared Queen's *Night at the Opera* to the Stranglers *Rattus Norvegicus*, started them singing, and the corridor outside the head's office brought back memories of detentions for the bad lads. By the time they reached the barriers and the sign saying *'Renovations, closed to Reunion'*, any tension had gone, and their conspiratorial connection was back in full flood. As a result, there was no way Sean wouldn't say 'Stuff that' and hold up the ribbon and Corinne wouldn't say 'Thank you kind sir' and slip under the ribbon, and no way at all they wouldn't head off to uncover what happened behind the forbidden double fire doors.

It was Sean who noticed the light under the sports hall door.

He poked his head inside. 'Look at this. It's the Black Museum.'

'Let me see.'

He held the door wide open for her, 'After you, madam.'

She laughed as she crossed the threshold, appreciating his courtesy, and looked around. 'A right old jumble sale more like.'

Sean stepped out into the hall, looking up and around him. He shouted 'Hellooooo Tennyson!' to hear the echo and turned to Corinne. He knew he had a look of childish glee on his face, but he couldn't help it, the familiarity of it all had hit him broadside on. 'It's even got the same smell. Can you believe it?'.

Corinne nodded. She'd got it too. 'What is it? Floor polish? Dust?'

'Knowing this place, it'll be asbestos.'

Sean took a deep breath, letting it transport him. It was a wet Wednesday in his second year, fourth year, sixth year and he was in there with his friends, laughing, running, climbing, competing; playing basketball, table tennis, hockey; being young and active, free-moving and engaged.

He moved deeper among the lumber, astonished at the range of the items there. It irritated him that it was stacked up with no order or system. 'But why would they keep all this in here?'

Corinne frowned. He knew she was trying to remember something, and he smiled to himself; her face was so familiar.

'I heard about this,' she said. 'It started as storage while they set up the Academy, then they had the new sports hall, so they carried on putting stuff in here on until they knock this one down. But now the deputy head's decided he wants crowdfunding for a social history display. He keeps going on about the "lived experience of the past".'

'We're history now? This is our childhood they're marketing.'

'Don't worry, they'll end up selling it all when he can't get the money.'

'Or slinging it into landfill when no-one will take it off his hands.'

Sean dragged out an old wooden vaulting horse. 'But I do know what the smell in here is. Desperation and Fear. Do you remember having to get over these things? Nightmare.'

'You were alright. You were a right little jock.'

'I was OK I suppose. Not like some.'

'Oi! My netball was legendary.'

He couldn't help himself. There was something about her indignation that melted him. He began to press against a door he had promised himself he would keep closed: 'For all the wrong reasons. Your trampolining on the other hand…'

Corinne frowned, surprised, 'You remember me trampolining? That was at junior school.'

When he looked back in later years on this evening, he would isolate this moment. There was a choice here. He could keep it as friends, and be nothing but light, and entertaining, and polite. They could have a lovely evening, and then she could go home to her house and he back home to Coniston. They would go on as they always had done, maybe with the odd email exchange that petered out in a few months.

Or he could take a second path, which could lead somewhere unknown, and dreadful, and wonderful.

There was no contest. So he took the first step on the second path. 'All that bouncing you had to do? So much to watch. Billy Bond used to sell tickets.'

She laughed out loud, mouth wide open in amazement. 'Bloomin' Bondy. I did wonder why there were always rows of small boys watching me practise.'

'Drawn by nature's goodness.'

'Get out. We were 11!'

'Boys start early. Well, some do. And you've always looked great.'

The second step. An innocent, generous compliment, which she could, if she wanted, notice as something significant far beyond that.

She blew out her cheeks, a little sad. 'Once, maybe. I got old.'

He looked directly at her and saw how she wasn't looking away.

He said gently, 'No. No, you didn't.'

He held her gaze this time for the third step. 'You still look amazing.'

His heart beating fast, not sure what kind of damage he was doing, but more alive in the moment than he had been for years, he reached out his hand to touch her cheek.

In her hesitation, in the confusion and the surprise this obvious intention caused her, he could see the decades fall away.

But she pulled her head back. 'You cheesy bugger. Is that why you dragged me off in here?'

'I don't know.' And that was the truth. From the moment he'd seen her with her friends when he arrived at the reunion, he'd been losing control.

'A bit of middle-aged torch lighting? What's the point?'

He shrugged, 'I guess it depends how bright the torch burns.'

'The second time round? You're joking, yeah? We were bad enough last time.'

'We were kids!'

'And now we're middle aged, married, mortgaged–'

'Miserable?'

'You speak for yourself, Mister! I'm happily married.'

He felt foolish, out of words, but it was also clear something was happening between them. At that moment he felt so much for her, and he would do anything to make it right.

She was far too light in the way she asked him: 'Are you miserable then?'

He wished that wasn't her question. Answering truthfully would mean a betrayal to Rebecca, which he had never made before.

'I'm alright. Ups and downs, you know. But I'm good.'

The lie lay flat and unconvincing between them. He could tell she knew there was more to the story, and it felt so foolish to be dancing around each other after all this time. He tried to step without fear out into this new era. 'Look, you know, back then. When you and I fell out. I never wanted to … '

But the words wouldn't come. Even now, when they couldn't be more grown up, when the chances to put things right couldn't be fewer, the words wouldn't come. There was far too much to be explained. For one thing, he felt so guilty; he knew how he had hurt her.

She was sombre, 'Never wanted to what?'

Was this to be the moment? In which he explained what had happened, and why? Explained a decision he'd taken so long ago? That he'd regretted so, so many times. That had broken the two of them up and driven them apart and kept them separate through all their best years. Was this the moment?

And then the gym doors flew open, and Mick Bluff banged in, the doors cannoning off the walls and bouncing off the walls to slam back into the door frame behind him.

15
THE FARADAY CAGE

Mick got back from his smoke with the Dillons in a grand mood, but when he saw a DJ playing Duran Duran's *Planet Earth* and realised that Sean and Corinne were nowhere to be seen, his buzz caught a sick edge. This was too quick – Sean looked happily married. Could he seriously be after her already? But Mick had seen a lot of happily married men behave very badly in Thailand and had been more than a bit naughty himself over the years, so the obvious conclusion was the sceptical one. He grabbed a couple of bottles of San Miguel from the trestle table bar and headed out of the hall into the school.

In widening circles, he combed the building. It didn't take long. Up and down stairs, along corridors, even checking darkened classrooms, instinct pulled him on and shortened his search, and he was soon in the sports hall corridor. He saw the light under the door and slowed himself down. He pressed his ear to the door, heard the murmur of conversation, and recognised Corinne's voice. Relieved, calming himself, waiting till he'd stopped panting, Mick painted on a jovial grin and flung the sports hall doors wide open.

There, springing apart as if they were in a sitcom, were

Sean and Corinne. The doors slammed shut behind him with a bang which echoed round the breeze block walls, and Mick advanced, scrutinising them. They looked far too serious to be having much fun, so he felt sure he'd got there in time. Pretending total innocence to everything, he widened his grin even more and flung his arms out in mock outrage. 'There you are! I thought I'd lost you.'

He noticed how Sean looked tired to see him, and that annoyed him, especially when he asked, 'Mick, what are you doing here?'

Mick considered, 'Just looking for my old heart breaker.'

'And who might that be?' Corinne said, amused.

'T.B.A.', said Mick. He was feeling a twinge of pain about all this, about the fact that the minute he turned his back they'd snuck off out to be alone together, but there was nothing he couldn't deal with. He looked from Sean to Corinne and pretended to catch their embarrassed manner in a way that implied he had only just cottoned on to what was going on. 'Ohh hello. Naughty, naughty. You've still got it, eh?'

Sean rolled his eyes, 'Yeah, yeah.'

But Corinne wanted things out in the open. 'What do you mean?'

Mick respected her for that, though he wouldn't play along too nicely just because it was her. He slammed Sean on the shoulder, 'He's a very attractive man, isn't he Cos? Don't you think?'

She shrugged. 'He doesn't look bad I suppose.'

'Fancy your chances?'

This needled her, 'Excuse me? I am married, you know.'

Mick grinned. He knew how this game went, 'I dunno. I haven't seen you for years and the first thing you do is tell me your problems.'

'It's not a problem! I've got a very good man and I'm very happy, so just … shut it!'

Sean looked at his watch. 'This reunion's done, isn't it? Do you two fancy going to the pub? I haven't seen the Rose & Crown for too long. If we left our cars and got a cab, we could have a couple of glasses.'

'Paul will pick me up so I'm OK,' Corinne said.

'Paul, hey. He's the one gives you grief, is he?' Mick pulled out his phone and squinted at it. There were no bars. 'No signal.' He looked around, up into the roof of the gym. 'Steel frame. It's a Faraday cage.'

'It can't be that bad,' Sean said.

'Depends on your network, I guess,' Mick said.

'What's a Faraday Cage?' Corinne said.

'When the phone signal hits the frame of the building, the electrical charge in the metal of the frame gets redistributed and it blocks the phone signal from getting through,' said Mick. He was trying to be impressive, so he was gratified when Corinne noticed.

'Where did you learn all that?' she said.

'Not here, for starters,' Mick said.

Sean leaned in confidentially to Corinne, 'He didn't learn anything here.'

Again, that annoyed Mick. 'I had a good time, though. A real good time, and that's what matters.'

'Is it?'

'Oh, don't do that. Let's go to the pub and have a proper night.' Mick put his arm round Sean's shoulders and looked at Corinne. 'Me and this bloke? We always had a laugh, right the way through.'

'I did remember to pass some exams though, Mick.'

'Bollocks to exams. I've done alright. Hey, you remember when we got Joe Belton drunk in that maths test?

Sean laughed. 'How could we forget?'

'The daft bugger fell off his chair,' Mick said.

'Cracked his head open on the way down.'

Corinne remembered the day. She and her friends had

watched the build-up in a fascination that turned into a slow-growing horror. It had started at dinnertime, out in the playground, with a quarter bottle of Smirnoff that Mick had picked up somehow. It went on through afternoon registration with Sean slipping him a paper cup with a straw, so that by the time Mrs Barnes had got there for their maths lesson Joe was swaying in his seat, smiling woozily at everyone as they laughed at him. Mrs Barnes came in carrying a gigantic pile of books and Joe had tried to get up out of his chair to help her. He misjudged it, knocked his desk over in front of him, recoiled, and slipped, and went flying backwards over his chair, slamming his head on the desk behind him. Corinne had been sitting close by and her stomach clenched at the noise of his head hitting the wood. The class had roared with a horrified laughter, and Mrs Barnes, the teacher, had yelled at him to get up. When he didn't, when he continued to lie on his side and hold his head in a foetal ball, she stood over him and told him to stop play-acting. He eventually lifted his head and Corinne saw first-hand the pool of blood coming out of the long cut on his other temple. He had been taken off to hospital for stitches, and, because everyone in the class had denied knowing anything, the head suspended him from school for a week for being drunk. If she thought about it, she could still feel sick for not standing up for him. 'Poor Joe. You were so horrible to him.'

Mick considered that. 'Yes, yes, we were. But there was something about the kid. You had to torment him.'

Sean agreed, 'You must admit, he did bring it on himself.'

'Boys are so horrible,' Corinne said.

'But we grow out of it,' Mick said.

'Do you?'

'Mrs Barnes went mental.' Sean said.

'But whoever listened to Mrs Barnes?'

Corinne watched the two of them fall about as they

mimicked Mrs Barnes teaching. She had to smile. They were cruel, but they were funny, and even now they had Mrs Barnes down pat. Corinne stopped smiling. A sadness and frustration were building. The missed moment with Sean a few minutes before was nagging at her, sparking irritation with the two of them. Always the same, even when they hadn't seen each other for 30-odd years, whenever they got together, Mick and Sean were bonded, off on a ride together which left everyone else behind.

She said, 'Well, if Joe turns up in the pub tonight don't get him drunk. I want to get home in one piece. Come on.'

She went over to the door and found the handle flapped loose in her hand. 'It won't open. Is it locked?'

Sean came over and tried the door. 'The handle's buggered. It's not catching.'

'Tennyson School. Crap as ever!' Mick said.

'If you hadn't banged your way in like a gorilla, it might still be working,' Corinne said.

Mick banged on the door and shouted, 'Hello?!'

'How are they going to hear us? We're three corridors away,' Corinne said.

Sean peered around the piles of junk, looking over at the far side of the sports hall, 'There must be a fire door?'

Mick leaped at that, 'Yeah. Come on. I want to go down the Rose-o. I'm thirsty.'

'Good boy.'

'Nothing changes. You two get together and it's always carnage,' Corinne said.

'Just like you two,' Mick said.

Sean cuffed him on the shoulder, 'Whatever'.

They headed off through the piles of boxes, threading their way through decades of history.

. . .

Over on the other side of the gym, Joe had sat, quiet and listening, throughout the last half hour. He'd heard Sean and Corinne talking, and he'd been interested, and a little relieved, to learn he, Joe, didn't seem to be the only one carrying a torch from his teens. He'd also read all too well how the dynamic had changed when Mick had come in. Again, who knew they would all be thinking like this? But then, when they started talking about him, Joe, he'd grown hurt, and angry, and offended, and then in an incredible reversion to his teenage self he'd grown weaker. As they'd talked about him drunk in class, there and then he'd renounced any idea of asking any of them about Suzy. What was he thinking? Street scum like him could never stand up to these people. He'd be like a worm in front of them. They'd laugh at him, or, worse yet, they'd pity him. He'd stutter, and his words wouldn't work, and he'd end up wishing he could wipe himself out from in front of them.

He'd tried to stop listening at that point to protect himself and waited for them to go. So, when he realised their search for the fire door would lead them to him, he got very alarmed. He jumped up, backed away, searched for an escape. It was no good. They had trapped him in a dead end of metal cloakroom stands and stainless-steel kitchen equipment.

With a sense of deepening dread, he subsided into waiting. As he heard them come closer, he felt a darkening of the air, a building of an oppression, a dramatic ebbing away of power. He climbed up on a desk, drew his knees up in front of him, wrapping his arms round them as though he were cold. As a last ditch, he prayed a simple prayer. Over and over he recited to himself: *'God is good. I am called. I am equipped. The best is yet to come.'*

It strengthened him, and so he could look Mick Bluff square in the eye as he led the other two round the corner.

Mick stopped, startled to see anyone there in front of him. 'Bloody hell! It's a garden gnome.'

'Mick,' said Joe

'Are you alright there, Joe?'

Sean came forward to see what was happening and laughed when he recognised him. 'Beltup? Is it you? How are you doing? What are you up to in here?'

'I was having a think.'

Mick said, 'Having a listen, you mean. You little tosser! Lurking around as usual. What's up, didn't you fancy the disco?'

Joe took a breath. He knew Mick was covering for his embarrassment about being overheard, and so he could understand and ignore it. He told himself he was a child of God. As good as anyone. Just don't let all that stuff in.

'I don't dance much,' he said.

Corinne came out from behind Sean and Mick, and Joe nodded at her. He did his absolute best to be respectable and polite. 'Hello Corinne, how are you? We didn't get chance to talk earlier – I'm sorry about your shirt.'

'Don't worry about it.'

Not sure what to do, aware of Sean's and Mick's eyes on him, he held out his hand for her to shake. Slightly put off balance by his formality, she shook his hand, and he went in to kiss her on the cheek, like he knew proper people did. But Corinne obviously didn't fancy that, and she dodged him while trying to hide the fact she was dodging him, so he ended up looking like an idiot. Then he felt her wriggling her hand free too and realised he'd been holding it too long, so he let go, noticing how quickly she stepped back.

Swallowing his hurt, he asked 'Are you well? How have you all been?'

Mick gave up on him and turned to consider moving shelves. 'Before we get into all that, let's get out of here, eh?

There was a fire door over here – do you remember where it was, Beltup?'

'No mate,' Joe said. Short and obstructive, because he didn't remember, because he was embarrassed about getting drunk in maths, because Corinne had hurt his feelings, and because he didn't like Mick Bluff already. But Mick threw him a stare. He had noticed his tone, and that made Joe anxious. He realised he was still scared of Mick.

Mick and Sean set off down the corridor of boxes. Corinne was about to follow them when Joe called her back. He had to make all this work.

'Hey, Corinne. Are you still living in Grimsby?'

'That I am.'

'I thought you were the travelling type.'

'I was. I went round the world twice, but I ended up a mile and a half from where I was born.'

Joe thought that sounded quite nice and said so. He thought of another question that proper people would ask each other, and Corinne answered it, and then she wanted to know a few things about him, and they ended up sitting together, both of them putting their feet up on a stack of old school magazines from the 1990's. They did all the chit chat Joe would have expected, and he managed to divert her and cover up his life, and he began to feel better. He told her about Jane Anson. She was interested, and, he noticed, didn't want to gossip about her, saying only 'poor Jane'. In fact, she was pretty nice all round, and much funnier than he thought she'd be, and she didn't ask questions he couldn't handle. Plus, on his side he felt he was handling it well. Making a good go of it all round

At a lull, he pulled out his tobacco pouch. He put together the makings of a rollie before remembering his manners and offering the pouch to her.

She hesitated, tragically guilty. 'Paul says I should know better, being a nurse and all that.'

'Well, do you? Know better?'

'I have a feeling I'm not going to.' But she was still hesitating. 'Have you got any mints?'

'Ah, go on. You can have a cigarette. Do you want me to roll it for you?'

'I'm not senile yet. Give it here.'

Deftly she made herself a neat cigarette, and he passed her his lighter. She lit it like an expert, and ended up smoking it with relish, even digging out an old silver sports trophy for them to use as an ashtray. He liked that.

'I feel dizzy. But I needed that,' she said.

'Ask if you want any more. I've got lots.'

'You might regret saying that.'

A movement caught her eye, and she nudged his arm. 'Look at those two.'

Far off, much deeper on into the sports hall, Mick and Sean were manhandling an old rowing boat out into the gangway.

'It's like Laurel and Hardy.'

'You don't hear about them very often these days,' he said.

'I know. And that's so wrong. We need to put it right.'

Joe liked the 'we'. He winced as Sean reversed into a long trestle table and jolted his back. 'It's a young town, Brighton. Kids don't know too much about the old films.'

'You should come round my house then. Paul's a mad fan. He goes to the conventions and everything.'

'Straight up?'

'We've got every one they made.'

Mick dropped his end of the boat and shouted in frustration.

She got up and stubbed out her rollie. 'I hope they don't need to move a piano. Come on.'

Joe piled in on Mick's side, Corinne with Sean. Between

them they pulled the boat aside, took down a teetering pile of empty plastic paint pots, and finally found the fire door.

A heavy padlock clamped shut the steel fast-release bolt.

'Great!' said Mick. He rattled the padlock. 'You do know this is illegal?'

'They'll have done it to keep out the yobs. Archway middle school in Cleethorpes got burned down last summer,' Corinne said. 'Are we stuck here then?'

'We can't be,' Sean said.

Joe was inclined to agree. Corinne was OK, but trapped with these two? No way.

'So, what do we do?' Corinne asked?

Mick pounded one last time on the doors and yelled, 'Hello! Hello!' before coming away in frustration. He gave Sean a look and took his jacket off, getting ready to run at the door. Sean grabbed him by the shoulder. 'Woah, woah, woah.'

'What?'

'A sheet steel door on a concrete floor? You'll break something.'

'It wouldn't be the first time,' Mick said.

'Come on, we're not that desperate. We can call someone.' Sean pulled his phone out. 'Yeah, OK. Same as you. No signal. Anyone else?'

Joe looked at his phone, alarmed to find it was dead. 'Battery's flat'.

Corinne shook her head. 'Mine's in the cloakroom.'

'No, no, mate, this can't be happening.' Mick said.

'There must be some tools in all this junk,' Sean said.

They turned to survey the overwhelming piles which surrounded them.

'Oh mate,' said Mick.

'Come on,' said Sean.

'That's quite a lot of stuff,' said Corinne. 'How big exactly would a pair of bolt cutters be?'

Acting together, in a move worthy of a silent film, Mick and Sean turned to pound on the door.

With one eye on Corinne, who, he'd decided, was definitely much more fun than he'd first expected, Joe held up a brightly coloured cardboard box. 'Anyone fancy a game of Hungry Hippos?'

16

THE CRUCIBLE

They found no bolt cutters and the doors stayed locked and, though they were sure someone would come, for the moment they had to wait. Though the evening was passing, and it would be getting dark outside, the amber light from the ceiling panels removed the passage of time in the hall.

Joe and Corinne sat on a long, low bench, lost in a conversation about games lessons from 45 years before. Of all the sports Joe had avoided at Tennyson school, volleyball was his least worst enemy. He knew he was only a crappy English kid with no muscles, a bad complexion and cheap plimsolls, tucked away in a corner of England where the sun rarely shone hot, where the sky was mostly grey with cloud and the sea usually brown with silt, but when he was playing volleyball, he forgot all that.

Something about the court, and the movement across it, the free-flowing nature of it, the fact they mixed the teams with men and women, that he'd heard it was a game the French and the Americans played, all made him feel like he was in playing ankle-deep in washes of deep, clean sand, wearing bright clothes of red, and green, and gold, blessed under tall pines filtering blazing sun, the blue of the Mediterranean or the Pacific at his elbow.

It was one of his great tragedies that Tennyson School had concentrated on football, which he was bad at and therefore hated, cross-country running, which made his lungs burn and he could never improve at, and cricket, when he couldn't hit, bowl, or catch a rock-hard cricket ball.

On the volleyball court he could run and jump and dive with intention and success. He knew the plays that would work. His own miraculous strategic mind would combine the team around him with the opportunities on the other side of the net. Serving into narrow gaps from the back of the court, setting up his side for clever flows of the ball, or leaping close to the net to smash the ball past baffled and wrong-footed opponents, he was energy and vision and deliberate direction itself. And yet he could only play once or twice a term, a few times a year, on those days when it poured heavy rain on an already waterlogged football pitch, or sleeted swathes of ice outside so even the crazy sports teachers wouldn't force them out into an east wind that cut at the faces, hands, and any bare legs. Instead, desperate for variety, perhaps dreaming of a better world themselves, they'd remember they had the nets and the balls and the rulebooks, and they'd get together a scratch game or two to fill ninety minutes till 3.30 pm.

Joe was remembering how it felt to be young and bouncing and flexible. How, when he played volleyball, he was made of a rubber that could shape and flow and direct itself, first over the court, and then across the rest of the afternoon. How he could stand tall and walk proudly for the rest of the day. Corinne, who seemed increasingly lovely to him, was very interested. She had enjoyed playing too, and they were having a real laugh about the one and only tournament. So, when Sean and Mick, both made jealous by this surprise bond, came over to sit with them, Joe was wide open and very vulnerable.

The problem was Mick and Sean were both bored with being in the gym. They had given up banging and shouting on the doors, they both were aware of each other's attention to Corinne, and, perhaps through a desire for a truce, perhaps because neither of them could face what a battle between them for this woman would feel like, or what it could uncover, they were beginning to feel mean.

So, like the smallest puff of storm cloud on a clear blue sky, Sean began to ask questions, and the evening began to sully.

'You know, I don't remember you from the sixth form. You vanished the summer we were 16. Where did you go?'

Joe half spoke, half sang a line from an old song about making a living out of playing pool.

'What are you talking about?' said Sean, giving Mick a quick look.

Joe grinned at them, expecting them to get the reference, 'You know. *Maggie May*? Rod Stewart?'

Sean shrugged, blank. Joe couldn't believe it. That was a song everyone knew, surely? But either they didn't know it, or more likely they knew, and they weren't going to play. Joe felt the first crack of discomfort. The truth about what happened when he was sixteen was unthinkable, so, panicking, he reached out to the first lie that came to mind, and so things began to slip away from him, and the entire evening began its slow decay into the day that would define the rest of their lives.

'I went on the road. This fair came through town, and I got a job with them. I stayed with them for a couple of years. Then I travelled about a bit. I had a great time, man, amazing. But that didn't last long. It was alright, but I wasn't getting ahead, so I woke up one morning and I thought I'd better get on with making some money –'

'- and you didn't want to steal it.' said Sean.

Joe took that like a punch in the face. 'What?'

Mick saw the signs in Sean and understood them well. He wandered over to dig through a great stack of old drama costumes and stage scenery. Apparently, he didn't share the desire to pick away at Joe, for which Joe was grateful. But Sean's jealousy had been piqued, sharpening his focus, and the questions kept coming.

Joe's old instinct to fit in came back, and he fell back into it without thinking. The best way to survive was to be like them all. Not so good as them all, that would make them challenge him. He needed to be in the same world as them, doing the same things, just not as well. So, he invented a life for himself he would have loved. A business manufacturing light fittings. A wife and two children. A nice little house, a nice new car. Nothing too flash, or too competitive, just enough to keep anyone happy.

But Sean wouldn't give him even that. 'Hang on a minute. When did all this happen? You've got this workshop now, but I don't understand. How did that get going? I mean – for one thing, what happened after this fair?'

'I started off with a market stall. I worked my arse off for a few years, till I got some money together. I bought into a mate's thing -'

'It's good you've done so well. Cos you were a little bit with the light fingers at school, weren't you? A bit of a tea leaf?'

That caught Joe by surprise: a shard, digging into him.

'Not really, no,' he said.

Over behind Sean, Mick pulled out an old cardboard cut-out of a medieval king in a peeling red cloak and a battered golden crown. He struck a pose with it and Joe saw a chance to change the subject. 'I remember that play! It was in our first year, wasn't it?'

But Mick had been listening all right and his memory seemed better than Sean's. 'A right little thief you were.

Always nicking. Then you burgled them multi-story flats. You ended up doing time.'

'Yeah, I made a mistake, but –' said Joe.

'There weren't no travelling fair. You got three years,' said Mick.

Joe hesitated. Ambushed, he couldn't carry this one off.

'Two,' he said.

'That's a pretty big mistake,' said Sean.

'The magistrate hated me –' Joe stopped, swallowed. 'I'm not proud of it. But I got it back together. Got into property at the right time –'

'Was this before or after you were homeless?'

Joe closed his eyes. He felt the beginning of everything he had dreaded about this evening. The old, unbeatable imbalance of power, which broke him before and could only lead to his being broken again today.

'Because I remember you down the underpass out the back of the railway lines. You lived out there, didn't you? Cardboard box and all?

'I –'

Corinne couldn't stand it any longer.

'Sean! Shut up!'

In an instant Sean became jovial again. 'Oh, I'm sorry, I was confused. Sorry mate, I was trying to get the order of things straight in my head. Cos your story doesn't add up. Hang on, you really are married? I'm not being funny but–'

'Sean!'

But Joe was in full flood now, beyond anyone's help. 'I am married! She's called Sarah, and we met on holiday in the Maldives, and we've got three children and we're very happy together …' and Joe knew he had lost them, that he had overreached. They knew him too well and knew his family and the street he came from and his old dad who dug roads and his mother who drank and beat him and whereas this lie might have worked elsewhere, these people could never believe something as good as that about him.

He turned away.

'Is he crying?' Sean asked in disbelief.

Joe wasn't crying, but it was very close.

Luckily, over in the past, Mick had found a distraction. He stood over a tea chest, staring at the contents.

'Bloody hell,' he said. 'Look at this lot!'

17
THE PHOTOGRAPH

'What?' said Corinne.

Mick plunged his hands into the chest and brought out fistfuls of old photographs. Glad of the shift in mood, Corinne went over, and not wanting to lose her attention, Sean followed.

'What are they?' said Corinne.

'Rogue's gallery.' Mick said.

Mick gave her a handful of photos, and Sean reached in past him to get a fistful himself.

Away over where he had been sitting with Corinne, Joe watched the three of them, the outsider again.

'There's one of the football team. Oh my. The shorts.' said Corinne.

'They're from the school magazine', said Sean.

'They go right back', said Mick.

They rummaged through, entranced. Mick held up a snap of a teacher in a deerstalker, holding a fishing rod. 'Remember him? Sniffy Smiffy?'

'I remember that hat!' said Corinne.

Sean wasn't interested. He was staring at one particular photo, and she could see it showed a girl playing netball. His focus on the picture, the way he seemed a little lost, made her curious.

'What is it, Sean? Show me?'

But he didn't.

'Is it me?' she said.

He didn't answer, didn't change the angle at which he held it, so she went over to look for herself.

The photo showed a teenager caught in motion. She was playing netball in the playground, wearing a red house tabard, with her hair tied back. She was leaping up to shoot, and the ball had left her hands, was on its way toward the net high above her. The speed of her had caused a blur in parts of the photo, but nothing could hide the look of excitement and fierce concentration on her face.

'Suzanne Devlin,' said Corinne, deflated.

'Give over. Let's have a look,' said Mick.

Sean handed over the photo. Mick studied it. 'Well, hello Suzy! Still looking good, I see.'

'She's so young,' said Sean.

'We were all young!' said Corinne.

'No, but … you know.'

'At least she never got old and knackered like us,' said Mick.

'You speak for yourself!' said Corinne.

'Let me see.' said Joe.

For, like a wolf in the night, like a salmon swimming home, like a wraith seeking the tomb, the mention of Suzanne had brought him across the room to their side.

Sean offered him the photo. His humiliation forgotten, for now, Joe took it and turned from them to get privacy. He closed his eyes a moment before he looked, tried to prolong this moment as long as he could, did his best to fix everything in his mind. The lighting, the smell of the sports hall, the three people around him, once known so very well, now strangers in their ageing bodies. The way his shoes were hurting, the anxiety churning in his belly. The beating of his heart, how his hands were cold, a little damp, how the fingernails he had been tearing at all evening were inflamed and throbbing now.

He turned the photo over and looked at the girl who had been his *terra firma*, the background to his wandering for the last four decades.

He saw, with tender curiosity, how she was nothing like he remembered. He saw how she was pretty, but differently to the pictures in his memory. Her thick curly hair tied in tight bunches, her skinny legs and arms, all the straight lines of her, marked her out as a teenager, still close to childhood, not like the grown woman he had created and loved in his heart. He had remembered her face wrongly. Over the years he had remade her into a conventional beauty. It was sad to lose the vision he had revisited a thousand times, and yet he was grateful to have the real her back again. Because it was her. The longer he looked at her the more he could see that, the more her face made sense again.

'Can I see?' asked Corinne.

'Mate?' Sean said.

'We've lost him,' Mick said.

Joe took a step, and another, and stumbled. He found another tea chest and sat down.

'Are you OK?' Corinne said.

He was still engrossed in the photo. 'I love that it's blurred. The thing about Suzy, she'd never stand still. Do you remember? She moved so fast.'

'Girl on the run,' said Mick.

'You can say that again,' said Sean. They both laughed.

Corinne looked at them, questioning. Joe caught the sense of something furtive, and he looked up. Were they all uneasy about something? But he had more on his mind. He peered closer at the photo, at a glimpse of a silver chain around her neck.

'I remember her necklace', Joe said. He looked round in disbelief. As though this would prove something to anyone who heard him. 'All these years, and I remember her necklace.'

'Oh, go on. Let's have a look,' Corinne said.

Joe surrendered the picture to her. She looked for a long time, before smiling.

'It's funny to see her look so serious. She was always laughing.'

'She was proper cheeky, that I do remember,' said Mick.

'I remember her funeral,' said Joe.

'Says Mr Cheerful,' said Mick.

'I wanted to go, and I couldn't, said Joe.

'Why not?' asked Corinne.

'His wicked ways,' said Sean.

'Yeah, alright,' Joe said. 'They'd locked me up down near Boston. but I heard about it because the cleaners in the remand home were talking about it.'

'How did they know?' asked Corinne.

'Pretty teenage girl dies in a fire? It made the teatime news, don't you remember? Especially when they said it was suspicious,' said Sean.

'I do recall, as it happens,' said Mick. 'You remember the photo of her they used on the telly? She looked so …'

'… Soulful,' they both said in unison.

They laughed, embarrassed to have been so open. Corinne looked from Sean to Mick, at their sudden reverence. 'Blimey. St. Suzanne. So, what's the big deal for you, Joe?'

Joe was wiser than he had been half an hour ago. He knew anything he gave Sean and Mick could be used against him. And besides, how could he ever describe what Suzanne Devlin had been for him?

'I didn't know her very well.'

Corinne frowned, 'You must have done. We'd been at school together ten years.'

'I knew her more at junior school. I didn't know much about her after that. I had my own stuff to do.'

He felt every word of his lie was visible, but Corinne only shrugged. 'Well, I loved her,' she said. 'She was funny. We sat next to each other in maths all the way till the sixth form.'

'I remember her coming out with us on our first date, don't you?' said Sean.

'*Saturday Night Fever*! I've no idea how we got in. We must have looked like kids,' said Corinne. 'She sat next to me and kept nudging me to snog you. You owed her so much, if only you knew.'

'Seriously? I thought I was in charge that whole evening.'

'Sorry,' said Corinne.

Mick slapped him on the shoulder. 'Run by a woman, mate. Dear oh dear.'

Joe had had enough of this. His mind was running on another, not even parallel, track.

'What happened with this fire then?' he said.

Sean wasn't happy to be brought to earth.

'I dunno. The Fitties wasn't it? Don't you remember anything?' said Sean.

'I couldn't find out what happened when I was inside, and when I got out no-one would talk to me.'

'Story of your life, eh, Belthead?' Mick said.

Joe let it pass. 'Why did they think it was suspicious? Where exactly was it?'

'Mate, it was 40 years ago. I've no idea.'

Sean kept sifting through the photos. He pulled one out with a laugh – a group of boys with fishing rods — and it sparked a boring story of a time he and Mick had gone fishing. Like heroes they'd got up before dawn to catch the tide, they'd cycled miles into town, in the rain, set up their rods on the north wall of Grimsby docks, in the rain, waited for hours, in the rain, and ended up catching not a sprat between them. Joe held on to his frustration and watched them banter about who was the hardest. When they started punching each other on the arm again he could wait no longer.

'You want to try digging the roads in January, lads. How did it start?' he said.

'"Lads"' Mick said.

Mick and Sean looked at each other, and Joe noticed even Corinne seemed surprised by his return to the subject. He was getting irritating. But he kept on.

'How did the fire start?'

'I don't bloody know. Some chalet thing.' Said Sean.

'What's a "chalet thing"?'

Mick sighed and shook his head. It was all too much trouble to excavate.

Corinne could remember. 'Yeah, it was definitely out on the Fitties. Her dad had bought one of them ones out near the yacht club. I think the power was a bit on and off, because I know they had all oil lamps. She was out there on her own one evening and she must have knocked one of them over. Poor lass.'

'Why was she out there on her own?'

He watched her as she tried to remember and tried to clamp down on his mounting anger. How was it these people had forgotten all of this? How many of your friends ever die? Like this? He would never forget hearing about Ronnie. He'd never forget the stained beige plastic of the table, the chicken curry he was eating, how the voice of the bloke who told him had grated away at him, flat and harsh and callous and savage as he gave him the SP of how she had messed herself, how her "mates" had turned over her room, how they'd taken anything of value (which boiled down to an old MP3 player Joe had given her) and left her all alone. How the floor had shaken and the table had rocked and the walls had fallen in on him until he'd had no choice but to give up and kick his chair back and tumble down onto the rolling floor and claw at his head with his hands until the staff came to put him in a restraint.

'As I remember, we were supposed to be having a party out there at the weekend. I think she was out there getting it ready,' said Corinne.

Everyone who grew up in Grimsby knew the Fitties. Built after the First World War they were a village of small chalets hidden out on the edge of town by the sea. Each chalet was different, and each owner would make it even more different, customising what they had with carved birds, or flagpoles, or gnomes or mermaids or plastic animals, flowers, parts of boats, cartwheels, seashell mosaics. There might be vivid gloss paintwork, sometimes in the black and white of Grimsby Town, or, because a lot of them were owned by out-of-towners, there could be splashes of the colours of football teams from Sheffield, Barnsley, Rotherham, even Leeds. Some were luxurious and modernised with carpets, smart Dralon suites, full feature fitted bathrooms. Some hadn't been touched since the 1920's, and, because they were well away from the town, the occasional musician, artist, or criminal would set up home there for a while. There were few roads, the only shops were in the nearby caravan park, and they'd occasionally get flooded by a big Spring tide, but most of all they were a place away from reality. When you were little, the Fitties were all about holidays. Joe could remember getting off the Number 8 bus from Scartho with his mam and dad. They'd walk like a proper family down the long approach road, down the roads between the chalets, then out the back. They'd walk through the trees, climb over the dunes on half-covered wooden slat paths laid in optimism over constantly drifting sand, and find a spot to pitch the red-striped windbreak. He'd wriggle out his clothes, and finally he could go out to the sea where he'd play for the afternoon in the delicious tension between the heat of the sun and the icy water of the Humber. The soft mud would squelch between his toes, and he'd look at the two forts out in the estuary and wonder how anyone ever thought they could invade England past them.

When you were older, you'd know the Fitties as the place teenagers had parties. At a Fitties party – and even Joe got invited to a few – people grew up years in a single evening. You could play punk records loud, and experiment with Carling and Blue Nun and Regals. There were first kisses, maybe more if things went well, or being sick as a dog out the back if not. Either way, there was no-one to stop you. It was no surprise Suzanne was planning a party there the weekend she died.

'You went out with her, didn't you?' Joe said to Mick.

'Suzanne Devlin didn't go out with people,' said Mick.

'Yeah, but I saw you kissing outside school loads of times. Did you use to go to the chalet with her?'

'No.'

'Who'd go out with her? Her old man was way too scary. You remember him?' said Sean.

'Right old hard case. Do you remember him chasing us? He ran all the way along South Sea Lane after us.'

'Why would he chase you two?' asked Corinne.

'No idea. Maybe he didn't like us,' said Sean.

'Who would?' said Joe, not quietly enough.

'What was that, Beltup?' Mick said, sharp and nasty. Joe changed the subject. A little.

'South Sea Lane comes up from the Fitties, he said.'

'So?' said Mick.

'So what were you two doing all the way out there?' asked Corinne.

'We used to go all over the place on our bikes. We went to Mablethorpe once!' said Sean.

'When you were kids. Not when you were sixteen,' said

Corinne.

Sean thought about it. 'I'd have been training. Mick used to pace me on his bike.'

'But why would Suzanne's dad have been chasing you?'

'How the hell do I know? He was a total psycho. I think we got mud on his carpet or something -'

Mick cut in with a glint in his eye – 'Hey – you remember Suzanne from when we used to play Kiss Chase? At junior school?'

Sean smiled affectionately. 'When we were eight, or whatever we were? She was proper game on, wasn't she?'

'"Fearless" is the word.'

'Right little Kiss Chaser she was. And she was fast. Even then.'

'Always got her man.'

Joe hated what they were saying. But it was a start. They were talking about her now. He had to go on. 'You must have been inside then?'

Sean looked at him askance. They all looked at him. He went on. 'Inside the chalet. You must have been inside the chalet if you got mud on his carpet. Or were you going round to her house?'

That got everyone's attention. Corinne most of all. Sean was amused. 'Bloody hell, Inspector Clouseau. Yeah, I went out to the chalet a couple of times.'

That surprised Corinne. A lot.

'What was it like?' asked Joe.

'I dunno. Brown. Dark. Chalet-y. How am I going to remember that?'

'But that's where she died!'

'Come on, what do you want? Floor plans?' Sean said. But all three were looking alarmed at Joe's rising anguish, and he realised he had to step away, calm down a little, or this was going nowhere. Besides, he had to accept, that was a fair enough question from Sean.

'I want to know what it was like,' he said.

'Did you really go round there?' Corinne asked.

Sean shrugged. 'Once. Twice. So what?'

'When?'

'I don't know. Me and Mick.'

'You never told me,' she said.

'And why would you be interested?'

'Hello. You do remember we were going out at that point?'

'Busted!' said Mick, with enjoyment.

'What does that mean?' asked Corinne.

'Nothing. He's being Mick,' said Sean.

'You do remember we were talking about running away and getting married in Venice?' she said.

'Weren't we sweet!'

'And that we promised to tell each other everything, everything we thought, every single day?'

'Good grief. Lucky escape, then,' Sean said.

But Corinne wasn't taking that. 'We were in love. Well, I was. But that's beside the point. Were you seeing her at the same time you were with me?'

'No. Not at all.'

She looked at him, long and hard. 'It's funny, isn't it? You don't see someone for all these years and yet when they look at you in a certain way you know what it means.'

'Oh really. What's that?' Sean couldn't help smiling.

'That guilty little smile? That "I'm a bad little boy but you love me anyway" smile?'

'I don't know what you mean.' His smile widened even further. He really couldn't help it.

'Liar, liar, pants on fire!'

He rolled his eyes. Caught at last. 'We did have a moment or two.'

Corinne gasped, then gave a short laugh. 'You little –' she said.

They were both grinning now, but Joe knew laughter in the dark when he saw it.

'Oh, come on. You knew I was a bit like that. Surely?'

'That you were a lying dog? If I'm honest, I did have my suspicions, but …'

'There you go.'

'Bloody hell Sean!'

Corinne was far more upset than she would have liked.

'Corinne, it's water under the bridge. It was years ago!'

'Whatever,' she said.

This was the least convincing 'whatever' Joe had heard for a long time. But he was joining the dots himself. 'Have I got this right? So you, Mick, were kissing her after school, and you, Sean, were round at her chalet? Were both of you going out with her that summer?

Sean and Mick looked at each other. And tried to explain. They weren't going out with her. Not as such. Joe couldn't understand what they were saying at first, then he realised they were both probably saying they were playing around with her. And she was playing around with them. Just teenagers messing about. Nothing, really.

There was one obvious question.

'Did you see her the evening she died?' Joe asked.

'No,' said Mick.

'No,' said Sean. 'Not at all. I hadn't seen her for a week – she'd stopped talking to both of us. She said she was seeing some bloke who worked down the Royal Oak.'

He looked at Corinne, who was stone-faced, staring into the distance. He moved over to her, but she held a hand up to block him. Sean turned back to Joe, his hands out, like he'd had a bad decision from a tennis umpire. 'Are you happy now? So that's enough Suzanne Devlin.' He seemed vulnerable, childish. 'Can we please talk about something else now? Like how we get out this bloody gym?'

18

THE TREE IN THE FOREST

In fact, there was no way out of the gym. There were no windows, and the doors were strong enough to resist being broken down by two men in their late fifties, no matter how determined.

Joe left them all to it early on, as they fretted about how long it would take before they were missed. He wandered off alone, going deep into the stacks of junk, and lay on his back on a stack of wooden decking in the middle of a huddle of garden rakes. The voices of the other three grew faint as he stopped listening. He stared at the grey breeze blocks of the walls, and the darkness behind the fluorescent light panels up above. The airy space above him reminded him of being in church. The steel girders under the corrugated metal roof felt like high arches, even the circular ceiling fans were like the painted plaster rosettes which covered the junctions of the arches in Brighton. He wondered how two buildings could take up such similar space but make you feel so different.

He had a pang of yearning for Brighton and the church. For the peace that fell on him as he walked into the building, and that armed him against the rest of the week. When you left the Sunday service there, the noise and the chaos of the streets hit you like a slap. You went from an hour or more spent in a place of love, where all you'd done was think about the best thing, the most good you could ever imagine, out into a grimy world where people argued and stole and cheated. Fighting without respite over things that didn't matter. A slice of heaven dropped in that church, every Sunday, just yards from the main road, if people would only realise.

As winter had left and spring had come in, and Joe had relaxed about being in there, the church had begun to feel like a forest. The high arches were like branches, cupping the sunlight which blazed through the stained-glass, laying it out across the people like the patterns on a woodland floor. Jesus had died on a cross, which some people called a tree. He died in agony, trading his life for ours, but this church forest reminded Joe of being a child, and playing in the ash woods around Scartho.

He lifted the photo of Suzanne he held across his chest and looked at her again.

If she'd have lived, she'd have put on weight by now, almost everyone did. She'd be dying her hair, having been through a hundred styles. She'd have settled down, found someone good for her, got married, gone on into her twenties, thirties, forties, fifties, children, grandchildren even. She'd have had jobs, got busy, good bosses, bad bosses, maybe been sacked, maybe been a high-flyer. Maybe divorced, maybe lucky and still happily married.

In some ways Joe was glad she wasn't still around. If she were he guessed he'd still be hanging around in the background, one eye on her protection. He felt the sharpness of regret. Though of course he had failed so badly the one time he could have helped. If only he could have been there. He would have sacrificed himself for her, no doubt about it.

Like a child, he played the romantic fantasy in his mind.

He'd be walking past the chalet, there by chance. He'd see burning, smoke, flames, and he'd be the only one in the area, so he'd kick the door down and run in. The place would be alive with flames, flashing sparks, wooden beams already glowing. She'd be unconscious from the smoke – or, better yet, trapped but awake, so she could see him there rescuing her. He'd free her from the wreckage, moving chairs, lifting beams, and he'd lead her out of the chalet to the fresh air, where she'd lean on him and, finally, learn she loved him …

These daft thoughts surprised him. After the last few years, he didn't think he had it in him to feel romantic about anything. In the chalet burning down, he saw more realistically their two wrecked families. Her house had burned down, but weren't all their houses burning down, one way or another?

He noticed how the idea of sacrificing himself to save her made him feel good, light, clean. Better.

Then, with a light "pock" a practice golf ball bounced off the side of a lawn mower in front of him and rolled back towards him.

19
THE BURNING TREE

There was a grunt, and a click, and a soft swoosh, and then another golf ball flew overhead and vanished into the piles. So, Mick and Sean had found the sports equipment section.

Joe got up and picked his way back through the piles of junk. Sure enough, they had set up a mini-driving range, with clubs, buckets of practice balls, and a clear fairway down the main aisle. He stayed hidden for a while, watching them. He had nothing to offer.

Mick, Sean and Corinne swung in turn, clearly competing, though each pretending nothing could matter less.

Mick took his turn, watched the ball fly with satisfaction, and went on with his story. 'I walk in this classroom, and I hear this bloke go: "I can't believe what's happened to Mick Bluff!" I mean, what? So I look like crap now?'

'You don't. You really don't,' said Corinne.

'Mmmm, I'll see you later. I look round to see who said this, and the thing is, it's this little skinny bloke, and he's totally bald.'

'With respect, mate …' Sean said.

'Mine's a razor!'

'Still no hair.'

'He's got this bald, shiny dome, like he was one of them aliens, not a single hair on his head, no eyebrows, no lashes, nothing – and he was saying I looked different? I see him, and I don't have a clue who he is. Not a bloody clue. I take ages to get it – Johnny Murphy!'

'John Murphy's bald? Shoot me now,' said Corinne.

'He's a boiled egg. And the bugger says I look different.'

She concentrated, and swung, and the ball lifted off and flew high out down the fairway. She smiled, happy. 'We've all got older. Of course we have. It was a surprise, and not all good, not going to lie. But after half an hour, didn't that change? Wasn't it amazing to see everyone again?'

Joe stepped forward. 'How did you feel when you heard she died?'

They turned to him, aghast.

'Will you stop that?' said Sean. 'You're really annoying me now. No offence.'

'What is it, Joe? Why are you asking all these questions?' said Corinne.

'I missed it all, you see. I wanted to know how it felt when you heard the news.'

'Can we get this bloke a bell to ring? *'Misery! Misery!'*' said Mick.

Corinne took pity on him. 'If I tell you, can we leave it alone? Honestly, it's getting a bit depressing.'

Joe nodded. 'Yeah, sure. Sorry.'

'OK.' She thought. 'It hurt. But also, it didn't. Suzanne dying, it didn't seem real. It happened, and it was shocking, but it didn't seem that relevant. You know what it's like at that age. You've just started out. You feel you've got so much time. Rivers and lakes and oceans of time. Everything's fresh. You feel so strong.'

'I didn't,' said Joe.

Sean was about to swing, but he had stopped, his attention caught by what Corinne was saying. 'Back then, I only remember it being sunny, even when it was raining,' he said.

He caught Mick rolling his eyes at Corinne. 'No, come on. Don't laugh, mate. You know what I mean.'

'Yeah, I remember,' Mick conceded. 'Your granny would die. Some old aunt. Stroke. Cancer. Heart attack.'

'Death by Woodbine,' Sean said. 'There'd be a funeral. You'd feel sad. You'd try to miss them. You would miss them. But it was nothing to do with you, and you'd go back to school, or go round your mates to play Subbuteo, and you'd forget about it.'

'Who ever thinks they're going to die when they're eighteen?' said Corinne.

'I still don't, as it happens,' said Mick.

'That's because you have an unerring ability to totally present your arse to the bleeding obvious,' said Sean.

Corinne considered that, serious now. 'When you're that young, you think you'll go on forever.'

Mick shrugged. 'And that is wrong because?'

'Everyone gets old. It's life.'

Mick shook his head. 'No, it's not. That's death, and I'm not having it. I go down the gym, I go running, I do some DJing, I feel great man. You lot want to sort yourselves out.'

Sean nodded, amused. 'DJing, eh? With "the youth". Nice. You know when it hit me?'

'Stretch waist trousers,' said Mick.

'False teeth?' said Corinne.

'Ha. Ha. Nope. Mirrors. In clothes shops. I kept getting surprised by who I was looking at.'

'Can't we get back to the good stuff?' said Mick. 'Throwing Rob Carter in the pond? That time Little Darren put dry ice bombs in everyone's desk?'

'Yeah, that was all good,' said Sean, but he wasn't smiling. 'I'm basically nearly 60. That's not what I had planned for myself, not at all.'

He looked round, saw their faces, and made an effort. 'Hey, speaking of good stuff, you liked a fire, didn't you?'

'Bloody loved one mate, and you know it,' said Mick.

Sean saw Joe's face. 'Calm down, Sherlock. I mean he liked a little bonfire.'

'Every chance I got when I was a kid. My most memorable –'

'– traumatising?'

'– maybe – one was that oak tree in Weelsby Woods, do you remember? It must have been three hundred years old. We couldn't get it to catch, not good and proper. We went back the next day, it was a work of art. Smouldering with embers. We tried to put it out, couldn't do it. I had nightmares for weeks, thinking the next time we drove with my dad past the gates the woods would be burned to the ground.'

Joe couldn't hide his contempt. 'You tried to burn down a three-hundred-year-old tree? Amazing, mate. Well done. What a dick.'

'Don't ever doubt me on fires,' said Mick, annoyed.

'Or tree art,' said Sean.

'Or piss art,' said Mick.

'And that is what I'm talking about,' said Sean.

They grinned and bumped fists, but Mick all the time was staring hard at Joe.

Uneasy, Joe changed the subject. 'So, who was this older man Suzanne was seeing? The week before the fire?'

'He worked down at the Royal Oak,' said Sean. 'He served all us kids. You could always get your snakebite off Alan. He was OK.'

'OK?' said Corinne. 'He must have been thirty. She was only just eighteen. Even then that was weird.'

'If he actually was dating her,' Mick shrugged. 'If you ask me, she was telling stories. I ran into him down the dole office a few years after and he told me all about it. He swore he'd never even served her, let alone been out with her.'

'If that's true, why would she say she was seeing him?' said Joe.

'She did like to feel important, old Suzanne,' said Sean.

'So why would she date you?' said Corinne. 'I can't see how that would make her feel very important. Or did it make her feel important to steal other people's boyfriends?'

'Be nice, Cos' said Sean.

'You weren't very nice.'

'I was young and foolish. What can I say? I'm sorry.'

'He was a bit of a shagger, we all were, no big deal.' said Mick.

'Oh, thanks mate,' said Sean

'Yeah, I get it.' said Corinne. 'And how did that work out for you Sean? In life, I mean. You haven't told us about yourself yet. Not properly. Lots of girlfriends? When did you get married? Was it for love? Have you been faithful? Does she mind you being a "bit of a shagger?" Do you ever wish you were less treacherous?'

Sean shrugged. 'I've never been unfaithful to her. Not once.'

Corinne looked at him, appalled. 'So, what was all that earlier on?'

'Corinne – I –'

'Seeing if I was still so stupid?'

'No!'

She absorbed his intensity. Nodded. OK.

'So. Staying faithful. How's that worked out for you?'

He exhaled, slow and heavy. 'You want to know? We've got a long and faithful and probably mostly averagely happy marriage and it's killing me.'

'Why would a happy marriage kill you?' said Joe.

'Pardon my assumptions here, Beltup,' said Sean, but am I right in guessing you have probably not got too much direct experience of relationships of the male-on-female kind?'

'We're not talking bag-ladies after your Special Brew,' said Mick.

'Of course I have,' said Joe.

'Real relationships. Hearing about their day. Doing the washing. Christmas card lists. Arguments in Tesco,' said Sean.

'Breakfast in bed. Having a laugh. Fixing the motor while she does the Sunday roast,' said Mick.

'Children,' said Corinne.

Joe looked at them all. They'd been living while Joe had bounced between strip clubs and the gutter, and he couldn't bear it. 'I've done that. I've got children. I am married, you know? I've got a boy and two girls, Jack and –'

'Poor Joe,' said Mick.

'Just shut up, Mick!' he yelled.

'Or?' Mick said. So, so quietly.

Joe fell silent. So that was it. The first cut of the knife, gently done. Joe understood Mick now. He was an expert in violence, with no need to posture, and he would take his time. But what about Sean? Some perversity pushed him on to provoke.

'So, what's the problem with you and your Mrs then?' Joe said. 'Is she too clever for you?'

Sean considered Joe and filed the attack away for later. 'Oh, she's too something alright.'

'That sounds interesting,' said Mick.

'It's not. It's the opposite of interesting.'

'It sounds boring then. Ah well,' said Mick.

'Mundane, unstimulating, tedious, dull, insipid, unexciting, stolid, lacklustre, prosaic. Are some of the words I'd use to describe my marriage.'

'Why do you stay?' asked Corinne.

'What's the choice? Really?'

'Come clubbing with me and I'll show you,' said Mick.

'No thanks.'

'It would definitely freshen your senses.'

'And I'd definitely end up breaking a promise I made in a church, in front of two hundred people, God, and my granny. Again, no thanks.'

'Church? God?' said Corinne. 'What's going on with you, Sean? It sounds like you need a break at least.'

'I'm trying to be good,' he said.

Mick grinned, 'It's so much more fun being bad.'

Sean looked at him, suddenly tired. 'Is it though?'

'Have you been bad?' asked Joe.

Sean turned to face him in disbelief. 'Who's ever been as good as they could have been? But never you mind. I'm trying. The important thing is we have a nice life.' He threw a sideways glance at Mick. 'I've made piles of money.'

'Not as much as me,' said Mick.

'Debatable,' said Sean.

'But provable.'

'Why would I want to prove it?'

'You wouldn't. Because then you'd realise I'm richer than you.'

'How do you know?'

'Enough willie waving, please,' said Corinne.

'Mine is definitely bigger than his,' said Mick. 'Your problem is you've only seen half the equation.'

'And that's definitely the way it stays,' Corinne said.

'Please!', said Joe. The frustration in his voice cut through and they turned to him.

'We've got all these photos, we're all together for the first time since school, we've got all night in here. If we all try to remember, look through these photos, maybe we can work out what was really going on with Suzanne. It has to be worth a go.'

Sean looked at him in despair. 'Will someone sit on him?'

'The thing is Joe, nobody cares,' said Corinne. 'She was a lovely girl, but she died 40-odd years ago, in an accident, basically at home. No conspiracy, nothing suspicious.

'But –'

'40 years. Please. Leave it. It's really depressing.' She tried to smile, but there was pain there too.

Joe looked between their faces. They all wore a similar look. He realised it was pain for him, and that drove him mad.

'But if it's all so long ago, why do you still care what Sean did to you?' He turned to Sean and Mick, 'And why are you two here fighting over Corinne?'

The silence which followed made him think he'd won. He went over to the box of school photos and dragged it out into the middle between them.

'Let's all grab some and see what comes up-'

'- no mate.'

'But –'

Sean stepped closer to Joe, in a move that reeked of fading patience and subtly rising anger. 'I came here to see Mick and Corinne. Mick and Corinne, they'll have similar reasons. The real question is you. Why did you get all dressed up in that brand new suit, which doesn't fit, by the way, pour on the aftershave, which you are supposed to use very lightly not sling on with a bucket, and come all the way from Brighton to this school building which, if I'm honest, can't hold many good memories for you? And why the hell are you so obsessed with Suzanne Devlin?'

So Joe told them. He kept the kiss to himself, but he gave them the rest. All about how he felt at school. All the pain, all the isolation – and especially all about the day he'd seen his dad digging the road, how everyone had laughed, and how

Suzanne was the only one of all of them who'd shown him any sympathy, through years at school.

Corinne got it, more than the other two anyway, and all three told him they were sorry if they'd behaved badly, but it changed nothing. He was still on the outside, and no-one wanted to talk about Suzanne.

It was Sean who summed it up. 'Joe, mate. I'm sorry you had a shit time at school. I'm still not sure why you're so obsessed with Suzanne, but, even if we wanted, what could we find out from here? We're locked in a gym with a load of old crap, and I for one am getting proper tired.'

Joe looked from face to face. They all agreed with Sean. So that, for the moment at least, was that.

20
THE OTHERS

It was later. There was silence from outside the gym, not a hint of music from the reunion, no sound from the outside world. They may as well have been immured.

Joe wandered alone among the corridors of junk. The other three sat separately, each downcast, each chased back into their memories.

Sean was reliving a blistering hot June day from long ago. Scared, sweating, he was running away from Bill Devlin's lock-up in the Fitties, dragging his bike through the green of trees, tripping over roots, slithering through long grass. Behind him a door slammed, and angry shouting came after him. He felt fear in his belly and acid in his throat. His bike was betraying him, catching in the undergrowth, and when the chain finally tangled in a net of thick briars, he dumped it without hesitation.

He made it through the trees, hit the grassy corner hard, vaulted a rusty old metal gate, and got out into the single lane road. There was a yell of 'Frigging in the rigging' and Mick Bluff hurtled in from his left like a pirate, jumping the drainage ditch and catching Sean up with no effort. He banged Sean on the left shoulder as he passed him on the right, and the two dug in to run.

To be safe, they had to get back to the line of trees far away on the horizon, back to the main road where passing traffic meant nothing bad could happen. The dusty strip of tarmac under their feet was called South Sea Lane. It cut due west for a mile and a quarter from the back entrance to the Fitties, dissecting the fields that lay wide open on each side, the fields that laid the two of them out bare under the big sky, and which offered no chance of concealment.

Sean could hear Bill Devlin pounding along behind them. Catching up with them was impressive for an old man, but Sean wasn't too worried; Bill wasn't fit, he'd get tired soon. But then he realised that wasn't good. The main road was a long way off, so if Bill got smart, he'd go back and get his truck. Sean and Mick needed to cover the distance before that happened.

Sean looked behind again, calculating. They'd ditched the fags in January and been training all spring, so they should be fine. The art would be to keep Bill dangling. If they could make him think he had a chance of catching them, they could string him along until he was stranded out in the open, then turn on the pace and leave him behind and trap him, unable to catch them up, too far from his lock-up to get his truck.

He punched Mick and nodded his head back at Bill and slowed the pace a fraction. Mick grinned, not understanding exactly why, but not caring. The knowledge they would mess with Bill's head was enough to make him happy.

They ran on for a time, cat-and-mouse, trying to keep the distance between them constant. But it was harder than it sounded while Bill lumbered like an angry ogre behind them. Sean risked a look and got a shock: there was no sign of the old man giving up. They'd misjudged how much they could play with him, and he was close, almost within grabbing range. Sean saw raw hate in his face, and scared now, he sped up. He passed Mick, who wasn't looking happy, having also learned the lesson that determination carries a lot before it.

The two teenagers concentrated on getting away. Running faster now, sound dropped away, and Sean fell into calm space. He felt the sun on his left shoulder, a faint sea breeze blowing on their backs. He noticed the smell of the cow parsley in foaming ranks on the banks of the dried-up ditches each side of them. He saw the dusty road stretching rod-straight ahead and felt a ten-minute chase which seemed like it would never end.

In later years, whenever he looked back at this moment, it went on for hours. A different person might count the mistakes he made to get this deep into trouble, and wonder what chance there was for salvation. But with each step Sean detached more, and more fear fell away. Over the years, his memory changed to reflect this. Now he looked back he saw it all from a distant height, as if he were floating in a balloon, or flying with the gulls, high above the three figures labouring across the landscape, soaring until the three humans below became nothing but slow-moving dots, an affectless scene in the vast flatness of the land by the sea against the horizon's curve.

Long after they would have thought possible, Bill gave up in a catastrophic commotion, his limbs flailing out of control as though the pistons on an old freight engine had all failed at once. Mick and Sean turned to watch him, bent forward, coughing and retching, still waving his fist in rage. As they watched, he reared up, cursing them still. Disturbed, they jogged backwards for a few steps, goading him, flicking him some Vs before turning to carry on jogging to safety.

It was a temporary reprieve, not the end of the story. All

three knew reprisals would come, but they dodged him well enough, and soon afterwards Suzanne died, and the world fell apart, and Bill's retribution got forgotten.

Run away and you'll be saved.

In his own corner of the sports hall Mick was thinking about his daughter Florence. About one particular morning a few months ago, when she'd held his hand and half run, half jogged to keep up with him. He had led her down dusty paths to the big swimming pool in the grounds of the hotel near his condo. He felt a molten shiver of pleasure when he remembered how she chatted to him as they went along. Such a sweet, sweet little girl. They slipped in the back gate of the hotel, dodged the ground staff, and walked to the poolside. The pool was busy with holidaymakers, but it was big, with room for them. He took her hand, they counted 1-2-3, and they jumped in together. The water was cool and deep as they dropped under the surface. The dust and the heat of the day left him. She bobbed up in her armbands next to him, laughing and splashing, and he saw she was safe before he dived under again, exhaling, expelling all the air in his lungs so he drifted to the bottom in the cool water that held him.

How hot the days could be in that country, how different Florence's childhood in Pattaya would be to his own. He wanted her to know what it had been like for him when he was very young. How swimming in the open air when he was five had meant the bathing pool at Cleethorpes, a shallow cement oval under a grey sky, filled with unheated water. You'd climb out, shivering, and run between the deck chairs of women in their flowery mini-dresses, men with rolled-up shirt sleeves, loosened ties and trilby hats, until you'd find your mam who would wrap you in a towel to keep you warm against the North Sea wind.

The bathing pool was long destroyed in a storm so Florence could never know it, but if she were here with him in Grimsby, she could still walk the streets he'd walked as a child. He wanted to show her his old house, the schools he'd been to, where he'd climbed trees. He wanted to take her to walk around Top Town, to cross the same road bridges and turn the same corners, to feed the ducks in People's Park, get chips at the Pea Bung, ice-lollies down Meggie's, get excited in the amusement arcades. Look out past the pier over the Humber to the Yorkshire coast, watch the ferries glide past, lie in bed at night in winter and listen to the dreadful moans of fog horns rolling in over the roofs of the town from the ships waiting on the muddy tide.

He was starting to doubt what he had done in leaving his family, but then he caught sight of Corinne, looking through a pile of old exercise books, and he knew he had not been misguided. Mick had more in common with Joe Belton than he knew. An old mechanic had said to him years before that nothing lasts forever, and Mick had spent years watching that come true. The people he'd met as he roamed the world, almost all had gone. Some dead, some made enemies, most, like Amita and Florence, left behind. But not Corinne Ayr. Through the army, the drilling rigs and the oil fields, all the bullying bosses, women and battles, the fleeing with his loot to the excitement of Thailand, as the seasons turned and he grew old, his feeling for Corinne stayed constant, burning quietly in the corner of his life.

He had a dream the night before he left Düsseldorf, on his way to Grimsby. He was with Corinne, in an old room somewhere. They were talking about nothing special, but something made him want to cry. She saw this, and whispered, 'Oh, come here', and put out her arms and gathered him to her and finally everything was good.

That was the dream, and it gave him heat in his heart, and patience over the evening. He had wanted her at school, but she had been with Sean, and, though he had watched Sean mess her around, the law of mates stopped any challenge. Now, so many years later, maybe two-thirds through his life, with only a few really excellent years left, things were very different.

So, as Corinne got up to wander off down through the boxes, and as he watched Sean shift in his chair to watch her go, he was calm and certain. He, Mick, was here for Corinne, and Sean should not try to upset that, or get in the way, or, worst of all, try to take her for himself.

Corinne turned corners, getting lost in the junk, and eventually she saw Joe in the distance. She was wary, but his position intrigued her. He was on his knees, bent forward and slumped over an old sofa, his head bowed, his arms out in front of him. She studied him, his bony backside in the suit, the price tag on the bottom of his shoes, his close-shaven hair, and the home-made tattoos on the backs of his hands. His surrender hit her most; he sprawled forward, loose and abandoned. She couldn't see the boy in him: that child was long gone. But in the trying, she nevertheless felt affection.

She stepped closer. His eyes were closed, and his lips were moving. She tried to listen, but he heard her, and looked up.

'I didn't mean to creep up on you. Are you OK?'

He got up, hurriedly.

'You look like you're praying!'

He shrugged, reluctant to answer, 'Yeah, I was. I started up on all that lately.'

'Really? So, what, you believe in God?'

He nodded, uncomfortable.

She didn't want to embarrass him, but she was curious. 'Can I ask what you were praying for?'

'This and that.'

She saw how his eyes slipped away from hers.

'If I were praying, I'd always ask for the winning lottery numbers,' she said.

'Hey, I do that too. A little prayer at the end. Can't hurt, can it?' His grin couldn't hide the fact he was serious about it.

'You've not won yet, I take it?' she asked.

'Not yet. But a tenner a week –'

'- a tenner a week? Are you serious?'

He shrugged, 'If He wants me to win, I need to be in the game.'

Joe wasting money he obviously didn't have made her obscurely furious. It took her back to how he was at school. Some people would never change. Joe would never get it right or do the sensible thing. He'd always be conned.

And the biggest con of all?

She couldn't help a sourness slipping into her voice. 'But honestly, how can you believe it? All that stuff about Jesus loves you? It's a fairy story.'

'It's no fairy tale. It's the truth. You should try it sometime. It would change everything for you.'

He'd stopped smiling, which annoyed her. 'I don't need to be changed,' she said.

But under his scrutiny, her words seemed to wriggle somehow. There was something off, and he could tell.

'Would you mind if I prayed for you?'

'Yes I would mind! I don't need that!'

'OK, OK, I'm sorry.'

He held his hands up to calm her. She hadn't realised she was being so agitated, and her own visceral reaction surprised her, 'You're all right. It's not for me, that's all. Each to their own.'

She didn't tell him the truth, that his offer felt too weird, far too intimate, and that made her feel sick. But the seriousness in him was heavy, and real, and it moved her to press him on why he had started this up, so late in life. So he told her all about how God was love, and how going to church made him feel loved. How his life had changed since he'd started going in there. How it made him feel like a better person. How it made him feel supported, like there was someone who constantly had his back. How he'd made friends there, how he felt people there cared whether he came back, and, he knew, would help him if he got ill, which, for a person like him, was amazing to have …

As he talked, she pictured herself chasing friendships and lovers through a hundred foreign beaches and bars in her twenties and her thirties. Coming back to Grimsby when her parents were ill. The long years in her forties without husband or children and believing she would stay like that forever. Meeting Paul as she turned fifty and thinking she'd found home. Which she had. A home with a 4D telly and a new kitchen and bathroom and a good car and a sun lounge and garden with decking for barbecues. All the basics for a sensible married woman without children. But the barbecue parties faded away and the kitchen always needed cleaning and the home soon clanged empty and hollow. She thought about sitting in front of that same telly through all the long silent evenings and weekends, with Paul ignoring her until he wanted her in bed.

Along with the other, far worse things he did.

A single vivid picture jumped into her mind. It was a bright snatch of memory. She was riding on her dad's shoulders. They were on their way home from the fish and chip shop round the corner from their house, and they were running back to mummy before it all got cold. Her dad held the bag with the fish and chips in one hand, held her feet with the other, and he jogged along, neighing like a horse, cantering along the cutting behind the shops. She had her fists buried in his hair and was leaning on his head, pressing into him to be safe, laughing and screaming with excitement, feeling secure and tall and powerful, not like a little girl, even a little girl on a horse. More like a giant on the back of an elephant heading home to a golden palace for tea.

Corinne realised she would never feel like that again, and sadness crashed over her. She couldn't help herself, because she didn't understand why that picture had come up now, but the sweetness and the love she felt in the memory of that moment was so awful she began to cry.

She noticed Joe had stepped forward, but he was hesitating, unsure what to do. How she hated a man who faffed, she thought, as her self-control collapsed. At least Paul never faffed.

She sat herself down on the sofa and made room for him to sit down beside her. After a while she leaned sideways into him. After a while longer she asked him why no-one loved her. He told her this probably wasn't true; he bet Paul did, and Sean and Mick were certainly interested, and there were bound to be more out there, loads more if she looked. That made her cry even more. After a while longer still, he put his arm round her shoulder, and she leaned into him in surrender, and he brushed her hair out of his face, and while he waited for her to come through it, he said a few words about her, under his breath, to God.

21

SEX

There was nowhere else to go, nothing else to do, so eventually Sean and Mick came along to find Corinne and Joe. It was a surprise she had been crying, and that they were sitting so close together.

Sean came forward, frowning, 'What's up, Cos? Is he messing with you?'

She glared back at him. 'He was praying for me.'

'Praying for you?'

Sean and Mick exchanged glances of clear disbelief.

Joe looked away, hurt by their contempt.

Corinne hated this. 'Don't you start picking on him! He's been nice. Which is more than I can say for you.'

She pulled away from Joe, sat up straight, wiped her face, and thought about this. She turned to Sean.

'You know, going out with you was probably one of the worst moves I ever made.'

'You say the nicest things.' Sean rolled his eyes at Mick. Women. It annoyed him to find Mick strangely unresponsive, but he didn't have time to think about that. He turned back to Corinne. 'Don't be like that. Fifteen to eighteen; we had as good a time as any couple could.'

She nodded. 'We had the best time. And that was the problem. You dumped me.'

'I didn't dump you. I went away to college. You stayed here. We grew apart.'

'You dumped me. Your first term, you came home, we had one row, and you dumped me on New Year's Eve. Just so you could go to that party.'

'Just because you'd been a nightmare all holiday and it was clear we had nothing in common by then.'

'Just because you wanted to sleep with Carrie Osmond.'

'Oh, come on. Someone had to end it – we were done. I happened to be the one who had enough balls to say something.'

'You know that's not the truth, Sean.'

He sighed. He did know, but he hated to admit he was lying, even now. He could still remember how it felt to be in his late teens. How horny he felt, all the time he was awake, and most of the time he was asleep. Lust was about the only thing he could feel all that summer after Suzanne dying, and he would lie awake in his bed worrying that some kind of demon had taken hold of him. Suzanne dying in the fire had knocked him off track. That summer he felt numb to everything and everyone – except Carrie Osmond. Carrie was the year below them at school, but at seventeen she looked like a Page 3 girl. The way her eyes would catch his in the school corridors made him feel sick with anticipation, in a way that being with Corinne had never done. The tension with her had bubbled away all summer, even during the fallout from Suzy, but nothing had happened. In late September he'd gone away to Loughborough, but he'd thought about her all autumn, even throughout the weekend Corinne came to stay in his hall of residence. By Christmas he couldn't bear it. No matter the cost, something had to happen between them. He loved Corinne or felt he did – he wasn't sure how you would know what love was when you were 18 – but Corinne had

had her long hair cut much shorter at the end of the summer and it had changed the way she looked. Short hair had made Corinne look ordinary, and he was only 18 and deep as a puddle and he wanted vivid and exciting.

Maybe after all this time it was the moment to be honest, and he wondered for a moment whether to tell her that. Then he realised saying he'd dumped her because she'd had a haircut would make him sound like a psychopath and he changed tack.

'It wasn't anything. I didn't see her again after that evening. It was just sex. She was bit mental, if you must know.' He wasn't about to admit Carrie had been so much more mature than he was, so clear and direct about what she wanted, that he had felt completely out of his depth. Just after midnight at the party she had taken his hand and led him upstairs into a back bedroom. The soundtrack was the Human League, Adam and the Ants, and Altered Images, the beat boomed and battered him through a thick fog of Stella and Johnnie Walker, and they had joined together in a frenzy. He had come back to consciousness midway through them having sex, and soon after they were finished, he had gone home and thrown away her number.

Carrie called his house once, but he got his parents to say he was out. He had never spoken to her since, but he had never forgotten the night either. Flooded with fear over what he had done, and guilt over how he had torched his relationship with Corinne, he ran back to Loughborough as soon as he could, even staying there through the Easter holidays, ostensibly to revise. There had been a long period during which he was terrified he would find out Carrie was pregnant, but as the months passed with no word, the fear receded. By the next autumn he felt safe, and vowed never, ever to be so stupid again. The spring after he met Rebecca and the direction of his life changed for good.

He came out of his memories to see the look on Corinne's face.

'Obviously it all meaning nothing to you makes me feel so much better,' she said. 'I was in love with you, in case you'd forgotten.'

'We were kids!'

'I'm serious. I thought we'd be together forever. I gave you everything. And you dumped me. That confused me so much. It devastated me. It took me years to go past it and trust people again. Years and years. I managed it though. I'm married now, after all. To someone who keeps telling me how much he loves me.'

'How lucky would you have to be for your first love to work out?'

'I blamed myself for a long time. I wished I'd pushed myself those last two terms and got better A-Levels. I thought for years if I'd got away to college I might have kept up with you. But now I look back, I can see how Suzanne dying upset you. We never stood a chance after that.'

Sean hadn't expected that, 'You knew I was upset about Suzanne?'

'You pretended you didn't care, but I could tell it had got to you. We were never the same after that. You just got so weird. But Suzanne dying was terrible, of course it was, I should have made more allowance.'

He shook his head, trying to process this news. She felt sorry for him and let him off the hook, 'It's OK. Now I know you were seeing her at the time? I get it, I do. Who wouldn't have been upset?'

Sean nodded, stared at his feet. 'It's all such a long time ago.' His voice was quiet. He looked up at her. He had to make one thing clear, at least. Out of kindness to her? Maybe. 'You know it wouldn't have mattered if you'd come to college? Once I got away to Uni, I felt the doors open. I felt my life begin. There was so much back here I wanted to leave behind.'

'Say what you mean, Sean.'

Sean realised how hard he had sounded. 'Not you. I didn't want to leave you. It was … You know. Mum and Dad. School. Grimsby. The fire, I guess. But when I got away, I changed so fast. There wasn't anyone could have kept up with me –' He cast her a shrewd look. 'You say you wanted me that much? Do you still? I don't know if I'll believe you if you say yes.'

She thought about it. Something had shifted for her as she had cried on Joe's shoulder. Something that had been frozen in her for far too long had thawed. She didn't know what she was going to do next with it all, but she felt freer. She looked at him, considering. 'You know what? And I'm not saying this to let you off the hook. You're right. I don't still want you.'

He crossed over to her and held his arms out.

'One last time. For luck.'

'Oh, for godssakes. Corinne?' said Mick.

'It's OK, Mick,' she said.

She hesitated, but Sean coaxed, insistent. 'Come on. For old times' sake. Cos?'

'For old times,' she said.

She allowed him to embrace her.

Mick watched them, his face stone.

22

THE CALL OF HOME

They held each other for a moment, until it became too strange, and they stepped away from each other.

'How did that feel?' Sean said.

'Wrong,' she said, sounding surprised. 'I felt nothing.'

Behind them, Mick got to his feet.

'Me too,' Sean said. I guess we're both happily married after all. There you go. Case closed. Friends?'

'Maybe,' she said.

Mick stepped forward. 'If you don't want her, I'll have her.'

'What am I now? A prize heifer?' She was so outraged she was laughing. 'You're all right, Mick. I'll manage.'

Mick grinned. He was used to resistance in the women he wanted, and it didn't bother him. 'You'd have fun with me at least. I'd help you remember what it's like being young.'

'I remember you being young. You spent most of your time outside the headmaster's door.'

'I never work too hard babe, you'll see.'

'"Babe". God, you were a nightmare. You used to scare me.'

Even Mick had to think twice at that. 'Little me? But I'm a friendly old thing.'

Corinne shook her head. 'You say that. You got in so many fights I thought there was something wrong with you.'

'I couldn't stand by if a mate was in trouble, that's true,' he said, more stiffly.

'But you started most of them! You remember Dave Derry?'

Mick wasn't sure where this was going, but he wasn't liking it. He was beginning to realise he might have a job on with Corinne. He tried to remember and failed. 'No.'

'Well, he'll never forget you. We were walking along home from school, minding our own business, when you ran up behind him, jumped on his back, dragged him on the floor, banged his head on the pavement, and ran off. For no reason at all.'

Mick had to laugh. That did sound like him. 'I was probably just being friendly. Saying hello and all that.'

'He didn't even know you! And he hadn't done anything.'

'I'm surprised he knew anyone if he was that unfriendly. Trust me, you've got to say hello to people in this life.'

'Don't give me that. You were a violent thug, and I bet you still are. Look at you. When did you break your nose?'

He shrugged. It had happened on a night some twenty-five years ago, when he and a mate had walked into the wrong bar in Archangel. There had been a roomful of Russian sailors against two of them, but they'd done OK, and if he was honest, he was proud of the mark it had left on him. 'I had a disagreement in a pub.'

'I have disagreements, but I've never had a fist in my face.'

'I've had far worse than that, don't you worry.' She was annoying him now. He'd have to bring this round soon, or he'd be getting angry, which wasn't a good look with any woman. 'You don't go in the pubs I do.'

'I've got more sense. Look at you. What does your wife think? You are married, aren't you?'

That made him miss a beat. 'Not as such. It's complicated.'

'Of course you're not married. So does Ms Complicated like it when you get violent?'

He paused. A long pause. 'She's called Amita. I just left her.'

All three of them were shocked. He liked them all a little more for that.

'Mate,' said Sean.

'I'm sorry to hear that,' said Corinne.

'I thought you'd be glad she was safe from me,' said Mick.

He saw that got to her, but that was irrelevant now. Why was he feeling so fragile? He needed to get a grip, to stop them feeling sorry for him. 'Don't worry, I've never hit a woman in my life. I've wanted to, but I never have. I left her, not the other way round.'

'Why would you do that?' Joe asked, annoying as ever. But Mick looked round the three faces, and saw their curiosity, and he had to unburden himself.

'If I'm honest, I don't know. A few months back I woke up. The sun was shining, and she was in the kitchen cooking breakfast. She was singing to Florence, our little girl. I lay there for a while and this funny feeling came over me. Ay, ay, I thought, morning glory, glorious morning – but it wasn't that. I had this weird feeling that everything I could see, everything I could hear, it weren't my life. Everything around me, it didn't belong to me. I felt nothing, not for either of them, not for the flat, not for lovely old Thailand. I went on for a while like that, thinking I was having a wobble and it would come back, but no. I got blanker and blanker. Amita got a right cob on, but I couldn't help it. Then, you know what happened?'

Mick looked around and saw, yes, they understood. Perhaps all too well.

'You got the invitation to come back here,' said Sean.

'To this reunion. And suddenly …'

'You knew where you belonged.'

'Yeah. Apparently I belong banged up in this gym for the night with you bunch of losers.' He laughed, but Sean didn't.

'So you left her? For good?' said Corinne.

'I left them. For good.'

'You left little Florence?' asked Joe.

'She'll be fine. She'll be better off without me. I'm not the stick-around type.'

'That's harsh, mate,' said Sean. 'Are you sure?'

'You got to face facts, don't you? Thinking about coming back here? It made everything out there fade away. There's something about where you grow up. The places. The people. What you go through. It hits you hard, and it hits you young, and it don't ever leave you.'

'Unfinished business,' said Sean.

'What?'

'Corinne, I mean,' said Sean. Mick gave him a warning look, but Sean ignored it. 'You came all this way to find out what happened to the love of your life.'

Mick couldn't read Corinne's face. Was there a hint she hoped that wasn't a joke?

'Mick?' she said.

'He's always been mad about you,' said Sean.

'Hang on –' said Mick.

She nodded. 'I know he was interested when we were kids. But …'

'Look at him,' Sean said. 'Look at his soppy face? All these years – and he leaves his family for you? You should reward him for his loyalty. Give him a kiss.'

'What? No!'

'Give him a kiss,' said Sean.

'Sean –' she laughed, flustered.

Mick tried to contain his growing interest. He realised how Sean's words were having an effect. How she seemed to be actually considering it.

Sean pushed again, 'Go on. Don't argue. Just do it.'

Mick saw her awkwardness and lifted his hands. 'It's OK Cos. He's being a twat.' He turned to Sean and punched him on the shoulder. 'He's good at that.'

'And you should know,' said Sean, the moment gone. 'Mate, are you sure about leaving Florence? Kids need their dad. If you leave her it's going to screw her up.'

'Debatable,' said Mick.

'Fathers aren't good,' said Joe.

'You said yours was,' said Corinne.

'He was top man until he died. I wasn't eleven, and he left me with my mam. That made me hate him alright.'

The other three looked anew at Joe. He had been silent for a long time, but this surfacing threatened a darkness no-one wanted. Corinne tried to head him off, 'I'm sorry to hear that. He's right, Mick. Dads are so important -'

'- you know when a young girl's been killed?' said Joe. 'The number one suspect is the father?'

'Well, of course. Keep it in the family. You men like that, don't you?' said Corinne. Joe threw her a glance and carried on, 'That's because the dad's normally done it. So where was Suzanne's dad the night the chalet burned down? Did anyone ever think of that?'

23

POWER OVER PEOPLE

Mick looked at Sean, saw the blankness on his face, and went first.

'And there's a question,' said Mick.

'I don't know, now you're asking,' said Sean, thoughtfully.

Corinne looked between them, staggered at the suggestion that Bill could have been involved. 'Oh, come on, why would he have done that?'

Sean considered, 'He shouted a lot. He used to knock her mother around, and her, from what she said. Maybe things got out of hand?'

Joe was on fire with this new direction. 'Is he still alive? When we get out of here, I'm going to talk to him.'

'I don't know, Joe. But the police would have interviewed him.' said Corinne.

'They'd have asked him every question in the book,' said Mick. 'Twice.'

'Yeah but –'

'And back then they didn't have to go light to protect his "rights" said Mick.

'Yeah, but –'

'It's a bit of a stretch, Joe,' said Corinne, doubtfully.

Joe turned to Mick. 'Where were you? You were seeing her, weren't you? Did you see her that night? Did the police talk to you?'

'Don't be daft,' Mick said. 'We weren't going out. We'd have an occasional bunk up.'

'How charming,' said Corinne.

Joe turned to Sean. 'What about you?'

'Get out of it,' Sean said.

'He was with me', said Corinne. 'That evening? The evening of the fire? We were together all the time. We walked out to Waltham. To the Tea Gardens.'

'Ohh, the good old Tea Gardens! That's where you were?' said Mick.

'Yeah. The Tea Gardens. I remember it well. Why?' said Sean.

'No reason.' Mick was mightily amused at this, and Sean's grin was breaking through his clear initial annoyance, but neither he nor Sean were letting Corinne or Joe into the joke.

Though it was irritating to her that the two men were always digging at each other, that there would always be constant tension and jokes she didn't understand, Corinne didn't really mind. It had always been like that between them. She could even see it as comforting.

Her own memory of the evening was misty, uncomfortable somehow. She put it down to the fact that around that time she and Sean had been learning how much fun it was to drink. She remembered wooden tables, and benches in long grass, and towering trees in a green dusk. There had been lanterns hanging in the branches and later on, when the moon came out, the round shadow of an owl high up and far off. Those days for her were full of excitement. She and Sean would soon be grown-ups, and soon they'd be going out to do things and make things happen. She thought they'd travel to visit the wide horizon of the welcoming world before, at some point still blurry, getting married, having children and beginning the shared life for which she believed they had both been born.

Sean broke into her recollection. 'What do you mean, keep it in the family?'

'What?'

'Suzanne's dad. You said he was keeping it in the family.'

'Well, they do, these guys, don't they? They pick on the women close to them. And never anyone their own size. Disgusting.' She was a little too vehement. Sean stared at her, and she couldn't meet his gaze.

Mick knew something was happening, but he couldn't see what, 'I knew a woman my size once. Olga the Shot Putter. Scary lady. Panzer Tank Mark 2.'

'Did she tell you what to do?' asked Sean, amused.

'Walk there, do that. Mysteriously I found myself doing exactly what she wanted whenever she wanted.'

Sean nodded, digesting that. 'Power over people is a strange thing. Hey Corinne, stand up a moment?'

'What?'

He was gentle. 'Go on. Just for a moment.'

Corinne was puzzled, but she went along with him, and stood up.

'Now sit down,' he said.

'Why?' she said, but she sat.

'Stand up,' he said.

'No. Sean, what are you doing?'

'Go on, it'll be OK.' His voice was low now, insistent, and commanding.

'No. You're getting weird,' she said.

'Stand up. It's safe.'

'Leave her, Sean,' Joe broke in. He didn't understand where this was going, but he didn't like it. Mick watched, keen-eyed, fascinated.

'It's OK. She's OK. Corinne – stand up please,' Sean said, and, despite herself, Corinne stood up.

'What do you want?' she said, anxious.

'There's a question. What do we want, Mick?'

'What a question,' said Mick, a flood of excitement filling his belly.

'Mick wants a kiss. Go over and kiss him,' said Sean.

Mick felt the happiness of complex friendship. He threw Sean a glance full of knowledge and darkness. He was more than annoyed to find Corinne wouldn't play.

'In his dreams,' she said.

Sean kept it going one more moment, 'What's a kiss? It's harmless.'

'Forget it,' said Corinne. She sat down, annoyed, the mood broken.

Sean wasn't stopping now. Mick watched him switch to light and good humour. The guy was good, no question about that. He was charming. People liked Sean. Almost everyone did. It was a miracle he didn't abuse that power more than he did.

Sean leaned into his theme, 'What is a kiss? It's something that can stay with you all your life. Who forgets the first time they get kissed?'

'Tell us about your first kiss, Corinne?' Mick said. They were back as brothers in a dance of flirtation with the girl in front of them.

'You perve. Why would I do that?'

'I want to hear about it.'

'It's private. You tell us about yours.'

'I'll tell you about mine,' said Sean. 'You remember Sally Grant?

'Yeah. Maybe.' said Corinne.

'Red hair? Tall, liked John Travolta and all that disco stuff? Anyway, you remember the summer we were thirteen? We all used to go back to school in the evenings and play tennis on the courts there?'

She shrugged. 'Not me.'

'OK. Well, I'd go with some friends, and she'd go with hers, but at the end of every evening we'd walk home together. I really liked her, and she really liked me, and we both knew it, but could I make a move? Could I hell. Didn't know what to do. So one evening she gets a puncture on her bike. I have a look at the tyre, and yep, it's flat all right. I say I'll try pumping it up, and she passes me her pump. I'm squatting down, pumping away, but getting nowhere, so she bends down next to me to see what's what. So, while we were down there, both squatting in the gutter next to her bike, we kind of collided, and I grabbed the moment and ended up kissing her.'

Everyone laughed at the picture, even Joe.

'Hey, that's, er, beautiful mate,' said Mick.

'Seriously?' said Corinne, laughing outright.

'It was heaven,' Sean said.

Even as they all laughed, Sean crossed over to Corinne, took hold of her left arm and pulled back the long sleeve on her dress. She struggled, tried to free herself, but he soothed her.

'Let me. Corinne. Let me do it. It's OK.'

His calmness overtook her. She stopped struggling.

'We're old friends. You can show us.'

He pulled back her sleeve, pulled it up past her elbow. Her forearm was covered with savage bruising.

'Bloody hell,' said Mick.

Sean reached for her other arm, gently dealing with her resistance.

'Give,' he said, and she finally held up that arm, rolling

back the sleeve herself. The bruising was even worse, and there was scarring up around the inside of the elbow.

'Is that a burn?' Mick asked.

24
THE SECOND KISS

Corinne looked around them, at the horror on their faces, and her face filled with shame.

'That was a hot saucepan.' She dabbed at her bruises. 'I'm clumsy. I bang into things,' she said. 'I know it looks bad, but I've got really delicate skin.'

A sadness fell on all three men.

'And this is the guy who you know loves you?' Sean asked?

'He loves me. So much. I don't doubt that.'

'Why would you ever doubt that with your fancy bruises and everything?' said Sean.

She looked between them all, saw their faces, and her flush of embarrassment deepened, until it squeezed her stomach and made her feel sick.

'But that's why he does it! He gets so stressed when he thinks he might lose me.'

'Do you have affairs?' said Mick.

She looked at him, outraged. 'No I do not! But I do know what it feels like to lose someone. You can't help it. You feel sick all the time. It's OK. I'm OK.'

Not OK enough for Mick. 'How long has he been doing it?' he asked.

'Not long.'

'How long?'

'A couple of years. A bit longer. I don't know. Honestly, we're really happy. He's had a lot to worry about, that's all. He's got anxiety. He hasn't got many friends. He argues with the neighbours.'

'He'll get anxiety when I see him,' said Mick.

'No, please. He'll kill me if he knows I told you.'

'It looks like he'll kill you, anyway.'

'Of course he won't! It's the story of me. It's my fault!'

Mick knew she believed that. He felt compassion for her, and rage. And he knew how his rage would play out. By the time they were out of the sports hall, it would have settled down into a steady bed of fire that would heat up the most heinous punishments for this man. But in the meantime, he enjoyed the feeling of volatility. 'That's it,' he said. 'First thing we get out of here, I'm going to see him with a hammer.'

'You'll see him with a hammer.' Her contempt was unexpected, and it knifed him.

'If he's lucky. Have you got any better ideas?'

'You're so, so stupid. It makes me weep.' And he saw how Corinne was indeed nearly weeping, mixed with her laughing at him, and he knew he would do anything in the world to stop this happening.

'So he can knock you around all he wants, and that's OK? No chance. No bloody chance,' he said.

'What's it got to do with you?'

Mick exhaled, battling to control himself. She'd asked a fair question, and how could she know the answer? He took a deep breath, nervous. But sod the others and what they thought. He needed to catch her up.

'We're talking about first kisses. I'll tell you about mine,' he said.

'Oh, please do,' she said. 'I can't wait.' She looked at Sean and Joe. 'And no, before you two ask, it wasn't me.'

Mick began a story he'd told no one. It was a story about a few minutes in his life that he held as close to him as a talisman. In those moments of four a.m. free-fall in a temporary bed; on long train journeys when he had forgotten where he was going, or why; being yelled at in the days he had bosses; when he broke up with yet another woman and he realised he was back to being alone; he would think of this moment and it would bring him hope. In this he and Joe were far more like brothers than he could have ever guessed.

His voice gentle for once, he told them about his first kiss.

'We were twelve, thirteen. It was snowing, icy. We had a real gale blasting in all week. The teachers didn't care, they chucked us out at dinnertime anyway, said it was good for us. For a couple of days, while it lasted, we'd all squeeze up together in a doorway to get out the wind. Fifteen, twenty of us, lads and lasses, jammed up against each other to keep warm. Everyone was laughing, talking, loud and fast. I guess we all knew what was going on. We were excited. Everybody rammed close. Boys next to the girls, all mixed up, all pressed tight. You couldn't move an inch if you were at the back. And a lot of them hands started to wander. One day this girl I liked – I mean really, really liked – stood in front of me. We were so close, pressed together. I dared to put my hand on her waist. I could hardly breathe. I remember, after a moment she leaned back against me, lifted her chin. I kissed her neck. Just brushed my lips on her neck. She didn't look round, but she pressed her cheek against my face, leaned back into me for a moment.

'That was my first kiss. Well. The first time I kissed anyone, anyway. And guess what …'

He looked around. At Sean, amused and intrigued. At

Joe, who wore an unreadable expression. And at Corinne. Who was aghast.'

'That wasn't me!?' she said.

'You just never knew it was me.'

'I can't believe you remember that!'

'I've never forgotten it,' he said, wary.

'I've never forgotten it either,' she said. 'But I've never forgotten having the measles, or the time I fell off my bike!'

'It wasn't like that!'

'It wasn't like anything. I can't believe you've brought it up!'

She was obviously horrified.

'Don't you want to give it a go then? Me and you?'

There was a long gap. But the look on her face was disgust.

'Oh Mick, I'm sorry,' she finally said.

'I'm not in love with you or anything. I just wanted to see you.' He knew he sounded like a child.

'That's so awful,' she said.

'What's awful, babe?' he said, a trickle of aggression now dropping between them.

But she wasn't intimidated. 'You're awful! Leaving your wife for a playground grope? I'm awful. Look at me. Look at my arms! And I deserve it. Who'd want me?'

He looked at her arm and saw the damage, and it moved him to love, and so he humbled himself.

'Make me an offer. I'll think about it.'

She knew the two of them were close to the bottom now.

'Well, I don't want you. I like my men to have more than two brain cells. Bloody hell! Stupid, stupid school reunions. Look at us. All of us, getting old, thinking we'd come back here and it would all be OK. It's pathetic.'

'So you don't feel anything for me?'

Corinne looked angry, and agonised, and Sean stepped

over, his hand lifted. 'Mick, mate, this is getting embarrassing.'

'I want to be clear, mate.'

'No. I don't feel anything for you. I really don't. I never have. I never will,' she said to Mick.

He felt the wave of inevitability that had lasted most of his life finally break. Marooned on the rocks, he looked around for help from Sean, who looked sad, and Joe, who looked scared.

He sat down, trying to control his breathing, as the tumult threatened to tear him apart.

'I came all the way from Thailand.'

'I hope you got a return ticket,' said Sean.

'Why don't you shut up?' said Mick.

'Sean, leave him alone. He's upset,' said Corinne.

'You know how to turn a woman on, don't you?' said Sean. 'A bit of grovelling, a bit of aggression? Exactly what they like. You've lost it, mate. You used to be cool.'

'What do you know about anything?' said Mick.

'Why don't you tell us some more about your poor broken heart?' said Sean.

Calm fell on Mick. He looked up at Sean, 'Just telling it like it is, old buddy?'

'You know me.'

Mick nodded. 'Telling it like it is. You're very good at that. You're a specialist. But there is one thing that you've never quite told as it is, isn't there? One tiny little great big awful thing that you've never quite told anyone how it is. Do you know what I mean? And now you've got Corinne wrapped up in it too. I can't believe she'd be so stupid, but there you are.'

Sean had nothing to say to that, as Mick knew very well. Mick knew he may regret this. Or maybe he wouldn't. Maybe there were some things that needed to be worked out. But he could see in Sean's eyes he had rattled him.

Corinne looked between the two of them in apparent confusion. 'I'm wrapped up in nothing. What do you mean?'

'Ah, it must be love,' said Mick, his sarcasm hiding his pain at the way Sean still got such preferential treatment.

'Oh, shut up Mick, will you?' she said, finally furious.

Mick shook his head. 'I dump me family and I come all this way to see her, and she's telling me to shut up?'

He tried to contain it but couldn't. Yelling, he stood to overturn the table next to him. A bookcase stacked with old computer monitors went next, slumping into a heap. A shelf of Pyrex from the chemistry lab cascaded onto the floor. For what seemed like minutes he hit and kicked out at everything around him, pulling down shelves, overturning boxes, toppling stacks of desks, undoing his wasted hope, smashing holes in the past.

To the three around, even Sean, it was terrifying.

Eventually he calmed and noticed the others again. It was the fact that he caught Joe having the nerve to look at him which bothered him the most. 'What are you looking at?'

'You. Mate.' said Joe. For a second it looked as though that "mate" provocation would earn him a beating. But Mick was spent for now. He turned and walked off down through the ranks of darkness, away from them all.

When the echoes died away, Corinne turned back to Sean. 'Well, Sean. What exactly is it that I'm wrapped up in?'

25
LOOKING FOR METEORS

He looked puzzled, and affronted. 'I've absolutely no idea. I haven't seen you for nearly forty years, remember?'

She studied him, studied the lines on his face. He seemed as puzzled as her.

'Seriously. I've no idea what he's on about.'

'So why did you want to come and see me after so long?'

'Morbid fascination?' Sean replied.

'Thanks. I'm not that bad.'

'You're not that good either. How did you, of all people, end up with a man who'd do that to you?'

And there they were, the focus skipping away from Sean's answer, back onto her. How did she always give up her power like this? Yet she had to justify herself.

'You wouldn't understand,' she said.

'Why do you let him hurt you?'

Being honest about this was hard.

'I guess I must like it,' she said.

'How could you ever like that?'

It was a genuine question from Sean, and she needed to do it justice.

'Not being hurt. I don't mean that. But that stupid game

you did on me? All that stand up sit down? You know where that goes. And when it's right, it's exciting.' She threw him a sharp look. 'Surrender. It's at the heart of love. You know what I'm talking about, don't you? You spotted it.'

'Maybe I do. But look at your arms. That's not love. It is only your arms, isn't it? '

'There's a lot of different ways to love someone.'

'The old Corinne – if someone tried to hurt her, she'd have had none of it. Certainly wouldn't have stuck it out for years.'

'I did stick it out for years.'

'What?'

'But you never came back.'

'Oh, come on!'

She didn't want to waste time on anger. So once again, she told the truth, shameful as it may be. 'I'm serious. I gave you my life. It took me years to move on. Years and years.'

'I'm flattered.'

'Don't be. It's imprinting. Baby ducklings do it with whatever crosses their paths. It means nothing. It's just a bugger to get rid of.'

He pointed out the obvious, 'You're married now. You must have got rid of it at some point.'

'So I did.'

'What happened?'

'I met Paul. I'd tried a sales job at that point. A direct marketing company over in Scunthorpe. I was awful in it. He was the manager. The way they ran the sales team, it was very theatrical. We had a lot of … rehearsals. On our own. He was trying to make me better. He just seemed kind, concerned, like he was going to look after me.'

'Always a winner. And it went wrong when?'

'It hasn't gone wrong. I love him, I do. I'm not always happy with him, in fact I can get furious with him, but that's OK.'

'But –'

'When he hits me, we argue, he apologises, he's sorry, and it's over. It's not too bad. We get through it.

'I think you've lost the plot.'

'I haven't. It works.'

'How could it ever work?'

'You know we've been talking about first kisses? There's your very first kiss – but then there's the first time you kiss someone new. That's almost as powerful.' She paused, considering best how to tell what she felt was a very confused story. A story she still felt had profound gaps in it, somewhere in its fabric. Logical gaps that, no matter how she turned her head, she couldn't quite see.

'We'd been working late in his office,' she began.

'Rehearsing.'

'Exactly. The office had a little garden, and it was warm, so we sat out there in the dark for a while. It was summer and we were looking for meteors. After a while he reached over and he pulled me to him and kissed me. The thing was, I didn't want to kiss him.'

'And that's why you were sitting there all alone in the dark with him.'

'No. I liked him, but I'd decided I always hurt men, so I wasn't going to get involved with anyone else. So I wasn't keen. I didn't let him kiss me. I even tried to pull away from him. But he pulled me to him, and he was very strong.'

She told Sean, and Joe who was still there, his head bowed, all about that evening, and the evenings and weeks following. She remembered how she'd felt. At that time of her life, she had been determined to be celibate. Men, and what happened between her and them, was too complicated. She had learned that, as someone got close, she would try to push them away. She never meant to, on the surface at least, but there would always be the pressure she'd feel, and a panic, and she'd pull away.

She had therapy in her thirties, and in her forties, which had identified the problem as a lack of trust caused by early trauma. 'Sean!' she'd thought when she heard this (and he had the good grace to look sad when he heard this). Yet therapy only went so far. Having the diagnosis healed nothing. The clarity she felt would soften when she got lonely and then vanish in the emotions of meeting someone new. Internet dating fed her sickness faster, and she burned through men. She grew so exhausted with dating. With the angry calls, the furious emails and texts, or the broken guys who kept on turning up for her in that shadowy, forlorn way. Let alone how depressed it made her, how painful it was to leave yet another person who was perfectly sweet but who had been foolish enough to fall for her. She entered each relationship in good faith, but perhaps after the first sex, certainly within a few weeks, the passion would ebb, leaving her with only a curdled depression that would build until she had no choice but to break off the relationship.

In her fiftieth summer she decided it was over. She was sick of causing pain. Finally, calmly, irrevocably, she decided she would be alone from then on. That was her first surrender.

So, when she met Paul a few months later, it annoyed her to feel such a pull to him. When she stopped struggling and let him kiss her in the garden, it seemed like a reward. Paul's mouth was warm, his lips soft and dry, his kiss tender. Even so, she hesitated. She pulled away and tried to end things there, but Paul wouldn't let her, holding her arms and, suddenly fierce, pulling her back to him.

That was her second surrender.

That night was one of the most exciting of her life. He opened the door to an experience she had never known before. It wasn't all good; in the weeks and months ahead, a devilish mischief entered their bedroom, but that never took over. If there was an element of repentance, of purgation for all her crimes, in the way she tolerated things going too far, well, there are worse things than repentance.

This third surrender made her feel good, and loved, and the pain which went alongside it all stopped it feeling claustrophobic. At 57 she was finally at a point of balance. A place where she could feel a kind of love and give a kind of love back.

She knew Sean wouldn't get it. She doubted anyone would get it.

'That doesn't sound right to me,' he said.

'Life is a compromise, isn't it?' she said.

Joe heard all this and watched Sean working to process where Corinne was now. Joe could see how he was trying to persuade her she was wrong to believe in a man who could beat her and burn her. Trying to save her, but with no clear direction, no clear idea of a path out. And from the footsteps in the distance Mick was coming back, no doubt to swing the conversation back in his direction for a time, which would probably lead to more anger, more battles between them all.

Joe felt so sorry for them. They were like children. Their pain, their longings, what drove them, their compromises, none of it seemed right. They were all trying so hard but were all so misguided: Sean hovering far above anything real or anything that could matter to him. Corinne trapped in a self-harming lie, and Mick bathing in an anger which could only consume him and lead him to darkness. None of them had any notion of the simple path to a good life that was always there for the asking. But Joe couldn't help them. They'd never listen to him. And he had listened long enough. He had to deal with what was inside him. He had to find the truth.

Mick arrived back, and the conversation fell away, and Joe took his chance to dive in.

'I've been thinking, and I can't explain it,' he said. 'Why

would Suzanne's dad want to chase you? What had you done?'

Joe watched the question land between Mick and Sean. Saw the tiny hesitation before they answered. The microscopic build in tension. A flood of adrenalin hit his belly. His instinct was right after all. There was some kind of guilt here: guilt to be uncovered and laid out in the light.

26
STOLEN GOODS

Sean and Mick told the story of the chase down South Sea Lane in such a way it made them and Corinne laugh – but when it came down to explaining why they were being chased, things got vague. Whether it was vandalism, whether Suzanne's dad had caught them stealing something, they couldn't quite remember. Foggy on the details, they accused each other of making things up. They wondered if Bill had a drink problem, they certainly denied there was anything significant going on.

'Did this happen before or after she died?' Joe asked.

'Before. Had to be,' said Sean.

'Why "had to be"?' said Joe.

Sean considered. 'Mick never went back after that night. I knew him a bit better, so I went round after Suzanne died. I didn't know what to say to him, but I had to go and see him. I can still see him sitting there. Filthy clothes, he hadn't shaved for a week. Red eyes. He hated me by then, but he cried to see me that day. He took my hand, shook it for ages for going round to see him. May your teenage daughter never perish in a fire, folks.'

It was a terrible image, but through it all Joe got a sense

of a performance. Sean was acting this, or presenting it as an offering.

'I thought it was the afternoon when he chased you?' said Joe.

'What?' Sean said.

'You said Mick never went back after 'that night'.'

Caught out, Sean struggled for words.

'Do you mean Mick was round there on the night of the fire?' Joe asked.

Sean missed a beat, and Mick saved him with a joke, but missed another beat himself and they all realised the moment for telling any lie had gone past and there was no option but to speak the truth.

'Yeah, I was there, OK?' Mick said, looking Sean full in the eye as he spoke. 'So what? I've got nothing to hide.'

He turned back to Joe and Corinne. 'I went round to the chalet to see Suzanne. But I left about seven. Got the bus to Scartho, went to my mate's house, sat and talked to him and his mum and dad. As I told the police. I went home at ten. Went to bed. The fire was at nine thirty. I was nowhere near.'

There was a moment of silence.

'You've got a good memory,' said Corinne.

'When you've sat in a cell for two days being asked the same questions, you do tend to remember the answers.'

That surprised Corinne. 'I never knew that. That they had you in I mean.'

'I wasn't proud of it.'

'I thought you'd think it was cool,' she said.

'It didn't seem right boasting about being hauled in for questioning when she'd just died.'

Corinne nodded, still sceptical. There was something amiss. And Joe agreed.

'So that's something to consider,' he said.

'Consider what? What are you on about?' said Mick.

'You've come over here with this sad story about leaving

your family, feeling all out of place, but how do we know you're not the big murderer after all?'

Mick's jaw dropped, and Sean laughed out loud. 'Woah, so it's definitely a murder now is it?'

Sean stood up, jovial and calming. 'Back in your box, son. We're getting silly now. I tell you what, I wish we had something else to do in here except talk. Talking's great, except when it isn't. Where's that Hungry Hippos?'

'Tell us about Suzanne,' Joe said.

'What about Suzanne?' said Mick.

'Tell us about you and Suzanne,' said Joe.

'There's nothing to tell.'

'I definitely disagree. When did you first start seeing her?'

'Do you believe this guy?' Mick looked around for backup and was surprised to find it wasn't forthcoming from Corinne.

'I do believe him, yeah,' she said. 'And there's one or two things I'm curious about as a matter of fact.'

'Where did you used to go with her?' asked Joe.

'I can't remember. Walks in the park. I don't know.'

'How often did you have sex with her?'

'You little pervert,' said Mick.

'He'll want all the details next,' said Sean.

'When was the first time? When was the last time? If you stopped, why did you stop?'

'None of your business,' said Mick.

'We've got all night. I want the details.'

'You're not getting them.'

'When did you start going out with her? When did you last see her?'

Corinne joined in. 'And what about her dad? Her poor, angry dad? What did you both do to him to make him chase you all the way along South Sea Lane?'

Mick looked from one to the other. 'I didn't kill her. No-one killed her. No-one even knows how the fire started! She died in an accident!'

'You would say that, wouldn't you?' said Joe.

Mick strode over to Joe and grabbed him by his shirt, hauling him up out of his chair.

'You want to shut your mouth, pal.'

'Ohhh … here we go,' said Joe.

Mick held Joe by the collar, turning and squeezing the cloth until Joe battled to breathe and stopped struggling, standing still and closing his eyes. Somehow Mick resisted laying him out. Throwing Joe away from him, he turned to control his temper. Joe got up and loosened his collar, rubbing his neck.

A long moment passed, and then Mick turned to Sean. 'Hey now Seaney. You're not saying much. Have you noticed, Corinne? Aren't you curious why Sean isn't saying much? He's normally got such a big gob.'

Sean shrugged. His voice was low, calm, as if nothing had happened. 'Joe's lost the plot, and you're losing your temper, same old same old. What's to say? I think we should all calm down, move on and talk about something else.'

'Come on, Corinne, does that ring true?' said Mick. 'Old Sean staying out of a wind-up? Aren't you curious about him? A little? You know there's something wrong with him. He's all murky, don't you feel that? Think back, we were all poor comprehensive kids together, none of our families had money – but remember those presents he used to buy you for your birthday? All those things? Remember how he always had money to take you out? Where did all that come from? Didn't you ever wonder?'

That resonated with Corinne. 'His mum and dad gave him it. Though I did think that was strange when I went round their house.'

'That's being polite. Their house was a pit, you know that,' said Mick.

That annoyed Sean, as it was meant to.

'Just telling it like it is, Sean. Your mum and dad were good people, but they didn't have a pot to piss in. So how come Corinne gets to go to London with you when she's sixteen, Paris when she's eighteen.' He turned to Corinne and thought for a moment. 'How come he bought you all those clothes?'

Confused, Corinne said, 'He had a pools round. I thought …'

Mick jumped in, 'Delivering pools coupons every Thursday? That job paid four fifty a week! That'll get you to London and Paris, sure it will. I'm not the only bad lad, Corinne, not at all. You want to think about it. Maybe old Goldenballs here isn't quite so golden after all.'

That sank in. Corinne spoke slowly, cautiously, 'Well, Sean. How did you afford to buy me all those nice things?'

'On his side now?' said Sean.

Corinne chose her words. 'No sides. But I am curious. Indulge me.'

'There's no big secret. I saved my money. I've always been good with money. Not like my parents, I–'

'Four pounds fifty a week?' she broke in. 'Do me a favour. I'm not a kid any more.'

'OK. I used to do a little shoplifting. To order. For kids at school. Most people wouldn't do it. In fact, they said I was bad for doing it. But when it came down to it, most of them wanted a new Adidas bag. Or a nice jacket. Shoes. Whatever.'

Corinne was finding this very hard to hear. 'People used to pay you to shoplift for them?'

'Yeah. And I got good at it.'

'And you called me a thief!' said Joe, unable to keep quiet.

Sean turned on him fast and hard. 'I thought we'd hear from you. There's a difference here, matey, a big difference in scale. I nicked some stuff from a few department stores. You got tooled up, went out at three in the morning, broke into peoples' homes, in the dark, stole things from their bedrooms when they were sleeping. My victims? Some pennies off the bottom of a profit-and-loss account. You go round and do a job, the people lose things they care about, they've had burglars in their house, worst case they'll have screaming nightmares for years. You're talking to me about crime? Forget it. Just forget it!'

Joe backed right off, scared of more violence, and, more than that, at a deep level knowing Sean's words were true. His own self-hatred kicked back in. Whatever he did, he was always worth less than these people. Stressed, and closing down, he fumbled out his tobacco pouch, rolled himself a cigarette.

Mick looked on, disgusted. 'No mate, we don't mind if you do.'

Sean looked up sharply. 'He's smoking? Have you got a lighter, Belthead?'

Joe froze, suspicious and defensive.

'Look at his little face!' said Mick, amused. 'It's OK mate, we're not going to hurt you.' He threw Sean an interested look, 'Are we?'

But Sean was concentrating on the lighter. He stood in front of Joe and held out his hand. 'Can I?'

Joe pulled out his Zippo, handed it over. He had a bad feeling. A bad thing was coming, but he couldn't yet see what it could be.

'I don't understand?' Corinne asked.

Sean nodded up at the ceiling, and Joe followed his direction.

'Look,' said Sean.

'At what?' she asked.

Joe followed his direction and realised his mistake. He felt sick. He had to do something.

Stepping away from them and scanning left and right, he headed for the nearest wall of the sports hall.

Then Mick understood. 'Smoke detectors.'

'A fire alarm!' Corinne said.

'We need something to burn,' said Sean, looking around. There was a lot of stuff around them, not much that was obviously flammable.

'Paper. We need paper.' he said.

Corinne and Mick joined in the search.

Behind them Joe was searching wildly along the walls, pulling down shelves, running between the stacks.

Mick found the box of photos. 'Here we go!'

'No! You can't burn them!' said Corinne.

'Not the photos – the box!' he said. He upended the box so the photos fell out, and ripped off a strip of cardboard. 'Here.'

The Zippo wouldn't light at first.

'I'm out of practice,' Sean said. 'Healthy lifestyle.'

He got there in the end and ran the flame under the cardboard. It ignited with a small pop. He blew on it and fanned it alight.

They all stood back, watching the smoke coil upwards to the ceiling.

'Oh my god oh my god we're getting out!' said Corinne.

'We might even make it to the pub,' said Mick.

'Do you think the sprinklers work? It's going to be so cold!' said Corinne.

'I'll swim if I can get out of this place,' said Sean.

The smoke went up, and up, coiling towards the detectors, when an enormous banging crashed across the hall. They whirled, and saw Joe, away down the hall by the doorway, swinging at the wall with a spade.

'What's that clown up to now?' said Mick.

He and Sean took a step, then another, trying to make out what Joe was doing. And then it became clear. He was attacking the fire alarm junction box on the wall. As they watched, he prized it loose, and hacked at it with the spade, smashing it up with a manic energy alarming to watch.

'What are you doing?'

All three of them ran to stop him, but it was too late. The box split into pieces, broken class and circuit boards hanging out. Joe dropped the spade, grabbed some cable cutters, went to work on the cabling.

'Stop it!'

There was a bang, and a flash, and Joe staggered back, falling into a pile of junk.

The box hung loose, cables sparked, then died out.

They stepped closer, taking in the damage to the box, each of them aghast at what it meant. Joe, forgotten, lay groaning on the floor. Above them the smoke drifted past the useless smoke detectors.

He looked up at them, scared.

27

195 LASHES

It surprised Joe that it was Corinne who was most angry.

'Why would you DO that?' she said.

He tried to look past her face of pure fury. His hands and his arms were vivid and throbbing from the pain of the electric shock. He wanted sympathy, consolation, someone to hold him as he went out on this dark journey into confrontation, but he knew now he was alone.

'We can't leave. We've not finished talking about Suzanne,' he said, his voice frail.

'You bloody idiot! We'll be stuck in here all night!'

For a moment Joe thought that was the end of the matter. Then Mick moved in. 'You stupid, stupid, stupid …' He kicked Joe in the stomach, once, twice, before Sean pulled him away.

'There's no point,' said Sean.

'I disagree,' said Mick.

'Leave him. It's not worth it.'

Mick gave a roar of rage that echoed up to the steel roof and stepped away to cool down.

'Knowing this school, the alarm's knackered, anyway,' said Sean.

'Is that all you can say?' said Corinne.

'Got anything better?'

She couldn't believe what she was hearing. 'I can't stand any more of this. I want to get out. I don't want to listen to this any more, I don't want to talk about that night any more. There's nothing else to say, alright? Nothing!'

It startled Sean how agitated she was, 'You were the one egging him on.'

'I wasn't egging him on,' she said. 'I felt sorry for him.'

'Do you still?'

She shook her head in despair. 'No. Yes. But some people bring it down on themselves.'

Mick stared at Joe getting up. 'This evening? It's a disgrace.'

Joe propped himself against a stack of fence stakes. It wasn't too late to salvage this. They would all calm down in a minute, and he could get to the point. He tried to explain himself, 'I wanted -'

Mick grabbed him again and put his face up close to Joe's. 'I'd be very careful how you proceed, Belthead. I'm in a bad mood now.'

'Don't, Mick,' said Sean.

'Why not?'

'Because …' but Sean couldn't think of a reason.

'I can't hear you,' said Mick.

A bubbling of fear began in Joe's chest. 'You want to know why I'm doing this? I'll tell you. We were eight or nine. We were playing Kiss Chase. She ran into me, and she snatched a kiss off me. She smiled and ran away –'

'– who did? Suzanne?' asked Corinne.

'Yes, Suzanne. I can still see her now. See the way she grinned back at me as she ran off. The look on her face -'

Mick rolled his eyes and looked at Sean, who nodded back at Mick, who began to pull two skipping ropes out from among the junk.

'You were all talking about first kisses? That was mine. You know what it was? A promise.' He stopped, distracted by Mick and the skipping ropes. What was this guy doing? Knowing Mick, it couldn't be good. Talking faster, he went on. If he could make them understand, he'd be OK.

'Her kissing me like that made me think I was the same as everyone else. It was a promise I'd have a nice life, be part of things. But that was a lie. There was you lot, at school always having a go. My mam, drunk every night. No food at home, no new clothes for school. No mates because I was weird. So I started to rob. Started breaking in places. I did them flats. But I weren't so clever at that. How could I be? So I get nicked. And then there was that first time in court? That's when I got blown away. That magistrate sending me away so soon. It's so hard to stay away from drugs in prison. It's so hard to keep straight when you get out –'

Something about Sean's face went sour as he said this. Joe stopped, puzzled. He had a sudden certainty that he had hurt Sean. But how?

'You'll not stop, will you?' Sean said, his face a mask.

'Stop what?'

'Banging on.'

In that moment Joe could have battered Sean. He tried to calm down. To be reasonable, but it was near impossible. On a rising tide of anger, he tried to explain. 'All my life I've had sod all. Except sometimes I'd remember Suzanne. Like you remembered Corinne. And you two know what went on that night – so tell me what happened!'

For the first time Joe saw how Sean and Mick had come closer, till they were looming on each side of him.

Sean looked at Mick. 'I've had enough of this one now, Mick. Have you had enough of him?'

'Very much so,' said Mick.

Sean turned to Joe. His voice was low, and reasonable. 'Get up on that chair, Joe.'

'What?' said Joe. He looked at Corinne. It was clear she didn't know what was happening. But he did. That sense of the world collapsing, the precarious safety wall between him and chaos falling down, it was all so familiar. A moment of pure panic hit him. He couldn't see where he was going, he didn't understand what was ahead of him, there were no guarantees of anything, the ground ahead of him could vanish, he could fall down a colossal sink hole …

'Go on, get up there.' said Sean.

'What are you talking about?' said Joe.

Sean lashed out at him with one of the skipping ropes and pain burned across his belly. Sean struck again and Joe tried to catch the rope, but Sean pulled it away so it scorched and twisted the skin of his fingers.

Joe felt the pain in his hand and looked at the two men in amazement. 'Oh, come on.'

He turned to appeal to Corinne, but she said nothing, and Joe didn't know why. Whatever was coming, did he deserve it? Did she think he deserved it?

'Up on the chair.'

'No chance –' and the skipping rope hit him full across his face. That was too much for Corinne.

'Stop it!' she said. 'Stop it! Have you gone mad?'

To no avail. Sean continued to lash at him, and Joe backed away, until Mick kicked a chair over to him. 'Get up on there.'

Shaking, terrified, resigned, Joe got on the chair.

'Take your jacket off,' Sean said.

Joe did so.

'Drop it.'

Joe did so.

'Now your shirt. And your trousers,' Mick said.

'No! What are you doing?' Corinne said. But Joe was past defiance. Familiar terror had taken over. He took off his shirt, kicked off his shoes, and dropped his trousers. He stood there, on the chair, naked except for his socks and boxer shorts.

'Undies on or off? What do you reckon, Corinne?' Mick asked.

'Keep them on, for god's sakes,' she said.

Joe tried to turn away from Corinne, to save the worst of his shame. He had always hated his body, and now he was in his late fifties that was far, far worse. No arms to speak of, skinny as a lat, with a pot belly. Who was he to think of fighting anyone?

Mick pulled out his phone. 'Are you on Facebook, Joe?'

He took some photos. '"This is Joe Belton, enjoying his school reunion."'

Joe was feeling it now. Hopeless and powerless. Just like the old days. 'Please, don't.'

'Stop it! Both of you!' Corinne was getting angry for him, but it wouldn't be any good, that he knew. They were off the leash now, and this had a way to run.

Mick tapped his phone. 'I'll save them for later. When I get a signal –' Corinne lunged for his phone, and he held it away from her. 'Ah, ah. Best not get in the way, love.'

They walked around Joe, looking him up and down.

'Looking good. Well. For a homeless.'

'Bit grown-in-the-dark, don't you think?'

'I love the tats, mate. Do them yourself, did you?'

Joe didn't answer, and Mick whipped the floor with the rope again, 'Did you?'

Joe nodded. 'Not all of them.'

'He got a bit of help to look that good. Nice one.'

They began to break him down.

'You're not married, are you?'

'No.'

'You don't own any lighting company, do you?'

'No.'

'Or a house?'

'No.'

'Married?'

'No.'

'Where do you live?'

'I'm in a hostel at the moment. I'm going to be housed. It's alright.'

For a moment he saw pity mixed with the contempt, and he didn't know which was worse. He thought that could be the end of it, but they weren't done. They carried on walking round him, and he waited, trembling. Their anger was still to come. He didn't know why that would be, what he had done to offend them, but then he never had known back in the day either. Yet he realised this time was different. Somewhere he could feel fear in them.

'You remember when you come to this school, from your junior school?' Sean asked. 'There was a rumour. They always said that, on the first day, the older lads hold you up and flush your heads down the toilets.' He looked around. 'You remember that? Well, that didn't happen to me. Or anyone I knew. Did it happen to you, Mick?'

'Not me,' Mick said.

'Corinne?'

'Of course not!' said Corinne.

Sean turned back to Joe. 'Joe? No lies now.'

It hurt Joe to admit it even now, but Sean wasn't going to let him off the question.

'Yes.'

'Yes what?' said Sean.

'Yes, it did happen to me.'

Sean sighed, and Joe realised that wasn't enough.

'Sean?'

But Sean stared him out. Until Joe understood what he wanted from him.

'Yes, it did happen to me, sir.'

Sean nodded, kind and understanding. 'Of course it did, Joe.'

'Why are you doing this?' asked Corinne, appalled.

'"Some people bring it down on themselves,"' he quoted her.

Corinne stared at Sean with contempt, but Joe knew it wouldn't be enough to save him. Sean caught him looking and yelled at him.

'Eyes front!'

Joe came to attention, and Sean came back to him.

'You're nothing, are you, Joe?'

'No. I'm nothing.'

'Just a liar and a cheat and no one to be listened to.'

'I'm a liar and a cheat and no-one should listen to me.'

'Ever.'

'Ever.'

Sean nodded, but he wasn't satisfied. So they carried on like this. They shredded his dress sense, his life choices, his character, his family – and then they got onto his faith. Mick went back to how Joe had been praying for Corinne earlier. He thought it made sense for a loser like Joe to have an imaginary friend who would help him feel better.

Joe wondered if this was where the fear was coming from. Did they feel judged by him? He was already learning that some people hated Christians. Yet he couldn't give it too much thought. They were grinding on with their mock interrogation, and he had to work hard to focus on what he was saying. They asked him all about church, how he got into it, what it made him feel like, but after a while their mocking and their malevolence became too much, and he felt knocked off track as his defences crumbled. His words felt hollow, his voice sounding thin and ridiculous as he tried to explain the visions he'd had. Worst of all he started avoiding saying the word 'Jesus', as it had sounded stupid and embarrassing. He felt that all his journey into the supernatural was as though he'd been gullible, conned. Real life included nothing supernatural. Real life was all about, had always been all about, standing on this chair, facing people like Sean and Mick.

He tailed off into silence, defeated and dried up as their glittering eyes mocked him. Thinking they surely had to let him be now, he moved to get down, but Mick lashed at him with the rope and so even at that point he had to climb back up and stand again, until Corinne looked up at him with sad eyes. 'Why do you take it?'

He stared out across the sports hall, trying to lose himself, trying to submerge himself somewhere to avoid the horror. He tried to take himself back into the refuge of the past. When he was ten, lying on the grass of the field behind the Rose & Crown after a game of football, watching the high-up, rose-coloured clouds drift into the quiet sunset. The first evenings at a youth club, when he'd worn the wrong new shoes and five button high waist trousers, and the wrong new jumper, but they'd all let him off because everyone was so excited to be there. Walking along Scartho Road when he was fifteen, thinking about Suzanne and singing 'You're the One That I Want'.

None of it sustained him. All those touchstones of his past seemed pale and grey, fading away, lost forever in the face of this attack.

The Devil was in them now. Unhappy with his answers, they flogged him with the skipping ropes, drawing blood across his back. Corinne cried out at that, but that didn't help him because her concern for him felt worse than being hit.

He prayed to Jesus, but no help came. He hung on to the idea he was doing it for Suzanne, but the last turn of the knife cut that support away. It came when they'd finished hurting and humiliating him, and Sean had thrown his lighter back at him. He missed the catch, which made them roll their eyes, and then Sean gave his final judgement.

'You poor idiot. You think Suzanne Devlin was some kind

of saint. You know she was sleeping with everyone she could by the time she was fourteen? We all had a go, didn't we, Mick? Some of us went back for more, some of us didn't, but she was always up for it. Saint Suzanne? You've spent your entire life pining after the school slapper who everyone had except you.'

Joe could take no more. He let out a long, low howl of pain. He doubled up, crouched on the chair, and Corinne stepped forward.

'Get down, Joe,' she said. He wasn't listening. He was wondering how he might kill Sean Garner.

'Joe? Come on. It's OK.'

Slowly, gingerly, he got down from the chair. She put his suit jacket back on his shoulders, but he batted her away. She tried again, putting her hand on his shoulder to reach him. He shook her off, retreating into himself.

Corinne looked at Sean as he laughed and chatted with Mick. She turned back to Joe, addressing him directly, but also speaking loudly, so that everyone would hear.

'There's one thing you need to know, Joe. What I said about Sean being with me the night she died? All that crap about the Waltham Tea Rooms, the lights in the trees? Well, I've been thinking and I remember now. He was there with me, but only just. I waited for him for hours, drinking cider on my own, feeling stupid, thinking he'd stood me up. He turned up just before closing time, and he told me I'd have to lie for him. I've told that lie ever since. If you want the truth, I don't know where he was that evening.

Joe looked up at her through his pain, and felt a burst of mad, crazy hope drench his wounded heart.

28
THE THIEF

They were scattered, in silence. Corinne was recovering from a lacerating attack from Sean. He said she was making the whole thing up. That her marriage made her want revenge against all men. She was sure of what she was saying: he had been late. He asked her to lie for him. Where he grew overheated and loose, she became calmer and more controlled. But inside, how she was glowing! She was molten with change. Speaking the truth had caused the rocky terrain of her last four decades to lose its form. There was a better life ahead of her, no doubt. It was far off, a dream of a better country, but she knew she was on her way.

Sean paced. The original anger at Corinne's betrayal had faded into wonder at how different their lives were back then. How much had changed in the world, and in him. He was also amazed at how Corinne was still overreacting to him being with Suzanne. It must have been a surprise for her – but, frankly, the idea that anything from twenty years into the last century could still impact anyone was absurd.

As ever, he was detaching, moment by moment, from the stress. Soon he was back in the Lakes, running along the towpath with Callum, thinking about the gin and tonic and roast dinner waiting for them – but he found he couldn't concentrate on the daydream. He kept getting tangled up over that Christmas run. There was something bad going on in the trees above his head. Something about a great branch falling kept distracting him, sending him off in an oblique anxiety.

Mick had listened to them arguing for a while, then he had shut off. The noise, the vehemence, Sean's posturing, the dislike it laid bare, it all took him back to a time when he would hear his parents arguing in the kitchen while he sat in his bedroom. The fact this meant he saw Corinne as more of a mother than a lover didn't escape him, and in different, less awful, times it would have given him a rueful smile. He had always been outclassed by Sean, always been the child to their married couple, even when they were all fifteen, and though he had hoped that would have changed, that he could have approached Corinne from a position of strength, the churning of rejection in his stomach proved it was no different. So he too escaped into his imagination. He sat in a corner, planning the greatest DJ set in the world, quietly tapping the changes from tune to tune on his thigh. He smiled to see the audience moshing in front of him, their arms outstretched and reaching up to him as he danced in the DJ booth, the audience and the DJ all connected, alive, everyone in the room experiencing the moment as one. Times like that felt, to Mick, like a foreshadow of something greater, a true taste of how heaven would be, if it existed.

And Joe. He may have been sitting astride the old motor mower, fiddling with his lighter, but his mind was in rapid, flickering motion. Renewed hope had given him an idea. An idea that led him off beyond the walls of the sports hall, flitting across strange starscapes of potential, sacrifice, and truth. He saw old spirits being laid to rest, tied souls being cut free. He witnessed the destruction of fiefdoms of sin, regret and misdirected longing that had imprisoned all of them in the past. He saw glimpses of something fearful on his near horizon, which echoed an ancient surrender, and promised delivery and freedom for all of them. He had a job to do. If only he could dare to get it right. How far would he, could he go?

'Where was you that night, Sean?' Joe asked. He felt stronger, more confident. 'How come you leave Corinne standing like that?'

Sean looked bored.

'Sean? What happened that night at the chalet, mate?'

Sean stared at Joe with an acid contempt. It was obvious he wasn't going to answer that question. Ever.

Joe ran the silver Zippo back and forth along his thigh, flicking open the lid and sparking it up in a single, deft movement. He held the lighter out, angled it this way and that, admiring the flame.

'You see this lighter? I got it from Suzanne. When we was eleven. We all went to a school trip to Flamingo Land. She won it on one of them grabbing machines in the arcades on the front. She couldn't believe it, she were jumping up and down yelling, she were that happy. She said she never won owt.'

'Why did she give it to you?' Corinne asked.

He flicked the lid shut. 'She didn't. I nicked it off her.'

'You have to laugh,' said Mick.

'It's the best thing I own,' said Joe. 'Why was her old man chasing you two that night? Go on. You may as well tell me now.'

Mick looked at Sean. It seemed to Joe that Mick wasn't

seeking permission. More calibrating what would happen if he told the story. It was clear he wasn't sure. Sean shook his head, but Mick went ahead anyway.

'What the hell. It was years ago. Who gives a toss? So. Me and Sean? We let old Bill Devlin down.'

'How?' asked Joe.

We were business partners,' said Mick.

'Excuse me?' said Corinne.

'Yeah, I know. Give us a break. We were kids. Kids with big heads. He heard about Sean shoplifting, so he asks him if he wants some proper work. Sean wasn't sure, so he got me involved. Bill got up to all sorts, out in that lock-up on the Fitties. He'd get naughty stuff coming in off the docks and he'd drive it out all over the country – but he wanted two fit kids with a bit of gumption. Me and Sean would go out and steal cars for him. Nice ones only. He'd have a shopping list. He'd hide them away in the lock-up until he could get them shipped out through the docks to Sweden, and then we all got paid.'

'You are joking?' said Corinne.

'Sadly not,' said Mick, enjoying her reaction. 'We didn't make that much because he was ripping us off, but we didn't know any better. We didn't realise he was having us, but we thought we'd have him anyway. He couldn't sell any cars if we didn't nick them for him, so we downed tools until he paid us more. He sacked us off, so we said we'd tell the police about him.'

'He didn't like that,' said Sean.

'You can say that again. We went down to the lock-up one day, and I have to say, he was perturbed. Definitely less than happy. Displeased even. I've never seen a man his shape run so fast. So that's why he was chasing us that day. Thank god he was an old man.'

'And did you tell the police?' asked Corinne.

'Of course not,' said Mick. 'We weren't stupid.' There

was a change of gear coming, and Joe paid even more attention. 'They did start asking questions though. Do you remember?'

Sean nodded. It didn't look like a happy memory.

Mick went on. 'All winter before that, there was this copper who was getting annoying. Ganniston he was called. He must have heard something about us and the cars. Wherever I went, he was always there. Always having a dig. So we decided we should get on their good side. Give them something else to look at.' He fixed Joe with a direct gaze. 'We'd heard you'd been burgling. Mr Ganniston, he was new, and dead keen. He was very interested in hearing all about what you'd been up to.'

'He bought us a breakfast,' said Sean.

It took a moment for Joe to understand. 'You told the police I'd been burgling?'

'That we did,' Mick said. 'Well. Sean did. He said it made sense.'

Joe stared at Sean. 'I did two years because of you?'

Sean shrugged. 'You had done the crime to be fair. We can't be having too much sympathy.'

Joe tried to process this. 'How did you know? I never told no-one.'

'One of the lads at school saw you crawling into a window back of Weelsby Street. But mate, a lot of people knew you were up to something. You started turning up in flash clothes. That silly hat you had. Not very Joe Belton, was it? So, yeah, I did have a word with Ganniston. He wasn't very interested at first, but I got him there in the end. If it was between me or you going down it wasn't going to be me.'

Joe couldn't believe it. 'I got sent away for that. It was very hard. People picked on me, but it wasn't like school. I couldn't get away. That time was the end of me.'

'Old Sean here, he does that,' said Mick.

'What do you mean?' said Sean.

'Look at the way he's smiling,' said Mick. 'He's so shady this bloke, don't you think, Cos? He comes over all jolly and cheerful when you meet him. But he's so deep, and dark, and shadowy. And right deep down in them shadows there's something not right. You know what I mean? Something twisted. Something horrible. Don't you think?'

'You want to shut up, mate,' said Sean, as he got up.

Joe stepped away from them, away down a corridor in the junk. There was a booming in his ears. Behind him he could hear Sean and Mick squaring off, but he couldn't make out the words. He passed on deeper into the sports hall. He needed a place to sit, a place to let his burden down for a moment.

He had always seen that first borstal sentence as a watershed in his life. Before he went inside, he stood a chance. After that, no. The court put a mark on him, and two years in the system ground itself into his bones. He never walked in the world the same again, and the world recognised that in him and responded.

It was a run of burglaries that did for him. The tower blocks off Albion Street were a terrible place to start, because there were only a few routes through each tower and there was no way out if he was caught, but he was young and stupid and had seen that as part of the deal. He'd found a broken service door near the bins that he could shove open, and, once in, the service stairwell took him to every level. It was winter when he started, and he'd wait for the nights where heavy rain came blowing in from the river, drifting across the town in sodden sheets, weather that meant most people were at home watching *Coronation Street* or *The Liver Birds* rather than looking at who was on the landings. He'd get into the block, slip up the stairs, and find a flat to open up. At that time of night, if the lights were off, they weren't going to be in bed, they'd be out on the evening shift, or down the pub. Either way, that was safe enough. Those council door locks were easy, and he found out he only needed a few minutes to lift any money left lying around.

Joe only took money. To sell things on he'd need people to buy from him, and by that age he'd realised he wasn't so good at people, at least not so good at making them like him, or do what he wanted them to. So he "cut out the middle-man", as he liked to think of it, and went straight for the cash. He looked for pensions, dole money, nicely stuffed brown pay packets, but best of all were the little nest eggs stored in the tea pots, at the back of drawers, in the fridge, even once in an old treacle tin in a still-warm oven.

He didn't do much with the money. He tried getting some booze a few times, which was stressful enough given his age, but it only made him roaring and chaotic before he threw it up. He bought himself a neck chain and a gold name bracelet, but that seemed stupid because he couldn't risk wearing it and he didn't like himself in it, anyway. He bought a lot of tapes for his cassette player, he got into all the new Two Tone stuff before anyone else at school, even got himself a fishtail parka and a pork-pie hat, but that wasn't a lot of fun with no-one else to do it with. He'd thought about saving it all up and getting a Lambretta now he was sixteen – there was a beautiful one all in dark red down in the window of Freddie Frith's – but he knew anything like that was pie in the sky – how would he ever explain a new scooter to either his mam or the cops?

So in the end he didn't know why he was constantly robbing like that, but he stopped worrying about it, got his head down and grafted. It became what he did. He started doing a few flats in a night, expanded into other blocks, and the streets round about, and the money piled up in the box under his bed. His method got better and better, growing from something like controlled terror to focused adrenaline, until he stopped fearing ever being caught. He saw himself as a ghost who would pass through the lives of the people he stole from. Pass through in such a tidy way that they might not even notice their cash had gone for days.

When the police knocked on his front door, he was so taken aback to see them he didn't even try to run. And then, finding himself in court, he could only think to blame his mam. She must have found the box and got it open somehow and told the police. But he could remember watching her in court, and she looked too embarrassed for that. She was there out of loyalty, even he could see that, and though she was doing her best to keep a poker face for the sake of all the busybodies, he could see she was upset, and hated all the people sitting there in judgement on him. He took the comfort he could from it.

The head magistrate, an old, pink-faced bloke with a bent back and watery eyes, had given him hope. He spoke so kindly to Joe, asked him all about his life, and why he was stealing. He listened so intently, and seemed so understanding, that Joe had felt he could speak truly about what had driven him to break into all those flats. He felt the magistrate to be such a sympathetic ear that, when he gave him the maximum sentence, the sucker punch took his breath away. He realised too late the twinkle came not from empathy, or compassion, but from the pleasure of extracting the most juice out of Joe that he could.

Then he arrived at the borstal, and the lights went out for a very long time. He didn't have time to obsess in the day, as it was all he could do to keep himself safe. In the evenings he would agonise on how he'd been caught. He'd retrace each night out robbing that he could remember, looking for mistakes. He avoided the worst of the drugs in there – all that came later, when he was safe on the outside – but there was something about the sweat, the dirt, the violence, and the refusal of hope which damaged him forever.

So now he knew. It was Sean who had told the police. He thought about killing him, but not for long. There in the sports hall, under the blank orange lights, the Holy Spirit came to Joe, and for the first time a sense of compassion for that entire time fell upon him. He saw a series of pictures of himself, a combined picture of his life. He saw himself out in the world, felt again the sadness of the Joe who thought he knew what he was doing all those years. He saw himself drinking, robbing, chasing women, flailing around with drugs, and gangs, and knives, and revenges, believing he was finally getting some respect, having large portions, not seeing how he was only slipping lower and lower.

He felt pity for the poor, lost man who had been in such pain without realising it all that time.

He gave thanks for God's patience in waiting for him to get up to speed. He prayed for forgiveness for what he'd done. He prayed for those victims of his crimes who were still alive. He prayed for Mick, and Corinne, and after a big old battle with himself, he prayed for Sean. And he prayed for himself, for the poor lost kid who had turned into this poor lost sod of a man. He prayed he might let himself be loved by God, and he prayed he might be of service instead of being such a total messed-up basket case. All in the Lord Jesus' name. Amen.

And yet, there was one thing still left to do. It nagged away at the corners of his consciousness. It would be with him soon, he knew.

29
RAMBLING OUT

In the hour or so since Corinne's rejection had shown him the stupidity of him coming halfway round the world, in the time since he had discovered his feelings for her were about as useful as mist, things had been shifting for Mick.

There was a rock-and-roll song they would all dance to in the lunchtime bops at junior school. He'd sung it a lot when he was a kid, and it had been running through his mind just now. No surprise, it was always useful when a girl turned you down.

I've been rambling out all my life
Happy with the pretty girls, never needed no wife
I stride into town, find the best one there
If she falls for me, well I don't care
I've been rambling out, rambling out, rambling out.

He'd loved that song. When he was young it summed up everything he thought a man could ever want.

When he got older, he realised there was another part to the song. The beat changed, and the singer's voice got sadder, and the words got more complicated. Like real life, he used to think:

Carol's the girl I'll give a shout

We'll be together tonight, tonight get busy
She's gonna be blue when she finds out
(Because they always do)
How I'll only ever be true
To my Lizzy

He liked that sadness, because he understood it, and it made him feel good. Corinne was his Lizzy, no doubt about it. Always there in the background, always available. The ultimate consolation. His ultimate home.

The story he told himself was one day he'd find her again, and she'd finally realise she wanted him, and they would be together, happy ever after. So in the meantime, he didn't have to commit to anyone else. In the meantime, he could go on enjoying life as he best wanted. Fighting, drinking, shagging, getting the best of everything.

But in the last hour another line from the song had barged its way into his head:

Feet of steel not clay, but I'm going no place.

He'd sung that so many times, but he'd never noticed the 'but' in that line. He assumed it meant that he'd stand strong and steady whatever challenge came at him. Now, that 'but' jarred him.

He realised there was another way of looking at those last four words. For so many years he thought he'd been in charge. That he'd kept himself safe. But all this time, had he been going no place?

Something was off. Deep, deep in the set-up of the whole thing, something was built badly.

He shifted, uncomfortable, wanting to find the angle to explain this. He looked at Sean and Corinne, and at Joe, who had arrived back looking like he'd seen a ghost. Interestingly, for once Mick didn't want to punch his lights out. He tried to find words, and couldn't, but he had to begin somewhere. 'Did I tell you I'd left my family?

Sean groaned. 'You did mention that, yes mate. Is there something new you want to tell us?'

'Maybe. Maybe not. Thing is, Amita, my Mrs, we're not actually married.'

'OK. Why not?' asked Corinne.

'If I'm honest –' He looked at their faces and he could tell they were curious already, and his hesitation made them even more so. He hated that. Talking about this stuff was weak.

He dug down inside himself, and surprised himself by what he found, hidden and fecund under a rich peat of lies. 'For a long time I've been telling myself I don't want to marry her because she only needs me for my money. If we get married, she's got her hands on that, and she won't need me no more. But I'm wondering now whether that's all of it.'

'What do you mean?'

'Am I lying to myself? She's always saying she loves me. Always. So why don't I trust her? Why don't I marry her?'

'Because you came halfway round the world chasing Corinne,' said Sean.

'And look how that worked out. I mean it mate. Why isn't Amita enough for me? She's not bad, really. She's pretty good in fact.'

'Strong praise,' said Sean.

Corinne rolled her eyes. 'Do you love her?' she asked.

'That's not such an easy question, is it?' said Mick.

'It should be,' said Corinne.

'I mean, I fancied her like mad. For a few years, anyway. We had a lot of laughs. We still do when we get drunk together. She's a good woman, works very hard. Very loyal. She's a good mother to Flo.'

He hesitated, aware how flat his comments sounded. 'It doesn't sound enough, does it? But you could make a go of it, lots of people would, and maybe they'd be right to. I've never been much cop at staying with women. But I don't want to be too hard on myself – I've never had chance to concentrate on them. I've always been too worried. I've always felt something was going behind me. Following me. I've spent more time worrying about that than anything else. Sorry, Amita. Sorry to all of them.'

He paused, and there was silence.

Joe asked his quiet question. 'When did you start feeling like this?

Mick knew without having to think. 'The weekend Suzanne died. I missed her, you know. I thought it would go away. But it didn't. Always after, I've been waiting for something to catch up with me. I don't know what.'

He had begun to pace, more and more agitated. He looked at Sean. 'What do you think?'

'Don't ask me, old mate. I can't help it if you're a screw-up.'

'I'm the screw-up? Me?'

'Don't go there. OK?'

Mick opened his mouth and closed it again as Sean gave him a ferocious glare.

A pregnant silence fell. The palms of Joe's hands were wet with expectancy. Until he realised the other three weren't going to say any more. Until he realised things were going to go back to how they were.

He couldn't let that happen. 'Did you light the fire in Suzanne's chalet, Mick?'

'No.'

'Did you, Sean?'

'No.'

'But you know what happened, don't you?'

'Even if we did, would we tell you?' said Sean.

'Mick?' Joe asked.

'What he said,' said Mick.

'Corinne?'

'I don't know, Joe, honestly I don't,' she said.

Moving like he had the weight of generations on him, Sean stood up. 'I've had enough of this.'

He started pulling out a pile of gym mats.

Joe stepped forward, alarmed. 'What are you doing?'

Sean didn't even look at him. 'We need to get some sleep.'

He carried on lugging the mats out, and pointed out some old curtains, high on a shelf, and told Mick to get them down for blankets.

Joe couldn't believe what he was seeing.

'No way. No way!'

Joe ran to Sean, trying to pull the mats off him.

Sean punched him high on his cheek bone, and pain exploded in his face. He lashed back, loose and sloppy, yet he managed to connect with Sean's ear. They fought, a scuffling, messy scramble, with Joe coming off worse, until he tripped and sprawled on the floor.

Weak and lost, he bawled back up at Sean, like a child. 'You can't sleep. Not now.'

But they were going to.

Corinne was upset, and, more than anything, tired. 'It's very late, Joe. Come on. It'll be OK. If we sleep, I'm sure we can get out in the morning.'

'No. No!'

He looked around wildly. Seeing an old Esso can by the mower, he picked it up. It was heavy with petrol and made a solid weapon. He swung it at Sean, and it landed square in his back. Sean stumbled and nearly went down, staggering away.

He recovered and turned, rubbing his back. His gaze at Joe had an alien coldness. But that didn't matter to Joe, who advanced, swinging the can.

'Tell me what happened!'

Sean dodged and dodged again as Joe flailed with the can. 'You little – pack it in!'

Moving past Joe's windmilling arms, he swung with all his weight. He punched Joe in the stomach, a clean blow, with all his rage, landing his fist full and square and intense in Joe's solar plexus. Stricken, Joe collapsed to his knees, trying to roar, gasping for breath, but still questing. 'You have … to tell me … what happened.'

'Nothing happened. Now go to sleep.'

Sean turned back to laying out the gym mats. To him, Joe was done.

Joe fell in a heap and struggled to breathe. The pain in his stomach made him want to throw up and to leave his body all at the same time. He closed his eyes, tried to let it go, tried not to pass out in a state close to delirium.

And lying there he realised what to do. His idea had crystallised. It was fearful, and savage, yet it used every scrap of his paltry self to its very best advantage.

30

THE SURRENDER AT THE HEART OF LOVE

Joe panted now, not from the fight but from the courage it took him to consider this next step. He held the idea up and tilted it this way and that, like a diamond dealer testing a suspicious gem. Whatever way he looked at it, whatever the light that refracted through it, whether guilt, loyalty, agony, grief, surrender, sacrifice, it seemed right. This idea felt inescapable, like the summit of his life, the very nub of him.

Joe got up. If he didn't do this, then what had his life been for?

Sean and Mick had laid out three gym mats and stretched out bundles of curtains for blankets. They and Corinne were sitting there, taking off shoes, outer layers, and getting themselves ready for sleep. Their conversation was low and calm, all concerned with pillows and comfort, and whether they all had enough blankets. It all looked domestic, a parody of similar scenes from so many other bedrooms across the country.

Slowly, quietly, Joe retrieved the petrol can from where it had fallen. He unscrewed the cap.

He called to get their attention. When he was sure all three were looking at him, he upended the can and dowsed himself with the petrol. Then he held up his lighter for them all to see.

'Tell me what happened that night!' he said.

A flood of adrenaline smashed across his entire body, and he felt more alive than he'd ever known himself.

Sean and Mick both leaped up, fanning out, their hands in front of them.

'Calm down, mate. Calm down,' said Sean.

'Take it easy man! What are you doing?' said Mick.

Joe shook his head. He felt calm enough. 'I don't want to do it,' he said. 'But then again, I do. Your choice. What happened that night?'

'Joe, please,' said Corinne.

Joe flicked back the lid of the Zippo.

'Woah, woah, don't!!' Both Mick and Sean were yelling now.

'Tell me what happened.'

Corinne took another step forward. 'Please, Joe. Please don't. I'm begging you. Please.'

There was a tenderness to her voice that puzzled Joe. 'Why do you care so much?' he said.

'Why shouldn't I?' she said.

'You didn't care much before, when I was up on that chair, stripped naked. You looked like you thought I deserved it.'

'I'm sorry,' she said.

'I didn't expect no better. Not in my heart. That's what happens to me.'

Sean stepped forwards. Joe saw with interest how he had completely lost his composure. 'Joe mate. I'm sorry you feel this way. What can I do?'

Joe felt a burst of irritation. How much more did he have to keep on saying this? He tried to master the irritation, but his voice cracked. He was not as calm as he wanted to be.

'Tell me where you were that night that you had to get Corinne to lie about it.'

'I can't remember. I'm sorry. I'd make something up, but there's no point. Put the lighter down. Seriously.'

Sean's face glowed with sincerity, and compassion, and, Joe noted, genuine fear. Joe tried to control his own emotions and did his best to speak calmly. 'No. I think it's time I did this. They treat me worse than a dog. Always have.'

'You said you've been homeless. That you aren't working. That can't make you feel very good.'

Joe shrugs.

Why don't I give you a job? I've got a big company. I can find something for you. I bet I pay more than Asda. Do you drive? I can probably find you a car too.

'You don't mean it, do you?'

'I do. Go on. Think about it.'

'No ta. I've had enough crap from people.'

'Please. Joe –'

'- you just need a bloody good holiday -' said Mick, glancing at Sean. Mick and Sean were beginning to circle Joe now, beginning to take charge, beginning to look for advantage. 'Why don't you come over to see me in Thailand? There's enough women over there to make anyone forget anyone.'

'Did being in Thailand make you forget Corinne?'

Mick tried to dig his way out of this gaping hole. 'Yeah, for a while.'

'Then why are you here?'

'Oh, come on man, I've told you about all that.'

'You said you felt Suzanne's death had chased you all your life.'

Joe looked between them all, as they stood frozen in panic. Petrol fumes were burning his eyes and the back of his throat now. Mick was closer than he expected, and he was somehow now holding a cricket bat. Sean bent to pick up a spade. They both stepped closer, one on each side of him. This had to stop soon.

'Is any of you going to tell me?'

'Stop him, Corinne. I can't,' said Sean. He took another step closer.

'Joe, please,' she said. 'Can't you forget it? Suzanne died so, so long ago. If you do this, you might kill us too, and even if you don't kill us, we'll never get over seeing you do this. Is it because you're lonely? We can be friends if you like.'

Joe looked round at them all, saw the hope in them. 'A job. A holiday. A friend. I can have all this if I stop asking about Suzanne?'

They nod. Mick stepped closer. 'Mate,' he said. 'Just calm –'

'Why the *hell* would I want any of that?' shouted Joe.

He held up the Zippo again, and amid their rising clamour, he spoke. 'Five. Four. Three. Two–'

'- Sean!' Mick said.

Joe looked at Sean with mild curiosity. 'So, it was you. I thought it was,' he said. 'One –'

'- OK. OK!' Sean yelled. 'I'll tell you what happened! Just stop!'

31
THE NIGHT ON THE FITTIES

So Joe lowered the lighter, and Sean told a story of temptation, betrayal, and corruption, of an irreversible loss of innocence. As Joe listened, his last few months in faith filtered everything he heard. Sean seemed blind to his own evil, even as he laid it out for inspection by all. Joe looked for signs of guilt and repentance and couldn't be sure. The words were there, perhaps, but where was the heart? He couldn't tell. There were complex circumstances, and so Joe grew to understand something of Sean's reasons for what he did. But understanding was not forgiveness for Joe, not yet at least. Though condemnation – or mercy – would be down to Jesus, when he met Sean on Judgement Day and looked at him with eyes of fire.

'It started after the Christmas party' Sean said. 'Our upper sixth year. Do you remember it?'

Corinne did remember it, as it happened. Yet there was a vast hole in her knowledge. 'But I was with you all night. How did you and Suzanne-?'

Sean nodded. 'Your dad came to pick you up early. He didn't like you being out after 11. I walked her home. I'd had some lager, I was feeling good, and I made her laugh. She kissed me for an hour outside her house. We got into bed pretty quickly after that. Me and you hadn't got so far. We were 'waiting'. I fell for her, to be honest. I was thinking maybe I should go out with her, not you. But then I noticed there were a lot of other lads hanging around her. She said she loved me. But she was definitely still sleeping around. Wasn't she, Mick me old mate?'

Mick nodded. It had been long settled between them.

'Mick was her second favourite. She liked me best. So that afternoon, the day she died, three o'clock, we were both of us there at the chalet with her. All spring she'd been playing us off against each other. Sometimes she'd choose Mick, mostly she'd choose me. It was me that day. Around teatime Mick realises this, goes off and leaves us to it. So, I got to have my evil way with her. But it wasn't sex I was after. I was there because I wanted to get her massively, staggeringly pissed.'

'What?' said Corinne.

'For a couple of weeks Saint Suzanne had been saying she was pregnant. And she said it was mine. So, all I wanted to do was make her lose the baby. It was more innocent days. The only way I knew was to get her as drunk as I could and get her in a hot bath. I filled her full of gin, got her up to her neck in bubble-bath, but nothing happened. Three hours later she was blacked out on the settee, and I was going to have a baby. She wanted to get married, you see. At the end of the summer, before I went off to college. She wanted to come to Loughborough with me. She'd told her dad, and he said he'd kill me, but she said it didn't matter.'

'That's the real reason he was chasing you!' said Joe.

Sean nodded again. 'She said she loved me. She said she wanted to marry me. He wanted to kill me.'

He stopped. For a long time. Joe lifted the lighter again, but Corinne waved it down. Sean would tell them what happened, she was sure.

Finally, Sean looked up, his eyes broken glass. 'So yeah, she was blacked out on the sofa. I was scared. I was desperate. I kicked over the oil lamp, smashed the glass, and made sure the flames had caught. I walked out of that chalet, and I never looked back. I cycled over to Waltham Tea Gardens in twenty minutes and met you and we had a couple of drinks and that was that. I guess I killed her. No, I know I killed her. And I'm sorry for that.'

There it was. The truth. Joe let it settle. He wanted to hear everything. He wanted Sean to empty out his dusty hoard of vile memories, he wanted to hear every possible angle on what happened.

'You know what she was like, the odds the baby was mine were tiny. She hadn't been to my house, you see, I was too ashamed to let her, but she thought my family was rich, because of all the money I was flashing about.' There was a flare of anger from Sean, 'It wasn't fair of her to pick on me because of that! If I'd had a baby that young it would have ruined my life. She deserved it really. And look – she was lying, anyway. She wasn't pregnant – if she was then we'd have heard about it in the post-mortem.' He looked round them all, truculent now. 'Yeah. So. I kicked the oil lamp over, and the fire caught pretty quickly. The curtains went up; I kissed her, though she was out of it, and I walked out.'

For a moment silence fell.

Corinne turned away and retched, once, twice. Dry, empty heaving.

Mick stared at Sean. 'Bloody hell, mate,' he said.

Joe finally felt anchored. 'You're a murderer,' he said. He turned to Mick, 'And you're a thief.'

And then to Corinne. 'And you. Why did you cover for him? You all knew something had happened, and you said nothing to anyone. You're all as bad as me. Or worse. After all, I've felt guilty all my life.'

Mick shook his head, with infinite sadness. 'We've felt bad. Trust me.'

Carefully, Joe closed the Zippo.

Sean hadn't finished. There was an even deeper pain upon his heart.

'The first kiss with Suzanne. It was amazing. Life changing. It was wrong; it betrayed you, Corinne. And very soon she'd cheated on me. I wonder, I'll always wonder, I guess, whether I'd have been so angry with her that night if we hadn't all been cheating each other like that.'

'I wasn't cheating anyone,' she said.

He shut his eyes, holding on through a flood of immense emotion. 'I remember the summer we started going out. Waiting for you outside school. Holding hands with you walking home. Did you know I'd stand for hours outside the back of your house, just to see you in your bedroom window doing your homework? I can remember it now. The trees around me, and you in the lamplight. I loved you so much.'

Corinne didn't know that, and even now, the knowledge moved her.

'Then I kissed Suzanne Devlin. And then the rest of our lives happened.'

Sean was finished. He put his hand out to Corinne, looking for some comfort. She shook her head, appalled. No more. Not ever.

He subsided, lost in thought.

Corinne reached forward to Joe and took the lighter out of his hand, 'You must be cold.'

She wrapped him up in the old curtains and sat down next to him. 'So now you know. Do you feel any better?'

Joe leaned into her, and she put her arm round him. He rested his head on her shoulder and shut his eyes, finding immense comfort in her.

She kissed him on the forehead. A small moment of grace.

32
REBIRTH

They found fresh clothes for Joe on one of the costume rails, and he washed off the worst of the petrol in the changing rooms. Mick switched off most of the overhead lights and they all slept. It was a sleep of exhaustion, in the half dark, bundled up in old curtains, rugs, lying on beds of gym mats, but despite all the events of the evening, the sleep came with a peace none of them had known for many years.

By contrast, Paul, Corinne's husband, spent a terrible night alone, eaten up by jealousy and the acidic fear of final abandonment. He drank the Glenfiddich she had bought him, sitting in front of the television until ten when he called her to check in. There was no signal to her phone. He believed she had turned it off and assumed the worst. Too drunk to drive, he had no choice but to wait. He watched old tennis matches on YouTube till two, fantasising all the time about her lovers from half a century ago, all young and healthy and golden, lovers who would break into the happy world he and Corinne had to take her away from him. Eventually going through to bed, he came to the point of feeling sick and worthless, weak and old. He tortured himself for the desiccation at his centre which meant he was neither kind nor interesting enough, nor strong enough or man enough to keep her eyes turned toward him.

He fell asleep around four, as the sun was beginning to show in the sky, and when he woke out of a hot and sweaty pit of bad dreams at eight, and saw she wasn't there, he could bear it no longer.

He got in his car and searched for clues. Driving through empty streets made his fears worse – how could he ever find her? – but going past the school at ten he saw a scattering of cars left still in the car park and seized on that as a sign. Caterers and sixth formers were going into the building to collect the remains of the buffet and disassemble the classroom displays, so he slipped in alongside them. Once inside with them he found he knew the caretaker from his pub and on the pretext of having missed the reunion he got him to show him around the rest of the school building. In his fevered state he was half expecting to catch Corinne and her lover there still *in flagrante*, and so, eventually, in the late morning when he did find her, it took him time to deal with the bizarre reality of the four of them sitting there, apart and in a sombre silence.

As Joe, Sean, Corinne and Mick walked down the long corridor back to the main body of the school, they were hungry, fractious and tired. Yet each one of the four felt the significance of transition, from the dark confines of the hall and what they had learned in the last fifteen hours, towards the wide opens of the outside world. At the end of the corridor the caretaker swung open the double doors back into daylight, and they passed through into the glass covered walkway to the rest of the school, blinking at the morning.

They dispersed in the car park more or less wordlessly. Paul drove Corinne off, and Mick and Sean each got in their cars. Joe refused a half-hearted offer of a lift from Mick and began to walk.

At the school gates he hesitated for a moment, then

turned right instead of left. He walked over the road, across a field which ran down to a plank bridge over a small stream, along the side of some allotments, and out into the open country. He needed space around him, the silence of the fields, and open sky. He wanted to give this day enough room to reflect its significance. As he walked, the calls of the birds high overhead, the roughness of the grass in the fields which caused him to stumble, and the low lines of trees twenty miles south and west, all brought his mind back to God.

He prayed for guidance and afterwards felt it was clear he had to take one more step. Not taken out of anger, or for revenge, but for justice, purely to make sure the entire process would run to completion and his duty could be discharged.

He asked God to forgive Sean for killing Suzanne, and before God he forgave Sean and Mick for all they had done to him. Then he walked back into the centre of the town and went to the police station, where he asked to speak to someone about an old murder.

The desk sergeant looked at him with weary distance and asked him to wait till an officer was free. He sat on a grey plastic chair in the reception, quiet on this Sunday morning, and read over the posters. He realised that Grimsby was in the grip of a knife and drug gang epidemic, which made him sad. He had hoped that was just everywhere else.

A plain-clothes officer in her late forties called him into the front office, where he told her his story. Initially sceptical, she grew attentive when he mentioned Suzanne Devlin. The officer had been at junior school sixty miles away in Spalding at the time of the fire, but she remembered the photo of Suzanne on the teatime news. She got a cup of coffee for him, took copious notes, went over the details twice, and called in a senior officer to whom Joe had to repeat his story a third time. Won over by the gravity of certainty that now surrounded him they took a formal statement and, upon finding out that he was homeless, they asked him to stay in town for a while if he could, or at least to notify them of his plans if he left. He was happy to do so and was happy to leave when they finished the interview. Telling and retelling the story had been exhausting, and he wanted to find a corner, where he hoped he could sleep for a while until the hostel opened.

He stepped off through the streets, past gangs of youths on bikes who looked at him curiously. He no longer felt intimidated by them, and this must have showed, because this time they stopped laughing, looked away and rode off rather than approach him.

33
KING MICK

Mick said, 'See you in the Wheatsheaf?' to Sean, got in his car, plugged in his phone, and drove off.

But when he got to the Wheatsheaf, he drove past without turning into the car park. He fumbled for his phone, found some lovely old reggaeton, turned it up loud, and rode on into town. He did a circuit of the town centre, past St James church. The bells were ringing as a handful of people left the Sunday morning service. They were dressed up for the occasion, many of them grey-haired, wearing respectable anoraks, jackets, the more affluent of them in smart coats. To Mick it looked like Marks & Spencer on tour. The way they took quiet leave of each other was so staid, it reminded him of people fifty years ago. Christ, that was all so boring, back then. He noticed how old they all seemed, even the younger ones. Amita was always trying to get him to go to church, but religion had to be nearly dead now. It surely wouldn't be too long before it was all closed down and people could get on with the party. That church would make a beast of a club.

He watched two young families, hugging each other goodbye, their children running round their feet. They didn't look like they had a lot of money, poor sods. He couldn't imagine a bigger contrast to Pattaya. From his DJ booth in the window of the bar on Walking Street, the people heading home from their night of worship looked gorgeous, wired, sexy, aggressive, loved-up, stoned, loaded, battered, androgynous, horny, ravenous. Five in the morning in Pattaya put on display all the iridescence of a rich and complex humanity set free to play, each person reaching for their own unique fulfilment under the cover of darkness.

Yet he saw something else here, in Grimsby, on the face of these grey-haired elders, these poor young families, and it was something that nagged at him. It was one particular emotion which he rarely noticed on Walking Street. Or anywhere he went, for that matter. More than anything, these Grimsby people looked happy.

The clang of the bells was beginning to do his head in, so he looped round the town centre one more time, reliving various long-ago nights out, and headed out along a surprisingly steel-shuttered and empty-looking Freeman Street.

He soon passed the site of the blocks of flats where, long, long ago Joe had begun his burgling career. He winced as he drove, but he couldn't feel too guilty about all that. It was typical of the silly sod to do something so reckless – but he had to admit he could see how getting banged up at seventeen could mess you up a bit. If he had the chance to do that again, knowing what he knew now about prisons, he'd probably not have dobbed Joe in. But then that would have meant he and Sean would have got done by the police, so he'd have to rewind a few of those choices that got them to that place. Which would mean redoing the choices before that, because everything all built on what had gone before – on and on into the past – until, before he knew where he was, he found himself back at the first day of Pinfold Lane infant school choosing not to sit next to this funny looking blond kid called Sean Garner.

He shifted in his seat, guilt spiking him, but he ended up

grinning. Yeah, so, what, was he supposed to erase a complete life? It couldn't be done. And why should it? Deal with it and move on.

'I've been rambling out all my life.'

At a gap in the buildings, he pulled into the kerb, and he looked across wide open spaces. They'd knocked the tower blocks down, leaving an empty wasteland the size of three or four football pitches, littered with rubble, fenced in with wire mesh. From the piles of bricks and the heavy machinery lying around they were building something in the space, but being Grimsby it might take a while.

He started the car and moved through the East Marsh, heading along to Cleethorpes. He parked up on the prom and looked out over the brown water of the Humber towards the thin, green line of Yorkshire on the horizon, some six or seven miles away. The river was busy with traffic. There were huge, block-like container ships, stacked up and heading in, and a white freight ferry on its way out to Gothenburg. For a while he watched an old man and his grandson mess about in the mud next to the waterline. They had a dog with them, a cute looking brown and black cross-breed which ran, scattering an indignant group of seagulls like spray while the little boy jumped up and down in excitement. The old man pointed with his stick and the boy got down on his knees, digging for some treasure in the mud, Mick couldn't see what.

There, on Cleethorpes prom, Mick felt the shadow of Suzanne Devlin leave him. Over the years he'd had the most awful nightmares. Night after night he'd seen her on hands and knees, clawing through the smoke, retching and choking, screaming in terror as the flames closed in. Imaginary pictures, made more haunting by being tangled up with the sweetest memories of the good times, laughing with her, and being naked with her. For all his bluster she had been his first. He would never forget that first evening they had been together, the way she looked at him as he unbuttoned her top, the way she rolled her eyes in mock irritation and helped him undo her bra, the curve of her breast, gentle in the twilight. He sighed. He liked her a lot, they'd had had such fun together, and he never understood why she had always preferred Sean. But people did prefer Sean, he had learned that, and somehow those people often ended up regretting it.

The idea of rewinding choices came back to him, as he thought of his life built, a brick at a time, on what had gone before. One by one he examined each brick and came to the question of why he was in Thailand. He'd always thought it was clear. The husband who wanted to kill him in Dammam meant it was wise to leave the Middle East, and he'd always liked the beach. Now, for the first time, he asked himself, how was it the guy was trying to kill him? Why had he got himself into that position in the first place? Where did that come from?

Rewind, rewind. That got him thinking.

There was an old, Victorian folly behind him called Ross Castle. It was a pretend castle built of stone, with a winding path up to the summit some forty feet above the prom. He'd loved it as a kid, had loved running down the spiral ramp, so he got out his car and trudged up to the top for old times sakes.

Mad King Mick, Lord of Ross Castle, boss of all he could see, leaned on the high wall of flints, wind in his face. He looked out over the Humber and replayed his life. The breeze blowing in off the sea tugged things apart, and the solid construction he had built of himself fell apart in his hands. It crumbled into a thousand pieces that tumbled about him, from which he could pull out the parts he wanted to keep, and from which he could lay out the true path of his life. How he had got to here from there. All the decisions at all the forks in the road, from major to minor. The decisions made from love, and which, he now realised, had always brought him happiness. And those decisions made from lust, or greed, or fear, which had always caused destruction or pain.

Eventually, in among the fog of whirling fragments, he saw the shape of something startling. He realised he only didn't want to marry Amita because he feared an evening visit from her brothers. But if they lived in England, then he wouldn't have to worry about that. And now this Suzanne thing was out in the open and Sean had finally put his hand up of his own accord, he felt a lot better about the old place. A whole lot better in fact. Joe would no doubt go to the police about Suzanne and at the very least they'd want a word, but that was Sean's train and Sean would ride it. He, Mick, wasn't there when it happened, and all he had to do was deny knowing anything and who could prove anything else?

The idea of coming back home took a firmer hold. He'd miss the DJ-ing, but maybe not as much as he reckoned. And once she'd bollocked him for slotting off like he had, Amita would love the idea. She had a friend in Scunthorpe who had come over with a retired trucker a year back, so that would help no end. Prices round here, he could buy them a serious house. Mad King Mick felt a whole lot less mad at that thought.

Later he drove round to the home to see his mum. She was in the lounge in front of the telly. He sat down in front of her, and she didn't recognise him at first, it always took her a while. In the end her face softened, and he told her his news.

'I've got a little girl now, mam. She's called Florence. I'll bring her to see you soon. And her mother.'

'That's nice. Did you get wed then?'

'Not yet, but we will be. You can come. Guest of Honour.'

Pleased beyond measure, Mrs Bluff reached out and gripped her long-lost son's hands. She didn't understand how there was a little girl now, or why, but she understood that her boy was smiling, and that he was coming home, and that made her happy.

34
CORINNE

'My hero' Corinne said to Paul, forcing herself to beam at him. 'I can't believe you found us! That's so amazing!'

He started the ignition and slammed the car into gear. He looked left and right, ignoring Joe walking alongside them, and pulled out onto the road away from the school.

'So it turned out to be a hell of a reunion.' she began, trying to ignore the obvious.

His voice was thick with emotion. 'Which one was it?'

'Which one what?'

'The one who kept you out all night.'

'Paul, for God's sake, we got locked in! You rescued us!'

'Was it the blond one? Sean? He looks your type. Muscle-bound and dumb looking. I hope you had fun.'

'Don't be so ridiculous-!'

'You -' he lifted his hand to cut her off '- make me sick.'

Neither of them said any more. He drove home and pulled the car into the drive, too close to the hedge on her side, so she'd have trouble getting out. Almost before the engine was off, he was up and out, slamming the driver's door behind him. She watched him open the front door and close it behind him without looking back for her.

The clench of anxiety in her gut led her to sit for a while. She knew the jealousy would boil away in him, even though it would get dressed up as worry for her. She'd never stayed out overnight before so she had no way of calibrating, but she was sure he would take a few days to come down from this. She'd have a day or so before he would hit her – the first stages were always verbal, as he bounced between stony silence and telling her how much she let him down.

She got out the car and went inside. He was already watching TV, so, exhausted by events, she went for a bath. It was hot in there, and she struggled to stay awake, so she got out, got herself dry, and lay on their bed. Her eyes closed, and she slept.

When she woke, she felt disoriented. A gale of applause came from the TV, still on in the lounge, although the long shadows across the wall told her hours had passed. Sitting on the side of the bed she felt heady, clogged with sleep. Outside the sky was peaceful, with layers of pearl and pale violet high and calm across the faint blue air. Yet here, inside her house, she could feel violence coming. Though it would have been far easier to stay in her robe, there was a tension in the unknown of the moment that made her get dressed.

She put her head in the door. He was turned away from her, in his chair, watching the golf.

'Is it good?'

He didn't answer, so she passed through into the kitchen and made them some sandwiches. After a while the kettle boiled. She made a pot of tea, found some Pringles in the cupboard and cut two slices of cake. She put it all on the tray with plates, sugar and the milk jug, and took it all into him.

'You must be hungry. I'm starving! I've made us some tea.' As she put the tray down on the coffee-table he glared up at her and she saw with a shock how his eyes were raw and red-rimmed. She couldn't acknowledge that, so went on. 'I've made cheese and pickle, and those are tuna -'

He threw the TV remote control at her. It whizzed past her face and smashed apart on the wall behind her. She couldn't help a scream of surprise, which brought a snort of contempt. He got up and stalked out past her into the kitchen.

After a minute or two she called out. She hadn't heard the back door, so she knew he was in there and that he could hear her. 'Paul. I've been thinking. There's something I need to say.'

There was no answer, but she didn't expect one, so she went ahead regardless. She talked about the love they felt for each other. She apologised for worrying him, and she explained again how the door of the old gym had been faulty. She told him she wasn't interested in Sean, and how much she loved him, Paul, how she always had done. How, when she met him, she was so lost, and sad, and she had always thought he had saved her life. She told him he meant so much to her. That of all the men in the world she had known, it was him she had chosen, and he had to realise how much that meant to her. She asked him to open his heart up to let her in, that he had to trust her. She would try do the same, and if they both tried hard enough, they could surely fix what was going wrong. But most of all she told him he had to stop hurting her.

She was surprised by how hollow she felt making these declarations. How, even as the words left her mouth, they felt too light, as though they weren't words that could belong to her. Perhaps they seemed insubstantial words to Paul too, because no answer came back from the kitchen.

She waited, wondering what it meant to be in love with someone. She and Paul had joked about having Big Love between them at the beginning, but it had turned sour on both of them, and she couldn't believe being married to her was making him happy either.

Something had happened in the Sports Hall. What had seemed a comfortable compromise for years now seemed different. How much sacrifice and surrender it all needed! Was it always bottomless like this? An endless war of attrition, only ever a forced coalition, a least-worst option, clung to as a fragile coral atoll in a dreadful, fast-rising ocean? Or could there be a happy place, where things were simple, and calm, and 'Big Love' actually became loving?

With all her being she longed for that second option. Which, she realised, is what had given her hope all these years. If you can imagine something so good, so perfect, then the thing you're longing for must surely exist, somewhere, somehow?

The silence dragged on.

After a long wait, she went into the hall, took up her bag and her phone from the table. She plucked the keys off the hook, oh-so-quietly, and walked out of the front door to the car.

As the engine fired, he appeared at the front window. He held out his hands in outrage and surprise. Viewed from outside the house the gesture was only comical. 'You silly thing,' his flapping hands seemed to say. 'Do you really think you can go somewhere without me?'

She backed the car out the drive and drove off down the road. She was heading towards the sea, but that didn't matter. She wanted space. Somewhere amid her long speech to Paul was the moment in which Corinne had stopped trying.

At the sea she turned left, and she drove for miles and miles, around and about. Yet whatever she did there was a gravitational pull she couldn't break. She'd get to the edge of the town and remember how he made her laugh, and she'd weaken, and somehow swing too far round a roundabout and head back in. She tried each of the three main routes out of town, and each time some sweet memory, some flash of regret, or sympathy for him, turned her round and pointed her towards home.

The problem was she had no plan to go forward. She had friends, but none she could land on like this. She had her own bank account, with some money in it, and her ISA, so the next few weeks, or next few months even, were fine. It was the future that would be the problem. What do you do with the rest of your life when you leave your husband at 57?

As she drove, she had relived the night in the sports hall. All the nostalgia, all the sadness of remembering Suzanne. Joe being tormented on the chair – and the petrol! Would he have done it? She had no reason to think he wouldn't. Then, the awful truth about Sean. His foul, evasive shadow lurching out into the light, something made real which she had glimpsed in the corner of her picture of him for as long as she could remember. She should go to the police about what he did to Suzanne, and she would, tomorrow, but for the moment it was monstrous and overpowering.

There was light too. She kept coming back to finding Joe praying, kneeling arse-over-tit on the tatty old sofa. It made her smile. He'd been so open about it all, so earnest. Whatever he'd found in the church in Brighton had taken hold of him, no doubt about it. But the petrol! How did all that work? Yet she smiled again: she envied anyone with that kind of certainty, but someone ought to tell him he didn't actually have to *be* Jesus.

So it may have been her subconscious at work, or perhaps it was sheer coincidence which helped her take her next step.

(What is coincidence, anyway? The ordering of life in a way that seems implausible without outside agency? The ordering of events that had to be accidental, but feels like it was arranged? The whole idea begs the question of what, or who, does the arranging.)

In later years she would know well the idea that the more you pray, the more coincidences seem to happen, but that was some way down the line. Besides, she hadn't been praying – not unless a life's longing counted. So, whether by coincidence or design, as she drove past St James' Church, the bells cracked and pealed overhead, and Corinne saw Kate, one of her oldest friends from school, walking down the path towards the six o'clock service.

Corinne parked and hurried in after her. Pleased – and surprised – to see her, Kate guided Corinne to a seat half-way down the aisle, by one of the tall stone pillars, next to a table of sweet-pea and acanthus. It may well have been coincidence that at this moment of her deepest need Corinne found someone who would lead her into church, but this evening, tucked up among the fluted arches and stained light, the alabaster and the everlastings, Corinne took her first step onto a trail which would last for the rest of her life.

She broke down in tears during the service, floods of tears, and Kate put her arm round her, and when she heard her story, she offered her a room for the night. That evening Corinne asked Kate why she went to church, and she took the time to talk to Corinne about Jesus, and what he'd done for everyone, and what believing this monstrously improbable story would do for her, Corinne Ayr.

It may have been another coincidence that, on the next Tuesday at this very church they would begin another term of the evening course which Joe had taken in Brighton. The course which explained the life and death and resurrection of Jesus Christ. How he came to be, what he did, and what that meant for the world. The evening course that, if you took it seriously, would crack open the fabric of reality and pull down the walls of your everyday life to reveal the love beyond, the love that created and fills the heart of everything.

It all sounded far too good to be true, but from the beginning she couldn't deny she found practical support there in the church. At first it felt as though she were leaning on a crutch. Kate put her up for a few nights, and kept Paul at bay when he found her, and backed her up when the police came to talk to her. Then others in the church stepped up to offer her a more permanent place to live. It surprised her at how generous they were to someone they hardly knew, but she was already learning how to be kinder to herself, and so she took that support without shame. What was wrong with accepting a little help? Over the weeks she realised the church had far more to offer, and eventually what she had perceived as being behind Joe's devotions became to be true for her too. She began to realise that for which she had longed for so long could be found in God – and then the Holy Spirit met with her directly, and it definitely wasn't too good to be true. Or, rather, it was both good *and* true.

She followed Joe in making that small hop of adjustment, making a commitment to believe. She too stepped over that low wall into the next field and began walking down that green hill into the next valley, and a better place in the world, and she never once looked back to her old life.

So the reunion's gift to her, the outcome of Joe's proposed sacrifice, the truth it forced, was freedom. From then on, she was free of anything that tied her to Sean, or to Paul, or to guilt, or to unrequited longing. Though she would remain single for the rest of her life, in the sense she would form no more romantic or sexual attachments, Corinne would be free to love and be loved by the people she met, and she would never again feel alone.

Then, when she died, some twenty years later, in a sunlight-scattered room in an old house on the edge of the New Forest, Corinne discovered how all of this was only the beginning.

35
SEAN

Sean didn't even pretend to go to the Wheatsheaf to meet Mick. He couldn't see the point. The only things left they had to say to each other were unspeakably raw. He drove back to his hotel, a big sixties job on the edge of a golf course, and packed. He had to get out of town, get back up north, head home before it all came down on him, because come down on him it must.

But as he packed, he forgot what had happened, and his head grew light, free, full of inviting pictures. Coniston calling. The garden, the goodness of the open air, the light off the lake, the kids. And Rebecca.

He slowed and then stopped. Rebecca. His elation fizzled into nothing. What kind of mad trip was he on? What was the point of pretending? It was all out now, so Rebecca would find out, and the moment she found out what had happened, everything was over. He'd kept it hidden for so long, kept things straight, put everything he had into being a good husband, a good dad, built a good life. All this, now, twisted into undoing, everything destroyed by a mad fragment with a can of petrol. It was, most of all, so unfair.

He cursed his own cowardice. He should have called Joe's

bluff. A loser like him would have chickened out, anyway. But it was Sean who had chickened out, and unloaded everything, and they'd all hung him out to dry. Even Corinne. Especially Corinne. He smarted as he remembered the look on her face as he reached to her at the end.

So now it was done. There was no way Joe would keep his trap shut, and they'd come for him soon. For a joyful, stupid minute or two he thought about getting on a ferry at Immingham, but reality bit back. It might well be a 40-year-old murder that should be buried under its own tumulus in the archives but give the cops a chance for an easy clear-up and they'd be all over it. He had nothing on his side. No passport with him, CCTV and number plate recognition everywhere, he'd probably not even make it home. Even if he dumped the car and got a train, his card would be tracked. Cameras at every cash point, helicopters with infra-red, a phone which was leaking his location, forget it. A guy like him would last two days.

Faced with all that, just make sure you get done what you need to get done. And there was one thing in particular he needed to do. After 40 years there'd be nothing to see, but if he didn't go there, if he didn't stand again on the actual axis of everything at the very moment his world turned, he knew he'd always regret it.

He showered, and dressed, putting on a T-shirt, joggers and his trainers. He cleared the room, checked out, threw his weekend bag in the boot. Somewhere within himself he was wondering if he might still try to run. But before any of that came along, he wanted to see what the place looked like now.

The chalet they had built on the site of the fire was now old brick, with woodwork and eaves painted in primrose yellow and duck-egg blue. He was surprised to see it looked friendly, and warm-hearted – he had half-expected to see that the fire had charred the earth. Two children's bikes leaned at the side of the house, a gas-fired barbecue waited under a neat tarpaulin, the grass was cut and flowerbeds tidy. Whoever owned this chalet kept it clean and lived an orderly life.

Yet in his mind's eye he could see the rusty old iron railing, the flaking wooden porch, Suzanne in fits of laughter at something or other at the front door – and the more he remembered, the angrier he got. There, in front of the chalet, twenty feet from where the fire had happened, there was no sign of any crime. In fact, there were no physical signs anywhere of what had once happened. Nothing was the same, there were no trails, everything had washed away, been absorbed into the earth and the air. Back then was another world. So why were they going to punish him for something that had long since evaporated like a cloud in the morning sunlight? How could they destroy his life for an event submerged in time? That simply didn't exist any more.

He needed to be with his family again, the three people here in the now who made everything right. To kiss Rebecca, to hold his children. To get past the chaff that so often blurred things when they tried to draw close. In that instant he felt such clarity that he loved them all, purely, truly. He felt the agony of how, inevitably now, they would be taken from him.

He got back in the car, and drove straight and fast out of Grimsby, heading for the M62 and home. He'd take his chances, that Joe hadn't gone to the police, and even if he had that it would take time to find enough specifics about his life to start the tracking machinery.

Three hours later, low on petrol, desperate for a pee, eyes gritty from concentration, he parked at Burton in Kendal services. He bought a coffee and a chicken wrap, served by a sleepy looking kid with dark hair that flopped over his forehead. How he envied the kid the peace of mind which meant he could take ages to make the coffee, and banter with his serving mate rather than look at Sean as he took his payment at the till. Savour your peace, sleepy kid, he felt, with no little hatred. Savour your peace, because it might evaporate forever in an instant.

He took the tray to a table in a secluded corner. A few tables faced a window leading onto thick green bushes and a distant view of the motorway. Feeling safe there he scanned local news sites on his phone for any clues of people out looking for him. Then he ate and relaxed a little.

That moment of calm cost him dear, because it meant he was off balance going back to the car. He came out the front door of the services, went around the corner of the food trucks, saw the police car parked ahead, saw how a police officer lifted his head to look at him.

From pure instinct Sean turned to run. Shouting went up behind him, and he realised once again what a coward he was.

He should have stopped – every part of anything reasonable would have made him stop – they couldn't be looking for him yet – the officer was probably just a traffic cop – but every single step he took was more suspicious until very quickly he had crossed the threshold and become someone on the run.

He was operating out of pure fear now, and the rip of cortisol made him fly. He sprinted across the lorry park, over the ramshackle grass and battered plastic benches of a forlorn picnic area and dived into the hedge at the side of the service station estate. He tore through the branches, bursting out and skidding to a halt above the M6 itself. There was no choice. He climbed over the lip of the parapet, dropped the eight feet down to the hard shoulder, and picked his moment to run between the oncoming cars. Safety at the central reservation for a moment, then another mad plunge between oncoming trucks, yelling in terror at the scream and skirl of the horns as they passed him, and then he was safe. He found a way to climb the low wall on the far side, and then he was off and into scrub woodland.

So, once more, Sean ran. He ran, and he ran, and he ran, and as he ran the machinery of the law came together, in determined men and women, first in vans and cars, and, when they realised how fast and how tricky he was, a helicopter sent up from the base in Manchester.

They found him twelve hours later, in pitch darkness, out on a hillside some fifteen miles away from the service station.

It was a still, silent night, not a breath of a breeze, no hint of wind. Any noise carried for a mile or more. The helicopter picked him up first, a black patch on the infra-red screen. He was sheltering, shivering and trying to sleep in a patch of sparse bushes. The pilot called the pursuing officers in. The thump of the helicopter blades overhead stirred him. Hearing the voice of the dogs across the moors he broke cover, running on across a moor dark with mere starlight.

He stumbled by chance into a builders' yard on the edge of a lake and the helicopter lost him for a time among the brick and the steel, but by then the dogs had a strong scent. Ferocious and terrifying, their barking desolate in the night air, they tracked him to his last hiding place. They found him at bay, crouched under a workbench at the back of a workman's hut, on the very edge of the vast, mirror-surfaced water.

He didn't fight them as they came for him. The one thing he said as they put him in the van was that it wasn't his fault.

He changed his mind about that later on, after a set of nightmarish visits from Rebecca and Billie. Callum wouldn't come to see him, which he found shocking, but Rebecca and Billie grilled him on every detail with a fearless and dreadful scepticism which flayed him until he was shamed enough to repeat the confession he had made in the sports hall.

When that wasn't enough, when the police case threatened to fall apart from lack of hard evidence and doubt over his mental state, he gave them more and more detail, insisting they proceed until they had no choice but to go ahead.

He was so volatile because there were two forces at war within him. The limbic drive to escape which had protected him through most of his life's difficulties, versus a more diffuse, more hard-to-handle instinct to Do The Right Thing. It surprised him when the second instinct drove him more. But he didn't actually feel sorry, there was no emotional weight to any guilt, it was all an intellectual thing. All he knew, in a blind, dull way, was that all this had to be endured before there was ever a chance he could feel well again. He wanted to be held up to the light as an example of how bad you could go. He wanted to suffer for what he had done, to burn from punishment, to be made pure from retribution, to recapture a long-lost feeling of freedom. He was satisfied with the life sentence he received in Hull Crown Court some nine months later. It put things in balance at last, and it left him free to heal.

After so many years bound by the coils of his lies, Sean needed to pay his dues. If he could get that sorted, then maybe he could repent.

36
THE ETERNAL

After he had been to the police station, Joe spent the rest of the day alone, walking the streets. He got back to the hostel just before the cut-off hour and rang the bell.

Mel opened the door, 'Oh no. He's back.'

But she couldn't stop her face crinkling in a grin. They held eye contact, a moment too long, until she dropped her eyes, embarrassed. A depth-charge of emotion bloomed inside him. He knew that look, and what it meant.

He stepped inside, 'How's it been today? Lots more poor people?'

'There'll always be poor people, Joe. You know that. I thought we were going to church?'

Seeing her walking down the corridor ahead of him sharpened each of his senses. He felt light, alert, more alive. He felt better.

'We'll do it next time.'

'"Next time". Are you planning on staying then?'

'Maybe.'

He saw a true vision, of Mel, and himself, Sean, and Corinne, and Mick. All the people in the houses around, in the town, the countryside around. The vision grew wider, and wider to encompass the country, the entire world. He saw how each person was on their own pilgrim journey. How some had to battle, some went through thickets, and wrong turns, but how each of them kept walking. And how each of those journeys in time would only end when they came before Jesus Christ, the eternal one.

He thought about his walk after coming out of the sports hall, how it felt to be out alone in the country, and he gave thanks. For the goodness of the trees and fields and sky. For the mud and the nettles, and the thorn hedges, and birds high above, and the distant hum of the traffic. For his breath in his body, for the way the earth went on supporting him. For the way the wind went on blowing at him, how the water always fell from the waterfall, regardless of what he thought, or did, or confronted, or turned away from. He gave thanks for how unstoppable gravity was. How the earth turned, and the sun rose, and the stars wheeled, every day for millions, billions of years, all without question. He marvelled at this universe which obeyed God's laws without ever hesitating.

If creation did this, so would he.

He gave thanks for his life so far, for all the barrage of memories of times and people and moods and experiences flooding over him. He gave thanks for the truth about Suzanne. He gave thanks for this coming new time, with everything it held for him now.

All this in an instant, as Joe looked at Mel, now collecting up mugs from the reception desk. She called over her shoulder: 'How was the reunion? Meet any old flames?'

He knew now: time didn't matter. God was real, and God was eternal, so all Joe's nostalgia, all the regrets, all the time they had all spent pining for the past – there was no need. Birth, life, death, murder, childhood, romance, passion, feuding, love – they were all forever there, each moment all held safely by a God who lives beyond time. He wondered – does every moment exist always? Either way, for the first time in his life he felt held forever, safe from loss in the hands of a loving father.

Joe felt the touch of an infinite compassion for all our poor, misguided struggles. He felt a mercy which can only come from a God who has created an entire universe to express his Love. He filled with joy as he finally understood: those sweet early memories, they weren't decaying images of lost times, they were promises of the heaven to come.

'I'm talking to you,' Mel said.

'Yeah, not too bad. No flames though. Are you going to make me a coffee or what?'

She was pleased with him, 'Make it yourself, cheeky beggar.'

He grinned, and they looked at each other in recognition and honesty, and this time they held each other's gaze.

One month after the reunion, at night, as the owl and the bat hunted overhead, Joe walked around Scartho, saying goodbye to the past, goodbye to the old hold it had over him, and saying hello to the future.

He was moving back to Grimsby, not from nostalgia which pulled him back, but from a rebirth of hope which drove him onwards. There was work to be had on the Humber Bank. The housing was at least half the price of Brighton. The people were warm and friendly, and he knew the place inside out. It felt right to be there.

Plus, there was Mel.

And if even there wasn't, it would be OK.

— END —

AFTERWORD

If you've enjoyed reading this book, then please do drop over to Amazon and leave me a review. I'm an independent author with my own imprint, operating outside any major publishing house, so every review really does help.

I've been creating fiction for over 40 years, and I still don't know where ideas come from. Things just pop up when I need them, and after all this time it's a reasonably dependable process. But while I was writing *After The Fire*, the question sharpened for me. Some scenes, some moments, some lines of dialogue, were arriving too fully imagined. I began to feel as though I was transcribing rather than writing. Which made me wonder who was doing the writing. Who, really, wanted this story to be told?

I'm not immune to how strange the supernatural sounds, and the details of Joe Belton's conversion to faith will seem esoteric, perhaps even deranged, to those who don't know Jesus, (though perhaps a little more familiar to those people who have already made that commitment themselves). What's more, I am puzzled by the way some of the visions in this book forced themselves on me: Sean watching the break in the trees on the towpath. Paul's arms flapping uselessly at Corinne through the window. The chase along South Sea Lane and the shift to the wider perspective there. Joe's voice as he tells of his night in the pub in Brighton. Sean on the moors. What eventually happens to Corinne. In no way that I recognise did I create these things. In some way I don't understand they were given to me.

There are more scenes; in particular one picture around Corinne that I loved, and feared, and which I chose not to include. It's a picture that arrived in a split-second, vivid beyond my understanding, and it has implications that pass into prophecy for us all. But prophecy is a serious business and I don't claim that gift, so rather than mislead I withhold. Besides, time will tell.

The book is pure fiction. I have lived in Brighton and Grimsby, but I was never down and out. I have a real family and real friends and we are all pretty happy. I did once go to a school reunion, but it was a very calm affair. The locations in this book are real, but the four characters in this story, and the details of their lives, are all invented.

Conversion to faith can be a messy business, and can overturn everything. Joe's solution to his problem is a pretty poor model for conflict resolution. Yet by his desperate actions lives are changed, some for the better, so I have to wonder: was God with him as he did what he did?

I think the answer is that God is with us in everything, and it's down to us to make sense of that as we can.

I hope *After The Fire* entertains. That's its first job. Without that it fails. I hope it moves the reader, and perhaps reminds them of the first time they fell in love. But I also hope that it leads some people to open their ears to that soft knocking at their hearts. Though you may feel Jesus is pursuing you as he did Joe Belton, he is gentle, and will never force his way. It's always our choice as to whether we open the door. If we do, then his promise is that he will come in, and he will sit down with us.

We can all know him, if we but choose.

Philip Gladwin, Grimsby, 2022

ACKNOWLEDGEMENT

To all those who helped me with this book.

To Fran and Nancy, who believed I could finish a novel when I thought I could only write scripts. Your support got me through.

To those who read earlier drafts and gave me much-needed feedback and encouragement: Austin Bye, Caroline Childs, Nicola Davies-Grant, Hilary and Charles Gladwin, Jonny Gumbel, Karla Hancock, Shirley Henry, Chris, Michael and Suzanne Hill, Jon Jeffes and Simon Thompson.

To all those script editors, producers and writers in television land who did their best to teach me how to tell a story.

To Patric Kearns and *Talking Scarlet*, who risked commissioning my stage play *Kiss Chase*, upon which some of this novel is based. To Marcus Hutton, Stephen Beckett, Jenny Funnell and Ben Roddy who first brought the central characters to life.

To the members of St Peter's Church in Brighton, where I met Jesus Christ. Thank you for the wonders I heard from you all. To Archie Coates, who led me to faith, and then prayed me out of a hole or two. Any muddles over the character and love of God in this book are down to me alone.

Finally, warm wishes to everyone at my schools, and Weelsby Road Methodist Youth Club, all in Grimsby, where so many of the story seeds were planted so long ago.

RESOURCES

If you're interested in what happened to Joe Belton when he met Jesus, then the simplest thing to do is to have a look for yourself.

THE BIBLE

In particular, look at the chapters, (also called 'books') within the Bible called Matthew, Mark, Luke and John.

They open the New Testament, and are four different angles on Jesus' life. I'm willing to bet you that if you take the time to get deeply into them they will change your life. They certainly changed mine.

There are many, many different versions of the Bible out there, all slightly different in the way they translate, or paraphrase, the original Hebrew, Aramaic and Greek texts, and there is bound to be one that speaks to you in particular.

The Message is a loose translation, more like a paraphrase. It uses modern American English, and aims to convey the energy and frequently very informal quality of those original texts to modern readers.

The **New International Version** (or NIV) is a very readable modern translation.

So is the **New Revised Standard Version** (NRSV). I'm reading the Anglicised version of that a lot at the moment.

For a more informal version of the New Testament try **The Passion**. It can be very vivid.

The **King James Version** towers above all other translations for the beauty of its language. It can be very powerful indeed, and it is the one that most older people recognise, but as it was first published in 1611 it can also be a bit of a battle to read.

APPS

If it sounds confusing, well, yes, there is a lot of choice. One way to get round that is to use the free **YouVersion** Bible app for smartphone and tablet.

This is a great app, which lets you bounce between a great many translations effortlessly.

COURSES

If you're the type of person who would rather investigate all this face-to-face, so you can debate in a group of like-minded people who are curious, or even sceptical, then you could try an **Alpha Course**.

This is a free, friendly course (one two-hour session per week) originally set up by Holy Trinity Brompton church in London, back in the 1980s. It now runs all over the world, and has had tens of millions of people take it.

It's the course Joe attends in *After The Fire*, and it's the same course I attended when I met Jesus. Most towns in England will have a church that runs it at some point in the year, and I believe it's often possible to find a church that runs it no matter where you are in the world.

Many places even have a version of the course that runs online, so as long as you have internet access you can attend wherever you are.

COMING IN 2023

AND
YET
Josser
Sometimes love slips
through your fingers
Philip Gladwin

JOSSER

CHAPTER 1

In those days it was all Formica, laminate and stainless steel. Flimsy partitions, chemical toilets, beds that folded out. Great parties in the summer, the nights spent chasing sleep, their rooms airless and stifling. December mornings eating fried bread, huddled close to the warmth from the blue Gaz bottle heater.

Outside home could be grass, or a car park, bare feet wet with dew in the morning, muddy in the winter and the spring. The first thing outside the van door was space, and freedom to play for Oli and her friends. Then a single braid of electrified wire. It ran in a huge loop to mark out the heart of the camp. In that movable compound the horses were set free to tumble and jink, cantering all day from end to end of their own playground.

On the perimeter of everything, a hundred or more caravans, trucks and bunk-wagons. They formed a sprawling circle, a spacious enclosure which held Oli's whole world.

Somewhere on the edge of it all, standing on the borderline between the great circle of home and the unknowable darkness of the outside world, would be the Big Top. Whether cramped in the inner city or embedded in the green woodland of a garden suburb, the tent was a citadel of red and gold, flags on the turrets rippling in the light breeze, as solid and stately and reassuring as a medieval castle.

The whole show would uproot every few nights, packing everything, driving to a new ground in another part of the country. When you're only in the same place for five nights every year there can be no roots put down on the earth. So their roots grew in the space between them. Show-business alliances going back a hundred years meant everyone was known to everyone. Marriages between sons and daughters of circus aristocracy ensured a new weaving of the braid of peace. Just as in a medieval village, loyalty was intense. The old and the ill were never cast out, instead given a caravan and self-respect with a job, be it clearing litter, washing or handing out flyers at the end of the show. The acts stayed a season or two, or three, then moved on to other shows, other countries, adding to the dense network of bonds and loyalties that stretched out from London to Los Angeles, Moscow to Buenos Aires.

For a very long time, this was all Oli knew, and so, until the man came for her mother, she was happy…

CONNECT

If you want to keep generally updated with what I'm writing, or to ask me any questions about *After The Fire*, or *Josser*, or the books and short stories coming after that, then you can connect with me at philipgladwin.com or at the And Yet website at AndYet.live

First published in 2022 by And Yet

AndYet.works

Printed in Great Britain
by Amazon

26915053R00158